CHAPTER 1

Imagine a perfect English country village and most (the place where I live. Goldenfields is about fifteen r .... coast, on the Kent Sussex border. On a clear day if you climb to the highest point of the surrounding hills you can just about see the glistening water of the English channel. At least that's what they say, although to be honest I have serious reservations. We have a village green, complete with an old traditional pump house. The main road that runs through the village doesn't get much traffic, thanks to one of our previous residents who was an MP in the eighties. I can't recall his name but he was tight enough with Thatcher that he managed to get her support for a by-pass.

The village has a pub, a post office, sorry, sub-post office, and some of the houses date back as far as the sixteenth century, complete with original oak beams and walls and ceilings that have peculiar angles. Trust me, I've been in several of them and there isn't a straight wall or floor to be seen. There are one or two more modern dwellings, and when I say modern I mean eighteenth or nineteenth century. None of the new houses can be seen from the green, and the council estate is tucked half a mile from the village centre, along with a school, a doctors surgery and any other monstrosity that could be seen as a visual blight on our 'perfect' community.

Pass through at any time of the day and you're likely to get held up by geese wandering across the road like they own the place. Well, to be fair, they probably have as much right to be here as anyone. At the bottom of the village there's a river and a large pond that the geese claimed as their own long before I arrived here.

1

The village is surrounded by fields and forests that stretch as far as the eye can see. The nearest town is about ten miles away. It sounds idyllic I know, but like most places there is always something unseemly lurking beneath the tranquil surface. We have our share of shady characters: I know because I've met most of them at one time or another.

This morning a few of us are meeting for drinks at the local tea-room. Apparently it used to be the village store until the owner realised he couldn't compete with the superstores. It works better as a tea room. The large front window overlooks the centre of the village. I don't mind sitting here at any time of the year watching the world go by.

Megan pushes open the door and I can feel all eyes turn towards us. It's usually the same old faces, mostly on Monday mornings and sometimes on a Friday afternoon. Today there is a new face lurking within the small group.

"About time too, we were about to send out a search party." Helen Pierce announces our arrival in her typical - joking, only half joking manner – that I don't mind but Megan seems to find very irritating.

"Sorry, had a few bits n' pieces to see too." Megan doesn't sound at all sorry, and as always, I wonder why she apologises if she doesn't really mean it.

We sit at an empty table and Melanie heads straight over. "Morning Megan, Harry," she nods and smiles and I can feel her eyes looking at me slightly longer than feels comfortable with Megan sitting right beside me.

"Hi Mel. How are you?" Megan returns the smile.

Melanie is about forty. She is slim with shoulder length hair and hazel eyes, and

2

it is quite obvious to even the least perceptive of us that she has a definite soft spot for me. And yet I can tell from the look in Megan's eyes that she is genuinely fond of Mel. Not an ounce of jealousy. Not one morsel. Even when Mel reaches down and runs her hand through my jet-black coat, Megan doesn't blink an eye.

"And how's my favourite boy today?" Mel asks, running her fingers along my spine, working up to my neck, making me shudder.

If I could answer her I'd probably say something like 'I'm good, but this is a little embarrassing.' But all I can do is gaze into her eyes. An involuntary wag of the tail wasn't something I'd planned, it just happens every now and then.

Megan orders a cup of coffee and Mel scurries away.

There are seven people at our gathering this morning, including myself and Megan. Helen Pierce is seated at her usual table by the wall, accompanied by Dawn Brown, Yolanda something-or-other – I can never remember her second name but it sounds foreign – and the new face. The new face is a man, which is very unusual as men generally try to avoid coming to these little meetings. Judging by the way these women are always fawning over me I can't understand why. Surely everybody needs a little attention now and then? The man appears to be a few years older than Megan, his face isn't too wrinkled, but his hair is missing in the middle, and it looks very weird having strips of grey covering the sides of his head. Nobody else appears to find it strange. Dorothy Barnstaple and Leah Derby are seated at a smaller table. I think they do this to avoid having to sit with Helen, who can be quite loud at times. They're slightly older than the rest of the group, so it's possible they are made to sit there because of their advanced years. I only mention this because Jasper, Dorothy Barnstaple's Poodle, was made to sit outside the tea room, and he was very old. Perhaps they'll make Dorothy and Leah sit outside in a few years time.

Mel comes back with a cup of coffee and a small bowl of water that she places on the floor beside me. She sneaks a quick stroke of my head and I glance at Megan to see if her face registers any disapproval. But there is nothing.

"This is Daniel," Helen announces.

Daniel stands and takes the two steps to where Megan is sitting. "Very pleased to meet you," he says, reaching out a hand.

"Megan, Megan Finch," Megan says, half standing as she takes his hand. "And this is Harry," she adds proudly.

He barely glances at me. I try not to let the fact cloud my judgement. Bald twat. I also pick up on the look he gives Megan. I have seen that look on a lot of faces - mostly men – upon meeting Megan for the first time.

"Harry and Megan!!" he says, a wide grin appearing on his face.

Megan strokes my head. "Yes, you're not the first to comment on it. My ex-husband's idea, he handed me this little bundle of fur and I picked him up and called him my little prince. Greg immediately came up with the bright idea of calling him Harry."

I've heard people comment on this a hundred times before. Apparently there's an English prince called Harry who married an American actress. From what I can gather they fell out of favour with the royal family and got sent to live in another country. The fact that everyone immediately associates myself and Megan with

4

these undesirables is a cross we both have to bear. I can't understand why, whenever I've seen them on the television they always seems very nice.

How long have you lived in the village?" Baldy continues, hovering over our table.

"Fifteen years."

"You must have been very young when you moved here," he says with a wide, toothy smile.

Oh, really! Pass me a bowl.

Megan laughs. "Not that young," she says, and sips her coffee.

I'm watching her closely now. It's been almost eighteen months since Greg walked out on us. Usually I don't refer to him by his real name, I've got a few other names I like to call him. I'm not given to violence, but I would happily sink my teeth into any part of him given half the chance. There is one part I would love to bite clean off. I shouldn't really hate him as much as I do, after all it was him who brought me into their lives. He walked out on us less than two months later. I presume he thought if he was leaving his wife for a younger model it was only fair to leave her something to keep her company. I suppose it's better than the parting gift Rita Blackman's husband gave her when he walked out on her and their two children: apparently he left her a dose of 'the clap' whatever that is, but it didn't sound very nice when I heard her explaining it to Doctor Roberts when I was sitting in the waiting room with Megan at the surgery some months ago.

Baldy finally relents and returns to his table.

"We were just talking about this spate of dog napping," Helen pierce says.

5

"Have you heard the latest?"

Megan shakes her head. "No."

"Two dogs in the next village disappeared three nights ago."

Everyone in the room tuts and shakes their heads. Megan reaches down protectively and tickles the top of my head with the tips of her fingers. My ears have pricked up at this latest piece of information. Usually I sit here day-dreaming while they talk about the weather or how long the grass has gotten on the village green, or something equally mundane. But this is serious news. Dogs being snatched from their owners has been big news for ages, but when it's this close to home...

"It's absolutely outrageous." Dorothy Barnstaple says. Dorothy has a plume of silver hair that she has tinted every Thursday without fail. Her voice sounds slightly different to the others. I've heard people talk like it on the television, mainly in period dramas. "If they catch them they should hang them up by their plums," Dorothy continues, "too many bloody liberals these days with their namby pamby views."

A ripple of laughter fills the room, and I gaze up at Megan hoping she will explain what they're all laughing at. But she is covering her mouth, presumably to stifle a laugh. Megan does this a lot. She has a laugh that can only be described as a cross between the sound of a machine gun and super-fast hiccups. I have rarely seen her expose this to anyone outside the confines of our house.

"You may well laugh," Dorothy continues, "but we are too bloody soft these days. They should bring back national service. That would sort them out."

I haven't got a clue what national service is, or was, but most of the room nod their heads in agreement.

The bell tinkles on the door of the shop and we all turn to see who is entering.

"Morning George," Mel calls out from behind the counter.

George Clarke is ancient. He's a thick set man who walks with a stick. He has a rugged face that always looks like he's angry at something, or someone. But George is one of the kindest people in the village. He certainly always takes time out to chat to me when he's out walking Winston, his beloved Spaniel. This morning George has a sad expression on his face; a look that doesn't appear to belong there.

"I can't find Winston," he says, his jaw locked in grim determination. But his eyes are glistening with the tears he's fighting to hold back.

Following the revelation about Winston everyone agrees to search the village and surrounding area. So now, myself, Megan and the man, Daniel, are walking up the narrow strip of tarmac that serves as a footpath up the hill out of the village. I don't know how he managed to attach himself to us, but I'm not happy. For a start he walks far too slowly, and far too close to Megan. He is walking on her left, closest to the road, which means I'm pressed up against the verge with its overhanging bushes and brambles. Normally this wouldn't bother me, but it was raining this morning and I keep getting slapped in the face by the sodden foliage.

"So what is it you do for a living Megan?" Daniel asks.

His words come in short bursts. A tell-tale sign that the climb up the steep hill is taking a toll. This fact makes me happy as he might decide to turn back, but instead he persists.

"If you don't mind me asking?"

"I'm a partner in a firm of solicitors, although I only count myself as temporary these days. I go into the office three days a week. Monday's and Friday's I work from home. How about you?"

"I was an accountant for a large oil company. I took early retirement last year. Sold my house in Croydon after my wife died..." he lets the words linger, obviously awaiting the sympathy that will follow.

"Oh, I'm sorry," Megan obliges.

Daniel waves a hand. "No, it's fine, really, I'm fine, now. We had almost twenty-five wonderful years together."

He sounds genuine, and for the first time I feel like cutting him a bit of slack.

We're about half way up the hill now. To our right, green fields lay silent beneath a cloudy September sky. About a quarter of a mile ahead at the top of the hill, stands the church, its faded sandstone blocks appear a strange shade of yellowy green as the weak autumnal sun filters through the branches of the tall Sweet Chestnut trees that form the boundary to the graveyard. Even from this distance I can see the spire reaching towards the heavens. I gather someone called God lives there. I've never seen him but he must be important because I've heard Megan shout his name quite a few times. Once - before Greg walked out on us, before I was allowed upstairs to the bedroom - I heard Megan shouting 'God' quite loudly. I've also heard her cry his name when she stubbed her toe, but as I say, I've never seen him.

8

Finally we reach the top of the hill.

"If we cut down past the cemetery there's a narrow footpath that leads back down to the village through the fields. If Winston's anywhere around Harry will find him. Won't you boy?" Megan says, unclipping my lead as we head away from the road.

I give her a look that says 'yes, of course I will'. But I am not at all sure about leaving her behind with this stranger. After all, we barely know him. Instead I stay a few paces ahead rather than run off in front as would normally happen. I can smell Winston's scent as I walk, but it's not fresh, more like a day or two old. A few of the other dogs from the village have passed this way this morning - along with their owners, and there is another strong odour that I don't recognise. A man. No, two men. Strangers, a scent that is quite unfamiliar to me. I never forget a smell.

"Go on Harry, search him out. Find Winston for us," Megan calls encouragingly.

I have reached a wooden style at the bottom of the narrow, muddy footpath that runs alongside the cemetery. The scent of the two men is strong here, and there are cigarette butts on the ground. I stop and circle the ground sniffing at every blade of grass. There's no hint of Winston, but I'll remember this smell if I come across it again. It's an odour I haven't encountered before: so strong that it catches at the back of my throat. I can only compare it to something Megan sprays on herself from a little bottle: Yet strangely different.

It takes almost half-an-hour to get back to the village. The man Daniel is trying to wipe mud off his shoes on the long grass verge. He's mumbling something to himself but he's fallen a little behind me and Megan, so even with my acute hearing I can't quite make out what he's saying. I feel a slightly wicked, comforting glow at his naivety: I mean, who wears city shoes to walk round fields in late September?

George is sitting on one of the benches that span two sides of the old pump-house. He looks lost. His features are set in grim determination, as if he's fighting against all his most natural emotions. It makes me feel sad just looking at him and I feel a strong urge to go over and rub up against his leg just to let him know he's not alone. Megan must feel the same because she heads briskly across the village green towards him. Daniel has caught up by now and appears to have attached himself to Megan's side.

"No luck I'm afraid," Megan says taking a seat on the bench next to George.

I snuggle up to his legs and he looks down at me. He has tears in his eyes, but the look on his face tells me that he's not about to let himself cry without putting up one hell of a fight.

George shakes his head slowly and says, "Thank you for looking anyway."

"Have you been back home?" Megan asks. "Just to make sure Winston hasn't made his way back on his own."

"Jill has been in and out all day," he says grimly.

Jill is George's daughter. I like Jill. She always make a fuss of me whenever we bump into each other. She carries little treats in her pockets too, which is always a nice bonus.

"Where did he disappear from?" Daniel asks.

10

George glances up at the stranger without raising his head. "Took him out across the fields this morning with the four-ten. I clipped a couple of rabbits up by the Beller farm and Winston raced off to get one of the buggers. Haven't seen him since."

I can tell from the look on Daniel's face he is struggling to comprehend what he's just been told.

"A four-ten is a gun," Megan informs him, noting his vacant expression.

Daniel nods as if he already understood . "Wasn't on a lead then?" he asks bluntly, and both myself and Megan glare at him.

"Can't keep gun-dogs on a lead," George retorts. There's a bitterness to his voice.

"No of course you can't George." Megan pats him gently on the arm. "I'm sure that's not what Daniel meant."

"No, no of course not."

Wicked I know, but I get a moment of pleasure seeing Daniel squirm. Humans are generally easy to work out their nature. Some of them a little harder than others perhaps, but people like Daniel don't take long to show their true colours. It's not that the Daniel's of this world are necessarily bad, but they are always looking to further their own interests. In Daniel's case I'm pretty sure his interest lies solely in Megan, and the fact that he has just let his mask slip, if just a fraction, only proves that I'm right and it won't take long for her to see him for what he really is.

Within a few minutes the rest of the 'search party', such as it is, has returned and are making their way slowly across the green to join us at the pump-house.

11

George looks up, more in hope than expectation. "No luck then," he says grimly.

"No, sorry," the group say almost as one. They all look sad, and a couple of them look genuinely exhausted from their impromptu exertions.

"We will find him," Megan says, and places her arm round his shoulder. "I'll go out again this afternoon with Harry and take a walk past Beller farm and into the forest. But I'm sure he'll be home before then," she adds quickly.

George looks as if he wants to say thank you, but is too scared to open his mouth in case he can't get the words out.

Dorothy Barnstaple and Yolanda sit themselves down on the bench. Dorothy snuggles up beside George and takes hold of his hand, Yolanda sits beside Megan, which is a bit of a squeeze as Yolanda still hasn't lost the extra pounds she put on last Christmas, even though I have heard her promise to do so on numerous occasions. To be fair, and without being too unkind, Yolanda could probably do with losing a bit more than a few pounds. But she has a lovely, round, almost oriental face and a beautiful smile.

"We are all here for you." Dorothy says, gently patting George's hand. "And as Megan says, we will find Winston, even if we have to search all night."

Whether or not George finds any of their kind words reassuring is hard to tell, but right at this moment – to me anyway – he just looks like someone who has lost the one thing that makes his life worth living.

CHAPTER 2

We're back home in less than two minutes. Our two bedroom cottage sits at the end of a short gravel lane that leads directly off of the main road, just across from the village green. In the winter the lane is full of deep pot holes that fill far too quickly with icy water. Our cottage is the last in a terrace of three, which affords us uninterrupted views across a valley of green fields to the west. At night, when the sun is sinking behind the tree-lined ridge three miles away, the colours are a cacophony of gold and yellow and orange: It truly is a sight to behold.

The row of brick cottages were built in 1903, and there's even a small plaque above our door to remind us of the fact. Above and around our front door there's a climbing rose that produces the most wonderful pink flowers twice a year. Megan is constantly moaning about the thorns tearing her clothes, but overall I think she would rather it was there than not.

The rooms inside our home are quite small, with low, oak-beamed ceilings and roughly plastered walls painted in subtle shades of grey and cream. Upstairs there are two bedrooms and a bathroom. Downstairs there's small front room with an open fire. I both hate and love our fire. In the winter it is nice to lay in front of it and feel the heat and listen to the sound of the logs crackling, but every now and then it spits out bits of fiery ash; I've had my fur singed on more than one occasion. The kitchen is at the side of the house, facing west over the fields. There's a large window over the sink and a solid oak door leading out into our little patch of garden. Last year Megan got a carpenter from the village to cut a small opening into the bottom half of the door: she calls it a 'doggy flap', which is very handy for me because when she's at work I can go in and out as I please. There's just about enough room in the kitchen for a small table and four chairs, and I have a large rug on the floor as this is the room where we spend most of our time. The house is also full of clutter. Personally I can't see why you need four-hundred little candles scattered around the place, or little sticks in vases that stink of various scents, but Megan seems happy to be surrounded with all this bric-a-brac, and if Megan is happy, I'm happy.

Megan boils the kettle, places my food on the floor in my special silver-coloured bowl, and prepares herself a sandwich. We have barely finished lunch when there is a knock at the door.

I don't look up from my bowl, I know who's there.

Stacy Sullivan has a very distinctive aroma. I love Stacy, which is just as well because although she's about ten years younger than Megan, and her skin is a different colour, they are best friends. Stacy is also divorced from her husband, Joe, and from what I can gather from their conversations he didn't leave Stacy for another woman, but a man. Apparently Joe and his new husband are currently engaged in a legal battle with Stacy for custody of their fourteen-year-old son, Liam. From what I can gather, Joe feels that as Stacy got custody of Poppy, their bull terrier, it was only fair that he gets custody of their son.

"I've just heard about Winston," Stacy says, stepping into the room.

I'm trying to rush the last bit of my lunch because I know what's coming. Poppy comes bounding into the kitchen behind her mistress, rushes straight over to my bowl and begins helping herself. Normally this is not something I would stand for, but for Poppy I tend to make an exception.

14

"I know, it's terrible," Megan says, filling the kettle. "Hopefully he'll turn up soon. I'm taking Harry over the fields by the Beller farm this afternoon. That's where George was when Winston disappeared."

Stacy takes a seat at the table. "What time?"

"Probably about two-ish."

Stacy glances at her phone. "If you can make it two-thirty I'll join you. I've got Mo Jones booked in at one-thirty, so I should be done in an hour."

Stacy is a hairdresser. I think most of the women in the village and surrounding areas use her because she usually comes to their houses rather than them having to go out. It obviously works because she's always very busy.

Megan places two steaming mugs of coffee on the table and sits down. "Yeah that should be fine. I've got some papers to catch up on anyway, so that should work out perfectly."

I let Poppy finish the remnants of my bowl and she thanks me by jumping up and resting her paws on my back. I have learned the hard way that although it's fine for Poppy to do this to me, if I reciprocate, both Megan and Stacy start screaming and hollering at me and Megan drags me off by the collar. I'm not sure if they realise there's only so much flirting I can take. Sometimes life seems very unfair.

"So," Stacy says, sipping gingerly at her tea. "I gather this new bloke was at the tea rooms this morning. What's he like?"

"Daniel, yeah he seems quite nice."

"Quite nice, or quite nice?" Stacy manages to make the two words sound

15

completely different each time she says them.

"He's retired. Widowed. Probably mid fifties, maybe a little older. Quite good-looking, although he's pretty much bald."

Stacy giggles. "You know what they say about bald men though?"

"They don't need a hairdresser." Megan says, and laughs.

"No seriously though," Stacy persists, "ten years older, not that much difference, and if he's already retired that probably means he's minted."

"Well feel free to have a go yourself as he sounds like such a catch," Megan says, smiling broadly.

"Me!" Stacey's eyes explode wide, like a startled owl. "With a geriatric! You must be joking."

"Oh but it's fine for an old bird like me?"

They both begin laughing quite loudly and I let Poppy follow me out to the garden to play for a while.

CHAPTER 3

By two-fifteen Megan has finished her paperwork. I'm still not sure why she calls it that because there is no paper involved, instead she taps away at a little black plastic thing that is never far from her side. I believe it's called an i-pad, and Megan tends to spend a lot of her day looking at it.

By the time we leave the house the sky has clouded over and there are few spits of rain in the air. It's getting colder too, which I'm happy about because the summers can get quite uncomfortable when you can't take off your coat.

We head up past the pub, up the hill past the surgery and school towards the little estate tucked away from the village centre. At the top of the hill there's a little narrow track that cuts along the other side of the hedgerow and leads along the top field before heading down again, thus avoiding the noisy children from the estate. It's a lovely walk in the summer, but when it's raining the ground gets very wet and muddy very quickly. I'm fine, but I think Megan finds it a bit of a struggle.

Stacy is already waiting at the wooden gate by the time we arrive. She's wearing a long green coat, green wellington boots and a big floppy black hat. I can't help thinking she looks a bit like one of the scarecrows old Tom Harris places in his fields to keep the birds away. Stacy lives on the estate, so it's only a two minute walk for her to get here. Poppy comes bounding over, her little tail wagging enthusiastically.

"I brought a brolly, just in case," Stacy says, waving a bright pink thing in the air.

"Me too." And Megan produces her own small, fat stick that she keeps tucked in the inside pocket of her coat. This thing still amazes me, it looks tiny and yet whenever Megan needs it she just tugs a couple of times and this great big canvas shelter opens up above her head. Personally I've never had a problem with rain, in fact sometimes it can be quite refreshing.

Megan unclips my lead. "Go on then Harry, see if you can find Winston for us."

There's a lot different scents hanging around on the ground, but no sign of Winston having been here recently, so I scamper on ahead, closely followed by Poppy. The ground is a well worn narrow strip of mud that runs close to the hedge.

To our left, the fields are a murky shade of green, and the other side of the hedge is the road that leads east, away from the village.

I follow the track, sniffing eagerly at the grass and bushes. Poppy has run off after a rabbit – which she has absolutely no chance of catching – and Megan and Stacy have fallen a little way behind. I can hear them chatting and laughing in the distance. As I reach the top of the hill where two tracks meet, I get my first fresh scent of Winston. The smell is strong enough that I know he was here today. I would imagine George must have walked up from the south of the village this morning, but what makes no sense at all is Winston's scent would take us down through the forest.

I bark a couple of times and wait patiently for Megan and Stacy to catch up.

"What have you found," Megan asks, breathing heavily.

I wag my tail and start to walk towards the woods.

Stacy is craning her neck, scouring the fields for any sign of Poppy. "Poppy," she calls out. "Poppy, come on girl. Where the hell has she got to?"

I'm torn between waiting for Poppy to turn up. and following the trail that seems quite strong at the moment, but if the rain gets too heavy it can wash a lot of the scent away quite quickly. I start walking into the forest, hoping Megan will follow.

"Where the hell has she got to?" There is just a hint of anxiety in Stacy's voice.

"She can't have gone far," Megan says. "Harry, come here boy." She slaps her thigh and reluctantly I start ambling back towards them. "Find Poppy boy."

Bloody hell. Which trail do you want me to follow? I know Poppy won't have gone too far and I'm reluctant to chase after her and lose Winston's scent. It is starting to rain increasingly harder and the sky has got quite dark. And just as I'm standing there pondering the situation, a little brown shape appears at the top of the field, hurtling towards us at a rate of knots.

Panic over, we set off into the forest.

The forest is huge: fourteen square miles of tall pine trees that line the hillsides around the reservoir. Cut throughout the forest are wide, treeless avenues called fire-breaks which are meant to stop fires spreading in the summer months. The twenty-feet wide clearings criss-cross through the entire forest affording a half decent walkway. On afternoons such as this, there is a lot more light too, because amongst the trees it looks quite dark right now.

Head down, nose pressed to the ground, I forge ahead trying to ignore Poppy who keeps running up and nudging me. I know she wants to play but I've got a job to do, and as the rain is getting increasingly harder I really don't want to risk losing the scent. I follow along the tree line, stopping whenever the smell is strongest.

As we reach the foot of the hill, where two fire-breaks cross, I pick up a fresh scent. I recognise the smell immediately, from the style this morning, only this time there is only one man. I stop and bark and wait for Megan and Stacy to catch up. As soon as they reach me I set off to the left, following the trail that circumnavigates the reservoir just a hundred yards down the hill. Through the trees it's just possible to see the water shimmering from the onslaught of heavy rain. There are a couple of row boats on the lake this afternoon, and I can hear the swish of rods. Greg brought me up here once and we spent all day standing by the water's edge. He kept thrashing about with his fishing rod, but didn't catch a thing.

Not that I minded, I was just happy to be there with him. The thought stings. How could he just walk out on us like that? Just as I'm starting to feel sad, a noise somewhere deep in the trees grabs my attention. I stop, prick my ears and listen.

"What is it Harry?" Megan is at my side, kneeling down to wipe some of the water off my coat.

Poppy must of heard it too because she rushes up beside us, a low grumbling sound coming from the depths of her throat. Her head is twitching from side to side, eyes darting about like a moth round a flame.

"Have they heard something?" Stacy asks, a tinge of nervousness in her voice. She gazes round, slowly. "Christ, I didn't realise how dark it was getting."

She has her brolly up and the sound of rain battering against the thin material is relentless.

I try and follow Poppy's gaze, but it's almost completely black within the trees, making it impossible to see if there is anyone there. Instead I ignore the sound of battering rain and focus all my attention towards where I heard the crackle of twigs. It could be a deer, there are plenty of them here, but usually they won't hang around if there are dogs about.

"Perhaps we should start heading back." Megan says.

I can tell she doesn't feel comfortable, but I don't see why, I would never let anything happen to her. I'd sooner die. And just as I'm standing there feeling all brave and protective a really strong odour suddenly hits me. Now I'm torn between following this pungent, fresh scent, and staying close to Megan. The scent wins, after all I can soon make it back if needed.

"Harry," Megan calls after me as I start walking away briskly, sniffing at the ground. "Harry!! Come back here."

But it's too late, I am now standing by a clump of thick gorse bushes that run alongside a narrow ditch at the edge of the fire-break. There's a wooden stake in the ground, with a thin, silver coloured wire attached to it. The overpowering stench of Winston and blood rises up from the ground. But there's another really powerful odour, a smell that's hung in the air for the last half-an-hour. At least one of the men who stood at the style smoking cigarettes before we got there this morning, was here later in the day. I would guess less than an hour ago because the aroma is very strong even after all the rain.

I start barking, and turn to face Megan who is walking towards me looking rather too angry for my liking.

"Come here now," she says, producing my lead from her pocket.

I wait for the snap of the metal clip, but as she leans over me, Megan stops, straightens and clasps a hand to her mouth.

Poppy scurries up and starts snuffling at the wire glinting in the bushes. Megan grabs her collar and eases her away.

"What is it?" Stacy asks upon reaching us.

"A snare." Megan spits the words out like she's just tasted something nasty.

"A snare! You mean..." Stacy leans down for a better look.

"That's exactly what I mean," Megan says, as if she knows what Stacy is about to say. "There's some fur here too."

Megan stretches out an arm, reaches into the gorse and grabs a small clump of

21

light-brown fur. Winston is chocolate brown with dashes of white. The fur Megan

is holding is a perfect match. Of course I already knew it must belong to Winston,

his scent here is overpowering. Megan holds the matted clump of hairs up in front

of her, twisting them between her fingers.

"Is that...is that blood?" Stacy asks, leaning in close to inspect Megan's

discovery.

"Yes, I think so."

"Oh, that's sick."

Megan stands up and climbs beneath the cover of Stacy's brolly. They huddle

close together, studying their find.

Poppy has jumped the narrow ditch and is sifting through the gorse. I can hear

her nose working overtime across the ground. Then, above the sound of the rain

spattering Stacy's brolly and Poppy shuffling amongst the gorse, I hear the sound

of a twig snapping somewhere in the darkness of the trees, not all that far from

where we are standing. Poppy hears it too because she stops, pricks her ears and

stares at where the sound came from. Then together we both start growling.

"Quiet," Megan commands. She squats down and grabs hold of the wooden

stake with the wire still hanging from it. She pushes and pulls, but the stake is

driven too far into the ground for her to be able to shift it.

"I can't move the fucking thing," Megan says through gritted teeth. "We can't

just leave it here." She gives it another tug and her hand slips. The razor- sharp

wire cuts into her finger. "Shit!" She jumps to her feet clasping her hand.

I hope the rain is making it look worse than it is because there seems to be a lot of blood dripping onto the ground. Poppy has jumped back across the ditch and planted herself firmly beside Stacy. Her hackles are up and her eyes are fixed on a single spot within the shadows of the trees. I can't see any movement, but I can sense something, or someone out there, lurking in the darkness.

"You okay? Let's have a look." Stacy takes Megan's hand and inspects the cut. "I think it looks worse than it is." She reaches inside her coat and produces a small square of tissue paper. "Here, hold that round it. We'll look at it when we get home."

"I'm not leaving that there," Megan says, and kicks out at the stake. It moves ever so slightly, so she kicks it again. Several kicks later Megan has managed to loosen the earth around the wooden peg.

"I think we really should get going." Stacy persists.

And then I see it, the dark silhouette of a man moving between the trees about fifty yards from where we are standing. This time I don't wait for Poppy, I just start barking furiously, hackles raised, fully prepared to protect us if anyone should come running from the shadows.

"Harry." Megan shouts, just as the stake breaks free from the ground.

"I think there's someone out there," Stacy says, pointing vaguely towards the spot both myself and Poppy are barking at angrily.

Megan rises to her feet holding triumphantly onto the muddy wooden stake, the thin strand of razor-sharp wire swinging in the breeze. "Okay," she says, "let's get out of here."

But before we can move I hear the sound of twigs snapping beneath heavy feet

23

heading straight towards us. Moving fast. All my instincts are screaming 'danger'. I have no intention of waiting until the assailant reaches Megan, so I leap straight over the ditch - closely followed by Poppy – and race through the dark shadows fully prepared to attack whatever is coming for us.

We zigzag between the trees barking and snarling for all we are worth. It's so dark though, and the strong wind is making the trees sway to the point where it feels the branches are reaching out for us. Whoever we're chasing is moving fast, heading down the steep hill towards the reservoir. In the distance I can hear Megan screaming my name at the top of her voice. I'm torn now, between continuing the chase and returning to Megan. Poppy is at my side, panting heavily. She pricks her ears at the sound of Stacy's loud whistle. We exchange a knowing glance and head back from where we came, satisfied we have seen off the intruder.

CHAPTER 5

Stacy lives on the new estate tucked just outside the village. The houses are like little brick boxes; they all look identical apart from different coloured front doors and little patches of garden. Stacy's house is clean and tidy but sparsely furnished. Joe didn't leave her with much money when he left so she only buys whatever furnishings she really needs.

We are all soaked through to the skin by the time we get there. I shake off as much water as I can, but this doesn't deter Megan from wiping me over with a dirty towel before I'm allowed to enter the house.

Stacy washes Megan's hand in the sink and produces a roll of bandage from one of the drawers. They both seem satisfied the cut isn't serious so Stacy makes tea for her and Megan and they both take a seat at a small, white Formica table in the kitchen. I lay on the floor beside Poppy, who has finally stopped pestering me to play.

"That definitely looks like it comes from Winston," Megan says, as she places the wooden stake with it's lethal wire and bit of matted fur on a sheet of newspaper on the table.

Stacy is rubbing her hair with a pink towel. "Yes, I know," she says sadly. "So what do we do now?"

"Call the police?"

"I don't think that'll do any good Meg', they aren't going to be interested."

"Well it's worth a try." Megan runs her finger cautiously along the wire. "I mean, look at it. Who the hell could use something like that? And if that is poor Winston's fur, then where is he?"

"Maybe it's worth talking to Tony."

Tony Skinner is what I believe they used to call, the local bobby. He's a police sergeant with a patrol car and a very large area to patrol: Most of his time is spent dealing with petty crime and minor infractions of the law. He's a tall man, with kind blue eyes and a very neat beard. I have heard Megan talk to Stacy about him on several occasions - usually when they are drinking wine in the evenings – and Stacy always seems to get very animated whenever his name comes up. One night I heard her tell Megan she wouldn't mind seeing what his truncheon looks like. I'm

25

sure if she asked him he'd show her.

"Of course, why didn't I think of that," Megan says, and laughs.

Neither me or Poppy get the joke.

"I suppose it's better if I leave this here with you then?" Megan taps the wire on the table.

"Oh shut up. We can hardly call 999, can we?"

"If you say so." Megan has a huge smile on her face.

"You call him then," Stacy says, and there seems to be a hint of annoyance in her tone.

"Oh don't be so touchy Stace'. I'll leave it with you and you can call the nice policeman and he'll come round and take down your particulars." But this time when Megan laughs she catches her hand on the edge of the table. "Shit!"

"Serves you right."

And for some peculiar reason they both start laughing out loud.

We walk home in the cold and dark. Megan lights the fire and has a bath and I lay in front of the fire trying to dry out.

By six-thirty we've had dinner. Megan is catching up with some work at the kitchen table and I'm in my basket when the door-bell rings. I bark twice, just to let any strangers know I'm here, and hurtle across the wooden floor to take up my usual position.

"Okay Harry," Megan says calmly, "Sit."

I do as I'm told, but I'm fully prepared for a defensive manoeuvre if called for.

Tony Skinner is standing on the doorstep trying to side-step drops of rain falling from the broken gutter above the front porch. He's wearing his uniform and a rather serious expression.

"Tony," Megan says, pulling the door wide. "Or is it Sergeant Skinner tonight?" she adds and smiles.

"Evening Megan. Sorry to come round unannounced. Have you got a minute?"

Megan takes him through to the kitchen and makes tea. Tony ruffles me under the chin on his way past, stooping as he walks to avoid catching his head on the ceiling beams. "How are you boy?"

I wag my tail by way of response. People seem to like it when I do that.

"I take it Stacy called you then?" Megan asks, filling the kettle.

"Yes, I've just come from there. I've got the snare in the car."

Megan finishes making the tea and joins the sergeant at the table. "You're taking it seriously then?"

"We always take poaching seriously." He takes a sip from his mug. "Problem is, there's very little chance of catching the buggers. But the least I can do is get the fur checked out to see if it belongs to the missing dog."

"Winston?"

"Yes, Winston. I'm sure you don't need me to tell you, but I'd be extra vigilant when you're out walking Harry at the moment. Obviously if there are poachers setting snares all over the place, that's bad enough, but with this spate of dogs disappearing from the area...Just be extra cautious, and if you do see anyone, that looks out of place as it were, don't hesitate to give me a call."

27

Megan nods her head slowly. I'm sitting beside her and she reaches down to stroke me. I'm not sure if this is to reassure me or comfort herself. "Some people," she says and shakes her head slowly.

"It's the countryside I'm afraid. It's always gone on and it probably always will. I've got a couple of names to check out; the usual suspects etcetera, and I'll certainly let them know we're watching. You might want to try and avoid that area for a while, at least until I've had a chance to have a chat with a couple of people."

"So what do you think they did with Winston then?" Megan sounds both worried and sad.

Tony shakes his head. "I really couldn't say. No animal survives for long in one of those things. They probably panicked and dumped the body somewhere. If they have any sort of conscience they might have buried him. I don't suppose we're ever likely to know. Sorry to put it so bluntly."

The thought makes me shudder. Poor Winston, trapped in that awful contraption, struggling for his life.

"Oh God, poor George."

"I'll pop by and see him tonight. I'm not going to tell him what I've just told you because that's just supposition. As soon as I can get someone to confirm what animal the hairs in the snare came from...well, I'll have to deal with that at the time."

"I have to go into the office tomorrow, but I'll pop in and check on him when I get home." Megan says. "I'm sure we'll all rally round as best we can." She glances down at me. "I'm not sure any of us will be a lot of comfort though.

Winston was all George had." And as she gently strokes me I can feel the sadness seeping out of her.

Tony stays for about twenty-minutes. As Megan's walking him to the door she says, "Oh, I forgot to ask, how's Stacy?"

I'm looking at her and she has a sort of twinkly smile as if she's just said something she might not have ought to.

"Err, yes, she's fine," the sergeant replies, and for some reason his cheeks start to turn a mild shade of red. "Why?"

"Just asking," Megan says, and gives him a huge smile.

CHAPTER 6

Nothing much happens the next day. I hate it when Megan has to go into the office. Normally I would take myself off for a walk around the fields, but for some reason I just don't feel like it. The weather is depressingly sombre, the sky is full of morbid grey clouds emitting a relentless drizzle, but also, if I'm honest, it's probably because I can't get the thought of Winston dying like that out of my head. I kept waking up in the night with terrible visions of him laying all alone on that cold, wet ground, struggling against the wire round his neck until there was no breath left in his lungs. Poor Winston. Instead I spend most of the day laying in my bed waiting for the sound of Megan's car coming up the gravel drive.

Megan is late getting home. I later learn from a brief telephone conversation she has with Dorothy Barnstaple, that she popped in to see George on the way home. No thought of coming to pick me up first, which is rather annoying, but I'll forgive her of course.

We have dinner and Megan takes me for a short walk round the village. It's still raining so we're back in doors within half-an-hour. By nine-thirty Megan collapses into bed. What a crap day.

Annoyingly, Megan goes into the office again the next day. I can't stand the thought of being cooped up again, and the weather has turned brighter, so shortly after Megan leaves for work I take myself off for a stroll round the fields at the back of the house. Normally I skirt round the edge of the fields, keeping close to the hedgerows. Arty Miller - the farmer who owns the land - won't tolerate dogs off the lead, even if they're with their owners, but for some reason he makes an exception for me. Megan did have a very prolonged conversation with him when I was about ten-months old. I remember it well because he spent most of the time staring at Megan's chest rather than at her face. Arty Miller must be at least a hundred years old, and he smells so bad that I remember thinking that some of his limbs must have already died and he just wasn't aware of the fact. When he smiles – which is all the time when he's talking to Megan – he displays five very brown teeth; one either side on top, and two clinging on for dear life at the bottom. He's always very pleasant to me, although I can't stand the smell for long.

Following a well-worn track takes me along the top field at the back of the houses, close to the village. From there I head down into the valley. To my right there's a about twenty-seven acres of ancient woodland where somebody has created a pet cemetery. A couple of my friends from the village ended up there but I don't fancy it much, it's all a bit dark and isolated for my liking.

I'm about half way down the field when something catches my eye in the woods. I stop and wait, crouching on the ground to stay out of sight. The minute he steps out of the trees I recognize him. Michael Totter is not a nice man. He's short, with black greasy hair and bushy eyebrows that make his eyes appear far too close together. He has very dark eyes that I find quite scary. I'm not the only one, I've heard Megan talking to various women from the village and they all seem to be of the same opinion. I got under his feet one night as he was coming out of the pub and he gave me a crafty kick and mumbled something under his breath. Megan didn't see what happened or she would have given him a mouthful, and I didn't make a fuss because I didn't want her getting into an argument with such a nasty piece of work.

Keeping low, I shuffle into the longer, wet grass. From this position I can just about see him, slowly trudging up the edge of the field towards me. He's wearing a green camouflage jacket, black woolly hat and faded blue jeans that are plastered in mud at the knees. He's holding a short piece of string, at the end of which two dead rabbits are swinging. As he's not carrying a gun I can only assume he's caught them some other way. It wouldn't come as a shock if it were Michael setting snares. If it was Michael who set the snare that caught poor Winston it seems strange that I didn't pick up his scent, after all, it's strong enough.

Before he gets too close I scramble into the woods. I can smell him as he passes, the stench of death, stale beer and tobacco clinging to him like morning dew to grass.

I let him get a good distance in front of me before I start to follow. He keeps close to the edge of the woods until he reaches the footpath at the top of the field. Here, he stops and tucks the rabbits beneath his jacket before taking a narrow alleyway down between the houses. The alley leads into the heart of the village and I hang back a little further because there's no cover for me across the roads. It doesn't matter because there's no cover for him either, so even when he's a few hundred yards ahead of me I can still see him. He crosses the main road, past the pub and up the hill towards the estate. I know where he's going, or at least I think I do. Michael lives about ten houses from Stacy, in a small block of flats at the far end of the estate. Confident this is where he's heading I cut round the back of the doctor's surgery and past the gardens that back onto an apple orchard to the east of the village. For some reason people don't like seeing me wander around without Megan. Once, someone had the audacity to clip a lead on me and drag me to the village post office. The humiliation, standing outside, tied to a chain-link fence until Megan got back from work and finally came to rescue me. For some reason Megan was quite embarrassed about the whole episode and kept apologising to the young Asian couple who work there. I couldn't see the problem, and I did get a lot of attention that day, so it wasn't all bad.

I run along the top of the orchard, enter the back of the estate through a small gap in the hedge, and wait. Michael arrives ten minutes later. There's still a bulge in his jacket where the rabbits are secreted, so at least I know he hasn't sold them on somewhere. If he sees me he doesn't pay any attention. I'm laying in the grass and there are several cars parked in a small bay in front of the flats, blocking his view. He walks straight to his flat and disappears through the front doors. Now all I can do is wait.

An hour later I'm still waiting. Another hour passes and I'm getting hungry. I've toyed with the idea of going to fetch Poppy, but it would be just my luck if he goes out while I'm gone, and I can't risk that. Thankfully I only have to wait another fifteen minutes.

He finally appears, still wearing the same dirty clothes, a cigarette hanging from his mouth and a small cloth bag in his hand. But there's something else, a bulge beneath his jacket that looks very peculiar. Whatever it is makes him walk very awkwardly. He sets off, taking the narrow lane leading west towards the forest and reservoir. I can follow from the field above the road, staying well back, but still able to see my quarry.

At the top of the hill there's a large wooden gate leading into the fields. I watch him clamber over and land in a muddy puddle the other side. When he's finished wiping himself down and cursing, he opens his jacket and pulls out the gun. Lots of people have guns in our village. They look like great big sticks, but they spit fire, make a deafening bang and kill things. I have seen Michael out shooting rabbits on several occasions: His gun has two barrels that can fire almost simultaneously; the rabbits don't stand a chance. I believe his particular weapon is called a twelve bore, and it has a very distinctive sound. To be honest they scare the hell out of me. But now my mind is racing. He's probably just after rabbits, or maybe deer, but what if he's got Winston tied up somewhere and he's taking the

33

gun to finish him off? There's no need for me to follow closely, not many people come this way so following his fresh scent won't be a problem.

I give him a good five minutes before I set off after him.

I've been following him for about ten minutes when I hear people talking. They're still a fair way off, somewhere deep within the forest, but my hearing is excellent and I can easily pick out two or maybe three different voices, none of which I recognise. From what I can tell, they're young men: Older people – especially males – tend to have a rather rasping, gravelly quality. I assume it's just lads from the village messing about in the trees. I know some of the boys like to sneak in the back way to the reservoir to do a bit of fishing, which is highly illegal of course, but I understand it's almost impossible to patrol the entire area.

Michael's scent is leading me towards the voices. So now I'm torn between pursuing him, and heading into a situation which could become extremely dangerous, or giving up and going home. The reason I say it could be dangerous is because I heard about some boys from the next village who tied fireworks to a dog's tail and thought it was hilarious to watch her run round in circles as the fireworks exploded. That isn't something I want happening to me. But as I'm sitting there deliberating I suddenly hear a lot of shouting and screaming and the sound of an engine. The shouting stops almost at once, but the noise of the engine carries through the trees for at least another two minutes before finally fading in the distance.

I wait a good fifteen minutes before daring to follow Michael's trail. There are no sounds now, except for the wind ruffling leaves in the branches overhead.

34

Even the birds seem unusually quiet.

Cautiously, I crawl across the ground, ready to bolt at the first sign of danger. Michael's scent leads me down the hill, closer to the water's edge. About fifty yards from the bank there's a wide track that cuts between the trees leading all the way round the perimeter of the reservoir. I know the bailiff, Geoff, uses the track to patrol the area looking for poachers. I also know he does this using a funny looking vehicle called a dune buggy. I've seen him driving it, and it doesn't leave very deep ruts in the mud, even when it's wet. The tracks that I'm looking at now are very deep, and fresh and the smell of diesel still hangs in the air. I snuffle round on the ground but Michael's scent stops here. Moving round in an ever widening circle, nose to the ground, produces nothing. Michael has just vanished.

I spend another five minutes scouring the area, and just as I'm deliberating about whether or not to follow the the trail of the vehicle, the sound of a gunshot somewhere in the distance causes me to jump in the air. Not just any gunshot mind you. I would know the sound of Michael's twelve bore shotgun anywhere.

Call me a coward if you will, but I wasn't about to hang around to see what he was shooting at.

By the time Megan arrives home from work I'm settled in my basket. I don't think I've ever run so far, so fast, and I obviously didn't pay much attention to where I was running either because the moment I jump up to greet Megan she throws her arms in the air and exclaims, "Harry, what the hell have you been up to today?"

It's only at this point that I realise I'm caked in mud from head to toe. Not for the first time, I wish I could actually explain my day to her, but instead I just hang my head in shame and wait for the inevitable bath that will undoubtedly follow.

Luckily for me, just as I'm about to be hauled up the stairs to suffer the ultimate humiliation, the doorbell rings.

"Stay there," Megan says, wagging her finger at me.

I have no intention of disobeying her when she's in this mood, so I do as instructed, pricking my ears up so I can hear every word.

"Tony!" Megan says, having opened the door.

"Hello Megan. You were on my way so I thought I'd better pop round and give you an update."

"Have you got time for a cuppa?"

I'm not entirely sure why she even asks him because I can tell from the tone of her voice she really doesn't want him to say yes. I know exactly what she wants. The moment she closes that door she'll be dragging me upstairs.

"Sorry I can't stop. Like I said, I just wanted to bring you up to speed. Those hairs that were in the noose from the snare, they belong to a fox, not a dog."

This information can't be right. My nose never lets me down, and I definitely picked up Winston's scent from the snare. Whoever Tony has asked for advice on the matter is clearly wrong.

"So it wasn't Winston then?"

Yes it was, I want to scream.

"It seems not."

There's a very peculiar tone to his voice this evening. I really don't know exactly what's peculiar, but something is most certainly not right. My inquisitive nature prompts me to poke my head round the kitchen door. Tony catches a glimpse of me over Megan's shoulder and smiles.

Megan spins round before I can retreat. "Get back in your basket and stay there," she hollers.

I do as I'm told. Although I really don't appreciate being shouted at in front of other people. I toy with the idea of slipping out the back while she's not looking, but think better of it. I'm in enough trouble as it is without making matters worse.

Tony laughs. "In the doghouse is he?"

"Yes. Yes he is." Megan says bluntly. "But if Winston didn't get caught in the snare, what's happened to him?"

"Could just have wandered off and got lost, or..."

"You think somebody could have taken him?"

"I really couldn't say, Megan. Best not to speculate. If I hear anything I'll be sure to let everyone know. Anyway, I don't want to take up any more of your time and I really have got to shoot off. I'll be sure to keep you updated. Bye."

I would much rather he'd have stayed: Anything to prolong my impending doom.

The front door closes with a thud and Megan appears at the kitchen door with my towel hanging over her shoulder and a seriously grim expression on her face.

CHAPTER 7

As if having to suffer the ignominy of a bath wasn't bad enough, today I'm being dragged round to Yolanda's house. Megan was on the phone for ages last night asking several people if they could take me for the day as she has to go into the office again. Three days running!! That's almost unheard of lately. Obviously I can't be trusted to be left on my own at the moment. Anyway, it transpires that I'm obviously not as popular as I once was because Megan made quite a few phone calls before she spoke to Yolanda.

So here I am, all clean and smelling of something disgustingly sweet that Megan poured out of a pineapple shaped bottle, all over me when I was in the bath last night. Whatever it was caused a huge amount of foam that took her literally ages to rinse away. I assume this is - in part at least - the reason for her bad mood this morning.

Apparently Megan's in such a rush that we don't even have time for our normal walk; instead she takes me down the fields at the back of our house and we come out at the bottom of the village. I'm not even allowed off the lead.

Yolanda lives in a huge house on the other side of the main road. It's only twenty paces from the edge of the village green to her front door. The house sits about half way up the green, and it looks like whoever built it had been in the pub most of the day because there isn't a straight wall, door or window in the place. The exterior is painted brilliant white, and there are lots of black wooden beams that intersect at various angles. Above the front door there's a small plaque that reads, 1689.

Megan escorts me to a door round the side of the house: I've never seen anyone

38

enter through the front.

Yolanda must of seen us coming because she's already standing with the door open when we arrive. I'm poised, ready to leap into action if the cat comes flying out. Yes, the elusive cat. I've never seen it and there's not a hint of it ever having been in the house, but I know there must be one because Yolanda was round our house one night with a few other women. They were all drinking wine and laughing and one of them started talking about a builder that was working on her house. One of the women said, "Yes he's hot," and someone else said, "Yeah but he's a cat person." To which Yolanda said, "Well he can come round and play with my pussy whenever he wants," and they all burst into hysterical laughter.

The bloody thing can't hide forever. And when it shows it's face...

"You're a life-saver," Megan says.

"My pleasure. Hello Harry. How's my good boy today?" She squats down to give me a cuddle.

I glance at Megan, still very aware – that for today at least – she certainly doesn't agree.

"Well I hope he is, because you weren't such a 'good boy' yesterday were you? I came home to find the house covered in mud, and Harry! Well, let's just say it took me almost half an hour to scrub him clean in the bath last night. God knows what he'd been doing all day?"

"Have you been a bad boy?" Yolanda says, in a voice which most people generally reserve for babies and toddlers. She ruffles either side of my neck with both hands and comes in for a full blown kiss on the lips.

Megan strokes me, but I can't feel any love this morning. "Behave," she says, gently pulling my head towards her. "I really can't thank you enough, Yo-yo."

Lots of people call Yolanda this, but she doesn't seem to mind.

"Hopefully I won't be back late. Bye Harry, see you later."

I get a few seconds to watch Megan walk away, but as soon as she disappears round the front of the house Yolanda takes me inside and closes the door.

The interior is pristine. I have been here on several occasions in the past, but I've never been allowed up the stairs to the first floor because there are luxurious carpets, apparently. I'm not sure what harm they think I'll do to their precious carpets. It has crossed my mind that the cat probably hides upstairs whenever I'm around. Anyway, I have to stay downstairs where the floors are all solid oak, except for the kitchen which has grey tiles that heat comes up through. Amazing!

We're standing in a wide hallway just outside the kitchen. There are coats hanging from hooks and a stand for boots and shoes. There's also several paintings; two of which look remarkably like a very young Yolanda. In one of them she has a white scarf draped over her body, but in the other one she's completely naked. It must have been several years ago because she's very slim and her skin looks all creamy and fresh.

"So what are we going to do today?" Yolanda asks, as she strolls into the kitchen.

I hope we're going for a long walk at some point, but I won't be holding my breath. I have learned from various conversations I've overheard that Yolanda prefers to take her exercise on her back. Some form of Yoga I presume. As

40

Yolanda is still wearing her dressing gown, I assume any hope of a walk will have to wait.

She boils the kettle, puts some very nice biscuits in a bowl on the floor for me, picks up her phone and taps at the screen. A second later she's speaking. "Hi, it's me. Can you talk?"

I look up from my bowl, intrigued by the change in her voice. The tone is much softer, huskier, almost a whisper.

"Okay," she continues in the strange voice, "I'm looking after Harry for Megan today, so apart from nipping out for a quick walk I'll be here all day."

Quick walk!! Well, I suppose it's better than nothing.

"Yes, yes of course," she says and giggles quietly. "Okay, well I'll be back by eleven-thirty so any time after then will be fine. I'll leave the back door unlocked." She pauses and laughs. "Well make sure you don't overdo it then, I want you fighting fit." Another pause, longer this time. "No, of course I'm sure. Yes, he'll be in London all week. There's some huge merger taking place so he's staying at the flat in Knightsbridge. Okay, see you then. Bye."

Yolanda leaves me to finish my bowl of biscuits and virtually skips out of the kitchen and up the stairs.

Half-an-hour later she appears wearing a navy blue skirt and black woollen jumper.

I'm delighted to say the walk is far longer than I was expecting. We start at the bottom of the village and end up doing almost a complete circuit of the surrounding fields. As soon as I'm off the lead Yolanda produces a bright red ball from her coat pocket and proceeds to throw it for me to chase for the entire duration of our walk. By the time we get back to the house I'm absolutely shattered.

Yolanda opens a tin of food and puts it in a bowl on the floor for me.

"You be a good boy," she says, and disappears.

By the time she returns to the kitchen she has changed into her dressing gown, and I can tell from the fresh smell that she's had a shower.

She grabs a bottle from the fridge and two glasses from a cupboard. "You have a nice sleep," she says, reaching down to stroke me on her way out of the room. As she exits the kitchen she pulls the door closed behind her.

Much as I don't appreciate being stuck in one room, having finished dinner I'm quite tired and there's a lovely thick, fluffy rug on the floor that Yolanda gets out whenever I come round. So I settle down for a nap. Sleeping has been difficult these last couple of days. I keep having nightmares about Winston struggling to escape from that snare. In my dreams I am racing through the forest to save him, but the mud is too deep and I don't seem to be getting anywhere. No matter how hard I struggle, I just can't seem to reach him in time. I wake to the sound of my claws frantically scratching the floor tiles.

Rain is spattering against the kitchen window. I get up and stretch, gazing out of the window at the gloomy grey sky. Any hopes of a walk later this afternoon are fast disappearing: Yolanda doesn't like the rain. I'm just about to lay back down when I hear it; a very peculiar sound coming from upstairs. I go to the kitchen door and press my ear against the narrow crack. Moaning. No, more than that. It takes less than a second for me to realise what's going on: Yolanda is being attacked.

I scratch at the door, but the handle thing has snapped it shut. Taking a step back I can see it's similar to the ones at our house: A bronze coloured bar about four inches long that curls down at one end. One of the few things Greg did for me before he left us was to show me some tricks. One of them was how to open doors using my paws. Ooh, that rhymes.

I jump up, hook my claws over the handle and let my weight slowly bring it towards the floor. When it's half way down I lose grip, the handle snaps back into place and my front paws land on the tiles. I try it three more times before I hear a click and the door springs open. Just in time by the sound of it, Yolanda is screaming and shouting quite loudly now. No time to waste. I race up the stairs without making a sound, because this carpet really is very deep and soft, and tear towards the room where the attack is taking place. My heart is thumping so hard it feels as if it's about to explode out of my chest. I'm no hero, but I can't let this happen without putting up a fight. The door's wide open so I don't hesitate. I can see a man's naked arse, and he's got poor Yolanda pinned to the bed and he's jumping up and down on her. She's screaming and shouting, putting up the best fight she can. Her bare feet are in the air trying to kick him away.

I leap from the doorway, any thoughts for my own safety pushed to one side, and sink my teeth into his big hairy arse. It's not even a bite, just a nip really, hardly got any flesh at all, just a bit of skin. You would have thought I'd just bitten off his willy.

Now all hell let's loose.

43

"JESUS CHRIST!!" He springs to his feet and leaps from the bed clutching his rear and dancing round the room like the floor's on fire.

"Harry, NO!!" Yolanda shouts. "Naughty boy."

Naughty boy!! Naughty boy!! What the hell are you talking about? I've just rescued you from this monster.

"Fucking hell. God, there's blood," he screams and drops to his knees the other side of the bed so I can't even get a look at his face for future reference.

Yolanda jumps from the bed, completely naked. Lots of pink, wobbly flesh hurtling towards me. "Harry, get back downstairs. Now."

She looks so angry I think she's going to hit me, but her outstretched finger just points at the door.

As I skulk back down the stairs I can hear him whimpering. "Bloody hell, God that stings. How bad is it?"

"I'm so sorry," Yolanda's saying. "Here, let me have a look. Oh it's fine. I'll get some TCP."

That's the last part of the conversation I hear. Now I'm far more concerned about the heavy footsteps heading across the landing from the bedroom towards the stairs. The thought of that thunderous look of rage in her eyes is quite scary. So I head off to my rug in the kitchen hoping that by the time she reaches me she's calmed down. All I can do is lay here confused by the entire episode. And there's still no sign of that bloody cat.

44

CHAPTER 8

It appears that miracles do happen, because when Megan comes to pick me up there is no mention of what happened earlier in the day.

"Has he been good?" Megan asks.

I've already adopted the position; back legs slightly bent, head down, tail firmly between my legs and eyes turned slightly upwards trying to look as apologetic as possible.

"Yes, fine. No problem at all."

And even when Megan is walking me away from the house I'm half expecting Yolanda to shout after us having just remembered what took place.

But that doesn't happen, instead we walk up the edge of the narrow slip road at the side of the village green, and stop outside the village store. Megan clips my lead onto a metal hoop fixed to the wall and I wait outside, still feeling confused, but also very relieved that I appear to have gotten away with biting a human. Not all dogs are so lucky, even if it is a mistake. I know at least one who – having bitten a horrible teenage boy – was bundled into the back of a car and never seen again.

Megan comes out a minute later carrying a loaf of bread and carton of milk. She's talking to baldy Daniel, who was obviously already in the shop.

"Yes, a few of us pop in for a meal on a Friday evening," Megan's saying.

"Oh, right. Is the food nice, I haven't had the chance to try it out yet?"

"Yes, very nice."

"Just feels a bit awkward, being new to the area. Eating out on your own I mean."

Oh really! I can tell immediately what he's up to. Most Friday nights we go across to the pub for a meal. Well, I say 'we' go for a meal, I don't actually get to eat there, but everybody makes a big fuss of me and I get to sit at the foot of the table and listen to all the gossip. Usually there's Megan, Stacy, Mel and Yolanda, but I have my doubts as to whether Yolanda will want to see me. Baldy Daniel appears to be angling for an invite and he's not being very subtle about it.

"Well, feel free to join us if you want. I'm sure the others won't mind."

I can't believe she fell for it. I can tell from her tone that she hopes he says no.

"Really? I wouldn't want to feel like I'm intruding."

"No of course not. We get there about seven-thirty."

"Well, if you're sure."

Oh please say no. Say you've now had time to think about it and realised it's not a very good idea. Or just tell him to fuck off.

"Okay, I'll see you then." Chance missed.

Baldy Daniel virtually skips up the road with a huge smile on his face, without having once even acknowledged my existence. I'm delighted for him.

We leave for the pub at five minutes to seven Friday night. Megan is wearing blue jeans and a thin, cream coloured sweater. It looks a little too tight, but I wouldn't want to be the one to tell her that. It's a pleasant evening; quite warm for late September, but Megan's mood doesn't appear to have improved. Ever since the day she came home and found me covered in mud she seems to have been down. Not many people would be able to tell there's something wrong, she covers it well, but dogs can sense these things, trust me. And there is definitely something troubling her.

Stacy and Mel are already there when we arrive. They're seated at a large wooden table on the lawn outside. To my amazement, Yolanda gets there five minutes later. She must have forgiven me because she strokes my head.

Most Friday nights the pub is very busy, and tonight is no exception. The perfect opportunity for me to do some detective work. All I have to do is keep watching men going back to their benches and chairs, whoever I nipped on the arse could be here, and when they go to sit down...

I can only assume Megan has spoken to them all about Daniel's imminent arrival because that's where the conversation starts.

"I didn't know what to say," she's whispering, her eyes flicking about to make sure nobody on the other tables is eavesdropping.

"No, would have been a start." Mel says, rather too bluntly.

The fact that Mel seems rather perturbed comes as no surprise to me. Mel uses Friday nights to vent any frustrations she may have with her husband, Ray. She loves him, that's made very clear, there are just a few things she'd like to change. Too many things for me to list, that's for sure. The main bone of contention appears to be Ray's complete lack of interest in exercise of any form – hence his burgeoning weight – and also his refusal to start a family. Apart from the fact that I like Ray anyway, I am in complete agreement with him regards to babies. Why

47

anyone would want one of those is beyond me: All they seem to do is make a lot of noise and poop.

"Yes, but you should of seen him. I don't want to use the word 'desperate' but..."

"So he's desperate as well?" Yolanda says, and laughs.

The others all shush her.

"Well, come on Meg', this is the one night a week we get to slag off all the useless men in our lives. The last thing we need is one of them infiltrating our little group." Yolanda pauses to take a large gulp from her wine glass.

"Okay, I'm sorry. He caught me off guard. What else can I say?"

Megan doesn't sound sorry, she sounds annoyed, and it isn't just me who picks up on it. This isn't like her at all.

"It's not the end of the world," Stacy says. "So, we have to put up with a man at our table for one night. You never know, it might make a pleasant change."

The others all glare at her in silence.

Daniel arrives at precisely seven-thirty, smelling of some awfully strong aftershave and having polished his head. I only say this because the light from one of the outside lamps is glinting off his dome and keeps catching me in the eye.

The following hour or so is spent listening to Daniel go on and on about his career; his dearly departed wife; his brother-in-law; sister-in-law and a thousand other things that have happened in his very long, dull life. I'm only catching little snippets of the conversation because there are more interesting things happening around me. Three men on a table close to ours are discussing the disappearance of Michael Totter. It transpires that he hasn't been seen for a couple of days, and although nobody appears in the least bit concerned about this fact, it doesn't stop them wondering. I think about that gunshot I heard and begin to wonder myself.

By nine-thirty it's getting quite chilly. There's a large, outdoor heater close to our table which affords some heat, but nowhere near enough to prevent Megan's nipples poking through the material of her flimsy sweater. Everybody has had a few drinks by this time, Daniel included. I've been counting and he's had at least four, very large gin and tonics. Over the course of the evening the sound-level coming from our table has continued to rise. Now it's got to the point where many of the people at other tables are glancing over disapprovingly.

"What time does Lance get home?" Stacy asks as she finishes her meal.

Yolanda looks at her slim, gold wristwatch. "Anywhere between ten-thirty and eleven." She holds out her arm and inspects the tiny hands of her watch. "Time for at least two more," she laughs, and all the women at the table join in. Daniel just looks bemused.

I catch sight of a man walking back from the bar with a tray of drinks, staring at Megan's chest. He stumbles on the verge, barely manages to regain his balance and his face goes crimson. When he gets back to his own table his wife has a face like thunder. Yolanda must have seen it too because she makes matters worse by bursting out laughing.

The others stare at her. "What's so funny?" Stacy asks.

Yolanda waves a finger at Megan. "You need to cover those up before they cause an accident."

Megan glances down at her chest, blushes and folds her arms quickly. "Bloody

49

hell."

The three men sitting closest to us have been staring over and whispering for at least half-an-hour. Even with my acute hearing I can't hear what they're saying, because someone turned the music up a little while ago and everybody at the tables started talking a little louder, drowning each other out.

Finally one of the three, a tall man with short-cropped hair, a metal stud in his eyelid and rather big nose, gets up and saunters over to our table. "Any of you ladies fancy a drink?" he asks, looking from Megan to Stacy.

"We're fine thanks." Stacy answers politely, but there is a hard edge to her voice.

He squats down and folds his arms onto the table. "What about you?" he asks, staring at Megan.

Daniel clears his throat nervously. "We're all good thank you."

Big nose, turns his head slowly. "Who the fuck asked you grandad?"

The top of Daniel's head gleams bright red and a vein in the side of his temple begins to throb beneath his skin. "They aren't interested." he says, with as much bravado as he can muster, and shuffles uncomfortably on the wooden bench. "We don't want any trouble..." his voice tails off. He's just gone up in my estimation though. Although he's clearly nervous at least he's trying to hold his ground.

"I just told you, we don't want a drink." Stacy doesn't bother keeping her voice quiet. "Now why don't you just piss off back to your boyfriends."

Yolanda, who is clearly quite inebriated by this point, bursts out laughing.

I'm the other side of the bench, to Megan's left. I let out a low, rumbling growl as a warning sign. Megan reaches down and places a hand on my back.

"Don't think I'm really interested in you anyway," he says looking at Stacy. "You're the wrong colour sweetheart."

It all explodes quite quickly after that. Mel slings her drink in his face and spits out the word, "wanker." Big nose tries to stand, Megan gives him a shove and he topples back into the flower bed. Daniel jumps to his feet, not sure what he's supposed to be doing at this point but clearly aware he should be seen to be doing something. The two friends jump up from their bench, covering the few feet from their table to ours in a split-second. Neither of them appear too intelligent. They are both wearing rather angry, vacant expressions. The weedier one of the two helps his friend to his feet. The other, stockier one - obviously bereft of a more practical solution - punches Daniel on the nose.

At this point I'm straining against my leash, desperately trying to get round the table and get involved in the action. But the lead is caught round the leg of the bench and Megan is shouting at me to lay down. People at the other tables are all staring but nobody seems to keen to intervene.

Daniel is clutching his nose, blood seeping between his fingers dripping onto his nice white shirt. He's cursing things like, "shit, damn and ouch," under his breath.

Yolanda jumps up from the bench and swings a fist in the general direction of the melee. She misses her intended target, does a complete pirouette and ends up falling flat on her face on the grass.

Megan has also stood up by this point, placing herself between the three men and Daniel. I'm going frantic, trying to get round the table. In fact I'm pulling so hard that the table actually moves, just enough to topple half the drinks on it.

51

Eventually I have to stop tugging because my collar is so tight it's cutting off the air to my lungs and I start making hideous choking sounds.

The original instigator has now been helped to his feet. His backside is covered in mud and there are dead leafs stuck to his shirt and jeans. He's still wiping Mel's Vodka and coke from his face with one hand whilst trying to shove his friend out of the way with the other. Megan is trying to ease the blood-stained Daniel round the table to get him as far away from danger as she can. Mel and Stacy are busy helping Yolanda to her feet. Clearly embarrassed by the humiliation of being shoved on his arse by a mere woman, big nose pushes past his friends and grabs Megan by the arm. At this point I'm going apoplectic. I'm trying to bark, but the only sound that's coming out is a strange choking, gurgling sound.

Then from nowhere another man appears. He's a fraction taller than any of our three assailants, with a tight, muscular frame. He's wearing jeans and a black v-neck t-shirt, the material bulging at the shoulders.

Big nose looks furious, he's snarling and spitting, eyes bulging. He steps towards Megan and raises his hand, fist clenched as if he's about to swing a punch.

"I wouldn't," the stranger says, grabbing big nose by the wrist.

"Get the fuck off me." He tries to snatch his arm away, but the stranger just twists his hand. Big nose screams and drops to his knees.

"Either of you two try anything and I'll break it."

The other two gape at him open mouthed. The situation obviously calls for an element of reasoning, something which neither of these two are equipped for. The skinny one swings a fist. Without releasing his grip on the first man, the stranger

52

ducks and pokes two fingers straight into the throat of his attacker. Skinny, drops to the floor coughing, gasping for air. The stouter fellow engages his brain cell and takes a step back, holding his palms aloft as if he's had a gun pointed at him.

"Now, you can all walk away like good lads."

Big nose, currently squirming on his knees with a pained expression on his face, turns his head to look up at this stranger who's got his wrist in a vice-like grip. He nods, immediately squints and sucks in air as even this subtle movement causes an excruciating bolt of pain to shoot up his arm. "Yes, yes," he whimpers.

The stranger releases him and takes a step back.

The three of them gather themselves together and stagger towards the garden exit. "You haven't heard the last of this," one of them calls out as they disappear into the night.

The hum of concerned conversation seeps through the night air from some of the other tables.

"Thank you," Megan says.

"No problem." The stranger smiles, more with his eyes than his mouth, and picks up one of the empty glasses that fell onto the ground when I tugged the table. He seems so calm that anyone just arriving on the scene would never guess what had just taken place. "How's the nose?" he asks, looking at Daniel.

"It really bloody hurts," Daniel whines. "I think it's broken."

Megan pats him on the shoulder.

"Here, let me have a look." The stranger takes Daniel's head in his hands, grabs a napkin from the table and gently begins wiping the excess blood from Daniel's face.

Daniel moans and says "ouch" about half-a-dozen times.

"No, it's not broken. You need to keep your head back and get some ice on it, but you'll be fine."

Stacy, who is never slow at coming forward says, "Thank you so much. I'm Stacy by the way...and you are?"

"Mark."

"Megan," Megan says, reaching out a hand. "Can we get you a drink?"

"No, but thanks anyway." He shakes Megan's hand and the rest of the women form a circle. It reminds me very much of a documentary I saw about the Serengeti; a pack of wild dogs had isolated a buffalo from its herd and surrounded it before closing in for the kill. And while they are all fawning over him, nobody appears to have noticed my lead wrapped round the leg of the wooden bench, pinning me to the floor, choking me half to death. I gasp for air, and some sort of gagging sound comes out of my mouth.

"I think your dog might be having some trouble," Mark says. He comes round the table, crouches down and lifts the heavy bench with one arm.

My hero. I stagger onto all fours and choke out the horrible tasting phlegm caught in the back of my throat. A few coughs later I can breathe properly. Mark is leaning over me, gently stroking my back. But now my airways are clear I can smell it. I turn and back away, hackles raised. There's no doubt about it, this is the same scent I picked up at the snare. This is the man who killed Winston.

CHAPTER 9

Megan is late getting up. I assume this is partly due to the amount of alcohol she consumed the previous evening, but also, I heard her crying most of the night. Megan almost never cries. It made me feel sad, so I climbed onto the bed and we lay there cuddling for ages. It was lovely, and I think she felt much better afterwards, but right now I need the toilet and Megan has fallen back to sleep. Reluctantly I'm forced to wake her by nuzzling my cold nose against her cheek.

Eventually, Megan forces herself out of bed and opens the back door to let me out. My relief is short lived because I haven't even had a chance to finish my wee when my nemesis appears. Megan has named him Houdini, after some famous escapologist. Houdini is a scruffy grey squirrel who torments me to the point of distraction. It started last year when I caught him helping himself to food from my bowl: The bowl was on the floor in the kitchen if you please. He just strolled in and started stuffing biscuits into his greedy fat face. I chased him into the garden, he scrambled onto the top of the fence, and just sat there watching me bark at him. Ever since then I've tried to catch the little bastard, without success. Now he's sitting on the fence post, confidently preening his disgusting grey fur. I can almost hear him laughing. I rush over, barking furiously until Megan opens the door and orders me to be quiet. As I skulk towards the kitchen door I can feel his eyes burning into me, and if he wasn't laughing before, he certainly is now. But I will get him. One day.

By mid-morning we've had breakfast and a nice long walk. It's a pleasantly sunny morning, if a little chilly, and although there are plenty of rabbits skipping round the edge of the fields, I just can't be bothered to take chase. I have much more important things to think about. I saw the way they all looked at Mark last night, and to be fair, until I realised the situation I was in the same boat, but the man is a killer. I'm certain of it. Anyone who could let an animal - any animal – choke to death in one of those contraptions is a monster, and I don't want Megan having anything to do with him.

After lunch Megan bundles me into the car and we head off. I have no idea where we're going, but it's usually somewhere very pleasant. I like to stand on the back seat with my head out the half-open window and my tongue flapping about like a stranded Salmon. I know humans like to see this because lots of people in the other cars wave and smile. As we hurtle down the road I have visions of a nice sandy beach, and maybe a quick dip in the sea. The only problem with swimming is, Megan always insists on giving me bath afterwards.

We've been travelling for about an hour before I recognise a landmark I've seen a few times before. Sitting on top of a hill, about a mile from the busy main road is a huge sandstone building, complete with ornate turrets and stained-glass windows. The building looks as if it belongs to another world and I crane my head out of the window as long as possible until it disappears into the distance.

I know where we're heading, and it's only another five minutes before we get there. As soon as I hear the tyres crunching up the narrow drive I start jumping around and panting excitedly. Megan says, "yes, you know where we are now boy don't you," as if she can read my mind.

Joanne, Megan's grandmother, is waiting with the door open before the car is parked.

"Oh my dear," she cries, throwing her arms wide to greet Megan as she approaches the front door. "It's so lovely to see you." She reaches up and grabs Megan by the shoulders and stands back. "You look absolutely stunning dear," she says, and pulls Megan in for a longer, tighter hug.

Joanne doesn't sound like anyone else I've ever met when she talks. I've heard other people call her 'posh', but I don't really understand what that means. She's quite old, small, round and frail, with thin grey hair that always seems to be perfectly combed into place. She has a jolly face, but the years have hollowed her cheeks and the skin now hangs around her neck like a limp lettuce leaves. She likes bright colours, and today she is wearing a dress that resembles a spring garden in bloom, the material floating loosely round her withering frame.

Having relinquished her hold on Megan, she ushers us into her little bungalow, pausing to stroke me affectionately as I pass. "He's grown since I saw him last," she says, and lets out a groan of disapproval as she tries to force her aching limbs upright having stooped to tickle my stomach when I rolled over.

Megan helps her to her feet and we go through to the lounge.

Together they make a pot of tea and we all sit in the lounge, which is the only room in the small bungalow I'm allowed in. The floor is dark Mahogany, but there are two deep, cream coloured rugs I can take a choice from. A solid wooden coffee table sits in the middle of the floor surrounded by a large crimson sofa one side and two matching armchairs the other. The sun is pouring through two patio doors that look out over the lawn and fields beyond. The garden isn't huge, but there isn't a blade of grass out of place. The borders are neat and weedless, with a variety of different coloured bushes that appear to have been planted with exact precision.

"How are you keeping?" Megan asks, sinking into one of the armchairs.

Joanne smiles. "Aches and pains and struggling to remember where I left something I only put down a minute ago, but apart from that it's all tickety-boo." She laughs and a drop of tea spills over the edge of the cup she's holding. "But what can you expect when you're nearly ninety?" she adds.

"The aches and pains I can believe, but your mind's as sharp as ever."

Joanne nods slowly. "Maybe."

Megan looks uncomfortable. She's fidgeting in her seat and nervously fiddling with her tea spoon, twisting it between her fingers.

"The garden's looking lovely," Megan says, peering through the patio doors. She lifts the delicate porcelain tea cup to her mouth and her hand is shaking.

"It is, yes. And the house is clean, the weather is lovely and my hip surgery has been put back another month because the bloody NHS is understaffed and overworked." Joanne sighs, reaches across the table and places her hand gently on top of Megan's. "So now we've got all the small-talk out of the way, perhaps you'll tell me what's bothering you?"

Megan smiles and shakes her head slowly. "I should know better."

"Yes you should."

Megan places her cup in its saucer. "Sorry. I wasn't sure I was going to tell you at all. I'm just being selfish, unloading onto you I mean."

Joanne smiles, and her face cracks into a million fine lines. Her eyes glisten with a sadness hidden somewhere deep inside her that nobody else can see. "You're the only family I have Megan. I'd gladly die right now if it meant you never had to suffer again. So whatever it is you're worried about telling me, don't be."

Megan's parents and older brother died in a car crash when she was eleven-years-old. Megan rarely talks about them, but I know the story from little bits of conversation I've picked up. They were on their way to fetch Megan from a friends house where she was meant to be staying overnight. She'd got scared, or had an argument with one of the other girls and called her parents to come and get her. Megan blamed herself for many years.

"Greg called me last week," Megan spits the words out.

I watch Joanne's eyes glaze over with bitterness at the mention of his name.

"That little bastard. What does he want?"

"I told you about his 'child bride'," Megan does the funny thing with both fingers in the air.

"The twenty-five-year-old twiglet? Yes, yes you did."

"Well, apparently she's pregnant."

"That doesn't surprise me. What did he expect was going to happen if he hooks up with a girl half his age? Serves him right. Don't let it bother you sweetheart; all those sleepless nights and dirty nappy's?"

59

"Twenty years, he's twenty years older than her." Megan corrects, as if this fact is quite important. "I didn't let it bother me. I really couldn't care less about him, or her, or their offspring for that matter." She pauses to take another sip of tea. "He wants the house."

"What! Your house?

"Yes.."

At last, now the reason for her bad mood these last few days becomes clear. No wonder Megan has been so down. And he wants to take our house away! Or worse. Is he expecting me to come as part of the package?

"Well he can't. I gave that to you as a wedding present." Joanne's cheeks turn a fiery shade of red.

"He's offering to buy out my half."

"Your half! There isn't any half. The house is yours. You are my granddaughter. He lost any rights he had when he left you for that little tart." Joanne places her cup back on its saucer with a hefty clatter. "Over my dead body."

"This is why I almost didn't tell you. I knew how you'd react." Megan gets up and goes round the table so she's kneeling beside Joanne. "I don't want you worrying about it," she says patting the old woman's hand tenderly. "I just...well I just thought you should know in case..."

"In case what? Megan. I will see that little bastard in hell before I let him take that house away from you." She eases Megan back a little, stares into her eyes and says, "It will never happen. I promise you."

Megan forces a smile. "I did half expect something like this. I just thought, well hoped really, that his conscience would get the better of him and he might just settle for a few thousand."

"Give him nothing."

"Unfortunately he has rights."

"He gave up any rights he might have had when he walked out on you. No Meg', he's made his bed, now he can lay in it."

"The law says otherwise."

"The law is not always right."

Not wanting to be left out, I creep over, place my head on Joanne's lap, and stare into her eyes. She gently strokes the top of my head and smiles, but I can feel her weak heart thumping away in her chest far faster than can be good for someone of her advanced years.

"Okay," Joanne says when she's had time to calm down. "Pay him off. Whatever he's asking."

"I've thought about that. To be honest I've thought about nothing else for the last few days. He's insisting he's not interested in me buying him out. He says it's the perfect place to bring up a family. Besides, house prices have soared, so even if I wanted to, I couldn't afford to pay him what he'd want."

"How much are we talking about?"

Megan shakes her head. "It doesn't matter."

"How much?"

"Probably three-fifty, for his half."

"Three-hundred-and fifty-thousand pounds!!" Joanne's eyes almost pop from their sockets.

"Exactly. Even if I could afford to buy him out, which I really don't see I should have to, he's absolutely adamant that he wants the house, not the money."

"Well if it comes to..."

"No," Megan interrupts. "I know what your about to say and that isn't an option. That's another reason I toyed with the idea of not telling you."

Joanne pats her hand. "I was going to say, if it comes to it we could always have him bumped off," and starts laughing.

I'm really not sure what they are both laughing at, it seems like a perfectly reasonable option to me.

Megan smiles and gets to her feet. "If only," she says, staring out at the garden.

Just for a moment I thought she was considering it, which would have been the simplest solution. But I can tell from her tone that having her ex husband killed isn't an option Megan is taking seriously.

We sit like this for a while, as the late afternoon sun slowly sinks behind the distant tree-lined hills. Me, not daring to move my head because I love the feeling of Joanne gently stroking me, Joanne enjoying the company, and Megan with her head resting on the arm of Joanne's comfortable armchair, barely able to keep her eyes open.

"Leave it with me." Joanne says defiantly when at last we get up to go. "I think I might have a way round the problem."

Megan starts to protest, but Joanne places a finger gently on her lips. "Not another word. Just promise you'll stop worrying."

We drive home in silence.

CHAPTER 10

The house seems cold and empty when we get home. Megan lights a fire, pours a glass of wine and we settle onto the sofa for the evening, watching the light from the flames dance around the walls.

I feel so inadequate. I want to help, but all I can do is nuzzle up to Megan, rest my head on her lap and hope that all this mess goes away. The thought of losing our home is killing her. I don't think humans are aware of this, but dogs can sense pain and fear and lots of other emotions; it's almost a smell, but not quite. I suppose you'd call it an aura, like an invisible cloud surrounding the body that nobody can see, but we can feel.

I close my eyes and picture Greg and how much I once adored him. That seems like a lifetime ago. Still, I can't believe he could be this cruel. Not content with casting Megan aside for a younger woman, now he wants to force her out of her home. I'm just enjoying the thought of sinking my teeth into his leg when a noise outside the window causes me to prick my ears. The unmistakable sound of feet on the gravel. But this isn't as solid as a footstep, there is no loud crunch. This is an almost imperceptible sound of someone lowering their foot to the ground, one step at a time.

I jump from the sofa, head for the front door and stand, listening. As soon as I'm sure, I start barking.

"Harry!" Megan says without raising her voice.

I stop, wait and listen. Silence now. Nobody should have occasion to walk past our house. The gravel drive only runs up as far as the fence to the back garden, beyond that is just open fields that are accessible from various footpaths in the village, but not through our property. The back door is closed, but Megan leaves my access hatch unlocked until she goes to bed so that I can pop in and out if I need to.

I push through the opening, trying not to let it snap back into place and make a sound that would alert an intruder. It's dark outside, the night air fresh and clean. But there's a scent hanging in the air that shouldn't be there. Slowly I tip toe round the back of the house. The fence is high, blocking my view of the driveway. I can hear the sound of cars passing through the village, and just about make out the low hum of chatter coming from the pub the other side of the green. I try and block out everything else and concentrate on whatever, or whoever is the other side of the fence.

"Harry. Harry, come on."

I can hear Megan making her way through the house towards the back door. She flicks the switch in the kitchen and light explodes from the window at the side of the house. Through tiny gaps in the fence I see a shadow duck down and the sound of a heel pressed into the edge of the gravel. Now I let them have everything I've got.

"HARRY!" Megan shouts, then screams almost immediately.

The other side of the fence I can hear someone running back towards the main road. I tear into the kitchen to find Megan standing clutching her hand to her chest.

She looks pale. When I run to her I can feel she's shaking.

It's gone nine by the time Sergeant Skinner arrives. He carries out a brief search of the area outside the kitchen window before joining Megan at the kitchen table.

"I don't know why I called you." Megan's says, looking rather apologetic for having bothered the police.

"Not a problem." Skinner assures her. "And you say you didn't see his face?"

"No. I only caught a glimpse of them. They were wearing some sort of hoodie thing, and their face was covered with a black scarf, maybe a balaclava. Oh I don't know. Sorry."

"What sort of height were they?"

Megan shakes her head. "Honestly, I couldn't say."

"It's just that, well, could it have been kids?"

"No. Definitely not."

"But if you say you didn't..."

"I know." Megan wrings her hands. "I suppose it was their stature; you know, big shoulders, heavy set..." her voice tails off.

"Okay, don't worry. I've had a good look round outside and there's no damage to your car, which is probably what they were interested in. Harry must of disturbed them before they had a chance to do anything. Good boy aren't you."

I lap up the adoration. I would of preferred it if Megan had opened the front door so I could give chase though. Kids or not, a quick bite on the arse would probably be enough to make sure they don't try that again.

"We've never had a problem before." Megan shakes her head slowly.

I can hear the sadness in her voice.

"I'm sure it's just a chancer. I'm on duty for another three hours so I'll keep my eyes open round the village and I'll take a drive past before I head home. How does that sound?"

"Thank you. And sorry, again."

I notice Megan double checks all the locks before she heads off to bed an hour later. I wait until she's fast asleep before going back downstairs. If they want to get to Megan they'll have to get past me first.

CHAPTER 11

It isn't often that I find myself hoping Megan has to go into the office to work, but it's nine-thirty in the morning and she's still here. Which almost certainly means she's working from home again today. That means another day when I can't go out to investigate. And there is a lot I need to know. Michael Totter still hasn't been seen around the village; there's no sign of Winston - although at least now I'm certain it was this Mark, person who's either killed or stolen him – and Yolanda's mystery attacker is still on the loose.

Megan takes me for a walk around eleven and we call into the tea room on the way home. It's busy this morning but I don't recognise many of the faces. The sun is out and the village gets quite a lot of visitors when the weather is nice.

Helen Pierce is sitting at a table talking to Dorothy Barnstaple. Every other table is occupied.

"Do you mind if I join you?" Megan asks.

"Of course," Helen says. She doesn't even wait until Megan sits down before she begins her inquisition. "We've been hearing all about Friday night." She doesn't bother trying to conceal her excitement. "Poor, Daniel, getting attacked like that! Apparently he was saved from a beating by some handsome stranger."

Mel appears at the table, note-pad in hand. "I filled them in with the bare details," she admits. "Coffee?"

"Please. And I'll have one of those cakes," Megan points at a selection of delicious-looking pastries in a large glass bowl on the counter. "I feel like treating myself," she adds, as if she needs to justify herself.

"So what do we know about this knight in shining armour?" Helen asks.

"He's hot," Mel says, probably a little louder than intended.

If only they knew the truth.

Megan smiles and nods her head in agreement. "I can't argue with that. Yes, he was very nice. I'm not sure what would have happened if he hadn't turned up."

Helen leans closer. "So what happened? How did it all start?"

"Some local lads had a few too many. Started getting a bit fresh. Daniel did his best to smooth things over, and then one of them said something to Stacy...something not very nice, and it escalated from there."

"Racist bastards." Mel interjects.

Megan nods.

Helen leans onto her elbows. "What did they say?"

"That's not important. Daniel tried to diffuse the situation, but it's impossible to reason with some people. As my grandad used to say, 'there's no arguing with stupid'."

"Poor man," Dorothy Barnstaple says. "I saw him in the stores yesterday. He has two black eyes and swollen nose. It looks like he took quite a beating. I asked him whether he'd spoken to the police and he said he didn't want to get them involved."

"It probably looks worse than it is. It was one punch on the nose."

Dorothy shakes her head. "Even so..."

"If Daniel wanted to take it further we'd all back him up," Megan says. "But to be honest I assume he's finding the whole incident a little embarrassing, I imagine he just wants to forget about it."

"Bloody thugs," Dorothy says. "And there's still no sign of poor Winston. I called in to see how George was doing yesterday morning, and I must say, he seems to have perked up somewhat. Not sure I'd get over it that quickly."

"He's probably hiding his feelings," Megan offers.

"It didn't seem like that. I was quite surprised. He dotes on that dog."

"People deal with their emotions in different ways," Megan says, and everybody at the table nods their heads in agreement. "Besides, there's no point getting too dejected until we know what's happened to him. He could still turn up. If someone has taken him it's not beyond the realms of possibility that they get a prick of conscience and decide to return him."

"These people don't have a conscience," Helen says, stirring her tea with more force than necessary.

If only I could let them know what I know. It's hard sitting here listening to them going on about Winston. It's harder still, having to listen to Megan and Mel cooing over this Mark fellow. I'll get to the truth if it takes all week. It's hard to see how Winston could have survived that contraption, and even if he had, and this Mark fellow was any sort of decent human being, surely he would have taken Winston straight to a veterinarian for treatment, and they would have contacted George immediately. Sadly, I'm certain this wasn't the case. If Winston is buried somewhere in the forest, I will find him.

Mel pulls up a chair and joins us at the table. She looks quite flushed from running around serving tables. "Anyway," she says looking at Megan, "I hear you had a spot of bother the other night."

Megan frowns. "News travels fast. It was nothing really. Anyway, who told you?"

"Stacy."

"What's this?" Helen asks.

"Stacy!" Megan says, frowning, ignoring Helen's question.. "How does she know?"

Mel smiles. "Where do you think she heard about it?"

Megan's forehead creases into lines as the penny drops and her face cracks into a huge, knowing smile. "I'll call you later," she says to Mel.

"Heard about what?" Helen persists.

"Oh it was nothing. I saw somebody outside my kitchen window Saturday night. Harry was going berserk...I probably overreacted, but it shook me up a bit. I think I just wanted peace of mind so I called the police and Sergeant Skinner turned up in his squad car. He took a look around and was gone within a few minutes."

Some of the other customers are looking over, trying to get Mel's attention.

"Ray." Mel calls. She waits a moment and then shouts, "RAY," again and smiles at the customers who are clearly becoming impatient.

Ray eventually appears from a room at the back. He doesn't bother trying to hide his annoyance at being disturbed. He limps from behind the counter, trying to force a smile. He's obviously in pain and the intended smile looks more like a grimace. He's put on a bit more weight since I saw him last.

"What's the matter with him?" Dorothy asks.

We all watch Ray as he tends the tables taking orders for tea, coffee and cakes.

"Oh it's nothing," Mel says quietly, waving a hand dismissively. "Apparently he caught his backside on some barbed wire when he was trying to climb over a fence. God knows what he was up to. I did offer to take a look," Mel prods two fingers into her mouth and makes a sort of gagging sound, "but thankfully he said that wasn't necessary."

Caught his arse on some barbed wire!! Really!! I watch him move slowly between the tables. Wondering.

We have almost made it back home when Megan suddenly tugs me across the road. I look up to see Mark, coming out the door of the pub.

"Hello," Megan calls, dragging me across the damp grass.

Mark pauses, looks up and smiles. He is wearing jeans and a large luminous yellow jacket. "Morning."

"Are you staying here?" Megan nods at the pub behind them.

"Yes."

I want to start growling but I know from previous experience this won't do any good. It would seem that humans aren't as intelligent as they would like to think. If they were that clever they'd be able to interpret the differing tones we emit. As far as I can tell there are three emotions they understand without too much trouble: Anger, sadness and happiness, anything else is lost on most of them.

"I didn't really get a chance to thank you properly the other night."

Megan is using 'that' voice, and twisting strands of her hair between her fingers. I think I might vomit.

"It was nothing."

"Are you working in the area?"

Even I can tell he's not in the mood to stay and chat.

"Yes. Environmental agency," he taps the letters on his jacket.

"Right, well thanks again. Maybe we'll bump into each other again and I can get you a drink. To thank you properly I mean."

He nods and smiles. "Yes maybe. Sorry but I'm late. Nice to see you again..."

"Megan," Megan offers as he walks away.

But he's not hanging around. He steps on the soft earth at the side of the grass verge to avoid having to brush past us on his way to the car park at the rear of the pub and calls out "bye Megan," as he disappears round the corner.

So not only is he a dog killer, but he's rude as well. All of this appears lost on Megan, who is currently standing on the spot staring after him like some love-struck teenager at a pop concert. His boots have left an imprint in the mud, and that gives me an idea. I casually amble over to the grass and cock my leg, but I don't really need a wee. Instead I'm studying the imprint his boot has made, trying to lock it into my memory.

When we do eventually return home there's a lot of crashing and banging coming from the back garden.

"How's it going?" Megan asks, pulling open the kitchen door.

There are lots of bits of wood and fence panels laying on the grass at the back of the garden. John Brown, Dawn's husband, is leaning against a fence post, sweating profusely. He looks a bit too old for this kind of work and his face is very red.

"Getting there," he says, wiping the back of his hand across his forehead. "Couple of hours and I'll be done I reckon."

I stroll down the garden to see what's taking place. The fence - which was about four feet high and I could just about clear - has now been extended higher by some sort of lattice contraption, making it a foot taller. Behind the bushes where the timber slats had rotted away, there's a new fence panel.

"Try getting out now," John says proudly, whilst patting me on the back.

I just stand there open-mouthed trying to take in the enormity of the situation.

"Tea?" Megan calls cheerily, clearly content with the progress and not a care for my feelings.

Just to add insult to injury out the corner of my eye I spot Houdini, sitting in the branches of next door's Birch tree. He's preening his tail, clearly ecstatic with what he's witnessing. I'm certain - if it was at all possible - he'd be giving me a wanker sign and laughing.

CHAPTER 12

Having spent all of the previous afternoon on her computer at the kitchen table, today Megan has left for the office. John had completed his work long before it got dark and he even had the audacity to whistle merrily as he loaded his tools into the back of his tatty white van. So this morning, as I listen to the sound of Megan's car pulling onto the main road, instead of a sense of freedom, I just feel trapped.

I traipse down the garden to survey my enclosure. The gate is secured with a padlock. The lattice thingy – which I now know is called a trellis – looms overhead, too high to jump. Every gap in the fence has been replaced with either a new fence panel or fresh timber secured with heavy-duty screws. It would appear my fate is sealed. It's a grey, overcast day and I wander back into the house to lay on my blanket and sulk.

I'm having a sip of water when I hear Houdini scampering along the top of the fence. I jump up and stare out of the window with both front paws resting on the window ledge. If the little sod makes a slip I'll be out there in a flash. I watch him move along the fence, pausing occasionally to wave his tail in the air like a conquering soldier carrying a flag. He reaches the new trellis work at the far end, but instead of jumping into the overhanging branches of next doors tree, he climbs down the fence and disappears behind a thick clump of Pampas grass in the right hand corner of the garden.

Now he's had it. I creep silently out through my door, and begin crawling across the lawn, keeping low on my haunches, edging closer to my prey. Any moment he's going to poke his head out, and this time I'm ready for him. But that doesn't happen. Instead I hear his dirty little claws on the other side of the fence and his head appears through the holes in the trellis at the top. I cock my head to one side, wondering how the hell he managed that. He certainly didn't get there by climbing this side of the fence because I would of seen him, and there isn't a gap big enough for him to crawl through. I know because I've checked. This has got me intrigued. The Pampas grass is wedged tight into the corner of the garden, but the bush is about four feet around, with long, coarse leaves that reach almost to the top of the fence at the highest point. I press up against the side fence panel and push my way along, careful not to let the sharp leaves scratch my eyes. The gap is tight - even for me – and now I'm wedged in here it's easy to see how John could have missed what I'm looking at. Buried in the darkest corner, just below the line of the fence, there's a small hole. There are deep scratch marks, and a strong scent of badger. I force my way closer and begin digging. Fifteen minutes later I'm free.

Very aware of the fact that Megan will start locking me in the house if I'm seen out and about again, I'm forced to take the long route round the village. This means chasing along the edge of the fields, through the woods and up the hill to the old church. I have to cross the road at the top of the hill. I'm forced to crouch down in the grass waiting for a break in the traffic for almost five minutes. But once I'm across, it's plain sailing. There's nothing but open fields and forest now, and I can easily find a place to hide if I run into anyone out for a walk.

It takes about twenty-minutes to reach the spot where we discovered the snare. I sniff the ground, trying to pick up a scent which is quite a few days old, but also searching for a boot print in the mud, and confirmation of what I'm already sure I know. Whatever rain we've had over the last few days hasn't helped. There are plenty of signs that people have been here, but most of the marks were probably made by Megan and Stacy, or possibly Michael Totter when I saw him here the other day. I pace the area in an ever widening circle, keeping to the side of the ditch where we all stood that first day. It's several minutes later when it finally dawns on me; whoever took Winston would almost certainly have had to crouch in the gorse bushes the other side of the ditch, there's no way they could have reached across and taken him. If the snare hadn't already killed him, Winston would have put up one hell of a fight. I leap the ditch and start scouring the area.

I discover what I'm looking for almost immediately. Half buried beneath the thicket of gorse - which undoubtedly saved it getting washed away by the rain – is a boot print. The print consists of several angled, symmetrical lines and a deeper, smoother indent where the heel dug into the ground. It matches perfectly with the boot print Mark left in the ground yesterday morning. It's all the confirmation I need, not that it's going to do me much good.

Feeling quite content that I've solved one mystery, I decide that as I'm on a roll I may as well try and find out what happened to Michael Totter. The fact that his personal hygiene leaves a lot to be desired is a bonus.

Even so, it takes almost an hour to pick up a trace of his scent strong enough for me to follow. Ten yards from the water's edge, half way up the bank at the base of an enormous Beech tree, I finally pick up his distinctive odour. By the look of the ground he must have crouched here for some time, leaning against the base of the tree. There are two cigarette butts on the ground, and some of the surrounding twigs have been snapped off half way up the stem. I can see clearly across the reservoir from here. There's a couple of boats in the distance and I can just about make out the gentle swish of their rods, carried to me on the light breeze. I can't help wondering why on earth Michael would have settled here long enough to smoke two cigarettes. It's not like he would be after shooting anything on the lake. Maybe he just likes to watch people fish? Nothing would surprise me after some of the things I've heard people say about him. Apparently he got arrested once when he took one of the lads from the village fishing. The boy told his father that Michael started spitting at him for no reason whatsoever, and when he told him to stop he tried to push him into the river. Perhaps fishing, or fishermen trigger some sort of psychotic spasm in his brain? The thought nudges me back to the moment.

Following the trail is made easier because there are scuff marks in the ground and little tell-tale signs in the scrub and low-lying branches; a snapped twig here, a flattened sprig of grass there. The trail leads along the top of the bank, skirting round the edge of the huge body of water. The reservoir gets increasingly narrower as the water disappears into the depths of the forest, until eventually there is just a

76

ten-feet wide river feeding into the lake. Once here, I can see right across the lake to the damn, almost half-a-mile away.

The reservoir is shaped like a long, triangular wedge: At least three-hundred yards wide at the concrete damn. To the left of the damn, where the lane leads in, there's a small parking area and timber building. A floating wooden jetty feeds out into water, with half-a-dozen row boats tethered to the mooring. Today there are three boats out on the lake and a couple of people fishing from the damn.

Where I'm standing the river is too wide to cross, unless I fancy a swim, which I don't, so I follow it back, deeper into the forest. It has started to spit with rain and the thick clouds cut out what little light would have otherwise seeped through the branches of the trees.

By the time I've reached a point in the river that I feel I can jump, it is quite dark. Not only that, but I'm starting to struggle with the trail. Cold drops of rain drip from the branches overhead, soaking into the thick layer of pine-straw.

I'm standing on the edge of the bank trying to decide if I can make the leap to the other side without falling back into the water, when something catches my eye. In the fading light it looks like patches of black oil. Closer inspection tells me what I was already starting to suspect: Blood, and lots of it.

Somebody has done their best to clean up what must have been one hell of a mess. The ground has been raked over by a boot or shoe by the look of it, but the rusty smell of blood beneath dead leaves and pine straw is strong. There are splinters of bark missing from the tree closest to me. And when I look closer I can see tiny lead pellets embedded in the wood about a foot above my head. The

77

surrounding area has been swept, probably with a large branch. Whoever was here went to a great deal of trouble to make sure their crime wasn't discovered. Now I just need to know exactly what that crime was.

The trail is easy to follow when I start moving again. There are spatters of blood every few feet, and shallow ruts in the ground that appear to look very much like the heel of someone's shoe or boot. Two, maybe three people dragging a body? I'm only picking up one scent, but the debris on the floor of the forest has been disturbed wide enough that I can imagine the scene: One person either side of their victim, stomping through the forest with a dead weight under their arms.

The further I move away from the reservoir, the darker it gets. It's raining quite hard now, and the trees are far closer together, the dense branches overhead thick with pine leaves, cutting out whatever sunlight is managing to seep through the heavy rain-clouds. The sounds of the forest can be unsettling at the best of times, but when you're alone every snapping twig or rustle of branches can be quite scary. Well it can for me anyway. There are lots of strange sounds right now, and most of them are causing me twitch nervously. I stop to consider exactly what I'm doing here. It is getting late, and if I'm not back before Megan, I'm in big trouble. The call of an owl somewhere in the distance warns me I'm not alone.

The trail has become almost impossible to follow. The rain is pouring down, soaking into the ground, the pine straw acting like a sponge, squelching beneath my paws. I've just about made up my mind to give up and go home when I see a mound of fresh earth that doesn't look like it belongs there. Someone has attempted to cover the loose earth with dead branches, but they must have been in

78

a hurry because they haven't made a very good job of it.

As much as I want to start making my way back, I know I can't leave until I discover what, or who is buried here. I drag the branches to one side using my teeth, and begin digging. The earth is wet and sticky and digging isn't made any easier because water keeps seeping into the hole I'm creating. But I'm relentless. The stench of death surrounds me, rising from the makeshift grave like a fine mist. Until I've unearthed the body I'm not leaving. If Michael Totter has killed someone and buried them here I want him to pay for his crime. An image of him springs into my head; crouching behind a tree, aiming his gun, those horrible dark eyes peering out from beneath his cap. I shake it off and continue clawing at the ground.

Thick mud and bits of twigs and pine straw cling to my wet fur, but I carry on regardless. Nothing is going to stop me. I'm almost frantic, ignoring the pain in my paws, paying no heed to the relentless deluge pounding me from above. I'm so engrossed in what I'm doing that I don't pay enough attention to the sound of flapping wings as some pigeons resting in the trees overhead suddenly take flight, calling out their warning.

My claw catches material and the overpowering stench of death hits me. I ignore the smell, stick my head in the hole and grab the wet cloth between my teeth. One good hard yank and the scarf Michael Totter always wears round his neck, slips from the pool of mud to reveal its owners slime-covered face. Those black eyes now lifeless.

Everything happened in a moment. A branch breaking under foot, too close for comfort. The bark of the tree next to me exploding, splintering minute fragments of razor-sharp bark in all directions. The unbelievable pain and the instantaneous sound of a gunshot. Me somersaulting, landing on my side and leaping to my feet in one, acrobatic movement. And now running, the wet rag flapping between my jaws. I'm at full speed when I hear more shots ring out. My is heart pumping so fast it feels like it will burst from my chest. But I'm not stopping. I can't stop. Branches snap against my face and side, debris scattering in all directions as I twist and swerve. And far behind me I hear someone shout, "Did you get it?"

"Yes. Didn't you see him jump?" He calls back proudly.

I don't know whether the voices stopped or just got so far far behind me that I could no longer hear them, but when my legs eventually give way and I collapse, I'm surrounded by silence. I have slumped to the ground at the foot of a tall pine tree. Drops of icy water cascade from the canopy overhead. The liquid washes over me and a dark river of blood slowly soaks into the damp earth.

I have tried not to think about death. I didn't expect it would find me so fast. I suppose I just hoped it wouldn't feel this painful and I wouldn't be alone. And as I close my eyes I only have one thought: I should be with Megan now.

CHAPTER 13

Megan

It's gone six and I'm stuck in traffic. It should take less than an hour to get home, but I left at four-thirty and there's no sign of the traffic moving any time soon. Harry will be frantic. I know dogs are clever, but some - Harry for example - are ultra-intelligent. I'm sure he knows how to tell the time. Okay, maybe his time awareness is dictated by things like food and the need to use the toilet, but he just seems so aware. I'll make a fuss of him when I get back, perhaps that'll stop him sulking because I've blocked off his escape routes out of the garden. That was an expense I could of done without at the moment but I didn't feel comfortable knowing he could get out. I don't know what I'd do without him.

Just as the traffic starts to move my ring tone explodes from the hands-free speaker, cutting off Adele, on the radio.

I tap the button. "Hello," I answer in my office voice, because for some reason the caller ID doesn't appear on the dash screen. I've spoken to someone at the garage and they've got it booked in for a week Wednesday.

"Hello Megan."

"Greg!" This is the last person I expect to be calling me. The last time we spoke he told me about the pregnancy and dropped the bombshell about the house. The conversation didn't end well.

I'm tempted to cut him off and go back to Adele, but the irony of listening to 'Someone Like You' blaring out of the speaker just as Greg decides to call is just too much to ignore. "What do you want?"

There's a pause, and I can picture his annoyed face as he takes a breath to calm himself down before responding. Greg always likes to be in control of his emotions, but it's a hard fought battle.

"My solicitor got the letter from fucking Joanne this morning. What the fuck is that all about?"

"I haven't got a clue what you're talking about." I tell him honestly. I'm happy that whatever Joanne had her solicitor send him was enough to cause this much agitation though.

"Really?"

"Yes, really. Perhaps before you go off the deep end you might want to fill me in. Although to be honest Greg, if she's managed to piss you off then that's fine with me."

"Careful Meg, you don't wanna turn into a bitter old woman."

Touché, and ouch. Bitter, I can take on the chin - although I'm really not - but 'old' touches a nerve. Greg always did know exactly which buttons to press.

"Just being honest with you," I reply, working hard to keep the edge out of my voice. I really can't handle him knowing he can still get to me. "But I suppose that's a concept you don't understand. Honesty never was your strong point was it?"

"And I suppose having Joanne's solicitor come up with some fake contract is?"

Fake contract! Now I'm really intrigued. What has Joanne been up to? I wouldn't put anything past her; she might look frail...well okay, she is frail, but her mind's sharper than an accountants pencil. I emit a long drawn out sigh. "Okay, just so we are very clear, this is the first I've heard about any contract. Take it or leave it. Now to be honest Greg, you're starting to bore me." I force a titter and add, "Just like having sex with you really." And before he can answer I cut him off.

I find it impossible to wipe the smile off my face for the rest of the journey. I can picture him standing there, open-mouthed, steam coming from every conceivable orifice, not quite able to forget my slur, but trying so hard to not let it get to him.

By the time I arrive home it's gone seven. I gather the clutter from the passenger seat, fiddle with the keys for the front door and wait for the inevitable excited yap-yap-yapping that always greets my homecoming. The door swings open and I stare into the silent darkness of the hallway. "Harry," I call, in my most apologetic tone. "Harry!!" I walk through the house flicking light switches as I go. Harry is obviously in the garden, probably hounding that bloody squirrel. I pass through the kitchen, throw three varying coloured folders on the table, and unbolt the back door. "Harry, come on boy. Sorry..." The garden is empty.

My first phone call is to Stacy. Harry loves playing with Poppy, if he's managed to escape he's probably headed down to theirs and Stacy has kept hold of him. I'm trying hard to tell myself that, but for some reason my hand is shaking. "Hi Stace'," I keep the tone light as I can, "Harry hasn't turned up at yours has he?" Please. Please. Pleeease.

"No. Sorry. Don't tell me he's escaped! You had the fence done yesterday didn't you?"

"Yes I did. Okay, no problem, I'll take a walk round the fields. He can't have gone far." I'm trying to sound like I'm not really that concerned - which at this moment I shouldn't be - except there's a horrible feeling niggling away deep down inside me.

"Give me twenty-minutes and I'll come with you." Stacy says, and I hear somebody in the background speak. There's a short silence and I can imagine

83

Stacy standing there with her hand over the mouthpiece as she speaks to whoever is with her. I can just about make out the words, "Won't," and "long."

"It's fine Stacy," I say, not wanting to ruin whatever plans she's made for the evening. "You don't have to. Really. He's probably chasing rabbits round the back fields."

"I know I don't have to, I want to. I'll be there quick as I can. See you in a minute."

I was going to argue the point but Stacy's already hung up. To be honest, I'm so happy she's coming over. The weather is awful and it's pitch black, I don't really feel comfortable traipsing round in the dark on my own. And besides, right now I feel like I need a friend.

Stacy arrives fifteen minutes later. She has brought a large torch and is dressed for the occasion in a heavy, waterproof jacket and green wellington boots.

We start in the back fields, trudging our way along the muddy footpath to the perimeter of the woods calling, "Harry," every few seconds. An hour later and it's too dark to see past the beam of the torch. The rain shows no sign of relenting and none of the hundreds of pairs of eyes caught in the beam of torchlight are answering our call, instead they disappear into the hedgerows as we draw closer.

"Okay," I say, gazing forlornly at the lights from the houses on the ridge at the top of the field. "We may as well head back."

Stacy puts an arm round me. "I've only got two appointments tomorrow, I'll cancel them and we can go out and have a proper look. We'll find him. He'll have run off over the forest or something."

84

I know her words are meant to comfort me, but they don't. I'm carrying round the image of that bloody snare we found, and I can't help wondering if Harry has fallen victim to one of those things. I try and push the thought away because it's just too horrible to contemplate. But I can't.

When we get home I'm still holding onto the hope that Harry will have turned up while we've been out. Those hopes are quickly dashed. Stacy stops long enough for a cup of coffee and we sit at the kitchen table trying to formulate a plan for the following day. We both agree to phone round as many people as we can, just to make sure somebody from the village who doesn't know who Harry belongs to has taken him in. It's not very likely, but for the moment it's all I've got, and I'm going to cling onto to that hope as long as possible.

A couple of hours after Stacy leaves I've had a bath and managed to get some food inside me. I didn't feel like eating anything, but if we are going to be out searching all day tomorrow I need to make sure I'm up to it, so I threw a few bits of salad on a plate and sat at the table picking at bits of tomato and cucumber whilst trying not to stare at Harry's empty blanket. I keep checking the phone, hoping someone, anyone, will call with good news. But it stays silent. I should really call Joanne to see exactly what Greg was going on about, but I know I won't be able to concentrate. Whatever it is can wait. I know I won't be able to sleep, so I've thrown on a pair of jeans and an old jumper with the intention of driving round the village, just in case.

I'm just pulling on my trainers when the doorbell goes.

It's almost eleven. My heart jumps slightly quicker than me leaping off the chair.

Harry! Someone has found him.

Tony Skinner is standing at the door when I open it. Tonight he's wearing his uniform and a serious expression that causes a stabbing pain deep inside me. "Hello Megan," he says gravely, and I notice that he doesn't look me directly in the eye for more than an instant. "Can I come in?"

I want to say 'No, whatever you're about to tell me, I don't want to hear it.' Instead I mumble something incoherent and turn towards the kitchen trying to fight against the feeling of nausea swirling in the pit of my stomach.

Tony waits until we're both seated before he begins. "I heard about Harry. I would of come sooner but it's been a busy night." He shuffles uncomfortably on his chair, twisting his keys nervously between his fingers. "The station received a phone call earlier this evening. The caller said they'd seen a dog hit by a car on the main road, just on the bend by the church."

I'm struggling to fight back the tears because I can tell from his tone what's coming next.

"I'm sorry Megan. They said it looked like he was already injured and was limping across the road when a lorry came round the corner..." his voice tails off.

Both my fists are clenched to my face. I can't stop the tears. "But it might not be Harry," I say.

"Probably best if you speak to Debbie. Just call the station and ask to speak to Debbie Martin, she took the call. She'll be able to answer any questions." Tony places a hand on my shoulder, but any attempt at comforting me is wasted.

"So where is he now?" I choke out.

Tony clears his throat. "That's the thing; according to the witness, the driver stopped and put him in the cab."

"So he could have taken him to vet!" I say hopefully.

Tony shakes his head. "Sorry Megan, but from what I've been told there was no doubt the dog was dead. I don't want to go into details..."

He doesn't need to go into details. My mind is working overtime, filling my head with all the gory images I'd do anything not to be seeing - but hard as I try – I just can't shake them away. "Why would anyone do that? Take a dead dog I mean." I'm suddenly very aware that I'm shouting.

"God knows. Could be any number of reasons. I'm so sorry Megan. I'll try and find out a bit more if I can. There might be some CCTV footage from one of the houses in the village, but even if we do manage to pick up a reg number, there's very little we can do about it."

"And what about this person who called it in? Could I speak to them?"

"They didn't leave a name. Again, could be any number of reasons." He attempts a sympathetic smile which - at this moment in time - is completely wasted on me. "Talk to Debbie," he says again, but his tone isn't filled with promise. "I really am sorry to be the bearer of such bad news. I know how much you loved him."

The word 'loved', used in the past tense causes an outburst of emotion that I would never have thought possible before I got Harry. I used to scoff at people who treated their dogs like...well, like one of the family. I never understood how anyone could let themselves get so wrapped up in an animal. Well I know now, don't I.

CHAPTER 14

The house is deathly quiet. Not a sound, apart from the hum of the fridge sitting in

the corner of the kitchen, beside Harry's blanket. The material is covered in black

hairs and part of me wants to go and lay down there just so I can feel close to him.

I shake the thought off: Even for me that's absurd. Instead I trudge up the stairs

and fall onto the bed. It's gone midnight and I was up early, but I know I won't

sleep tonight. There are too many signs of Harry everywhere. Before Greg left us,

Harry was never allowed upstairs. Greg's idea, not mine. 'I'm not having that

bloody animal traipsing all over the carpets with dirty paws,' was Greg's favourite

line. The first night he moved out I took Harry up to bed with me. He's been a

permanent fixture ever since.

I must have drifted off eventually, because I wake to the sounds of early

morning traffic travelling through the village. It's almost five-thirty, and a

smattering of light is already seeping through the curtains. Just for a second I have

this unbelievably wonderful thought that it was all just a nightmare. Harry's not

dead. Any minute now he'll come bounding up the stairs, soaking wet and covered

in mud, and instead of shouting at him to get off, I'll grab hold of him and cuddle

the hell out of him. The thought disappears in an instant. My pillow's still wet from

last nights tears. And that disgusting, empty pain, like someone has literally

reached inside me and grabbed a handful of intestines, still burns just a painfully

88

as it did last night.

I get up and shower. I brush my teeth. Drag a comb through my hair. I make a cup of tea and do all the banal, daily rituals that can be carried out on autopilot. Today I was supposed to be working from home, but I just can't bring myself to think about work at the moment. I know what Tony said, but I can't just leave it at that. What if...and I mentally slap myself for even considering the thought. If I could just speak to the person who witnessed the accident. Just to make absolutely certain there hasn't been some sort of mistake. There, I've done it again. Stop. No, I can't stop. I don't want to stop hoping because once hope is gone all I've got left is reality, and right now reality is a bastard. And then, from out of nowhere, I have a compulsion to go and speak to George.

It's not even seven o' clock by the time I begin to walk down the hill. The traffic is very light along the main road at this hour, but I greet the passing of every large vehicle with a look of disgust. The rain has stopped, which is just about the only good thing I can say about today.

George lives in a tumbledown cottage at the foot of the village. I can see light bursting from at least two of the downstairs rooms long before I reach his home. I knew he'd be an early riser.

A strip of narrow concrete snakes its way towards Georges front door; overgrown bushes and grass drooping over the path under the weight of last nights downpour. There's a steep bank at the end of the garden that falls twenty feet to the river below. As I push my way past the soggy foliage towards the front I can hear gushing water. Usually I would find the sound of running water quite soothing, but this morning I barely notice it.

George answers the door the moment I knock. His face doesn't betray emotion. He hasn't shaved for a couple of days, and his stubbled jaw is locked grimly into its usual setting. "Megan!" he says, clearly surprised to see me at this hour.

"Sorry," I mumble, still not entirely sure what compelled me to make the journey. "I just..." An involuntary tear trickles from the corner of my eye and George stuns me by taking a step forward and folding his arms round me, pulling me in for a long, silent cuddle.

I cannot think of another time in my life when this would have felt appropriate. I don't know George that well. Sure, we've spoken a couple of times, but I wouldn't consider him as anything more than an acquaintance. If that. I've always thought of him as a stubborn old man who belongs to a bygone era, and almost certainly has no wish to adapt to modern life in any shape or form. And yet here we are, two people fused in a moment of grief. Neither of us say a word, because no words are required. It is the strangest moment, and yet somehow it just feels so natural.

When we're eventually seated at a rickety wooden table in the living room, cum kitchen, cum dining room, George stuns me with a smile. Well I say smile, and I know that was the intention, but it comes out looking more like someone suffering from constipation. "I heard about Harry," he says, and wraps his shrivelled fingers round my left hand.

"I don't know why I came." I say honestly.

The smile turns into a grimace. "When I came home from the war," he begins,

90

and there's a misty, faraway look in his eyes, "people would come up to me and slap me on the back. I'd walk into a pub and people wanted to buy me a drink. In their eyes we were heroes. Maybe that was true for some. For most of us the reality was quite different. Most of us were not much more than kids, sent to fight in a foreign land. We knew we were fighting on the side of the righteous, but that doesn't make things any easier when you're lying all alone in your bed at night with the screams ringing in your ears... We'd seen and done things that nobody should ever have to live through. In those days there wasn't such a thing as PTSD, you just shut up and got on with it. The only people you could really talk to were those who had been there with you. They were the only ones who truly understood."

It was quite a speech from someone who had barely spoken more than three words to me in all the years I'd lived here. Perhaps he said it partly to put things in perspective, but I like to think it was more about our shared pain.

Although I stayed for over half-an-hour, not many words passed between us. And yet it never felt uncomfortable: We were just two grieving souls who had come together in a moment of need. I was so glad I came.

By the time I leave George's, the village has woken up. There aren't many people about, there never is, but most of those I do pass stop to offer words of comfort. News travels fast. Good or bad.

Yolanda is coming out of the village store and calls across the road to me. "Meg," she yells, waving her hand as she makes her way hurriedly across the

91

green.

She rushes straight up to me and gives me a great big hug. "I heard about Harry. I'm so sorry."

I put on a brave smile, even though I can feel my eyes glistening with tears because every time somebody offers any comforting words it reminds me of the stark reality of the situation. I try to keep telling myself Harry was just a dog, it's not like my husband just died, or God forbid a child, but it doesn't make the pain go away.

"I'm having a few of the girls round later this morning for coffee. Please come if you feel up to it. About eleven o' clock!" She pats me on the shoulder and smiles. "You don't want to be stuck in the house on your own all day."

I watch her cross the road, carefully picking her way round the edge of the damp grass in high-heeled shoes, and a little voice inside my head screams, 'how the hell do you know what I want?'. And that just makes me angry because I don't want to be this bitter woman who resents everybody else just because they don't understand.

When I pull open the front door there's still a little part of me hoping Harry will come bounding up the hall. Of course that doesn't happen. His lead is hanging on the hook by the front door and I grab it on my way past, just so I can hold onto something of his.

Stacy arrives at nine-thirty and I realise I haven't called her to bring her up to date. So on top of everything else, now I feel guilty because she's cancelled two clients and I know Stacy isn't in a good position financially. She really can't afford to be turning work away. So I have to sit her down and relay all the information Tony Skinner told me last night.

"But why would anyone put a dead dog in their lorry?" Stacy asks, looking bewildered. "It doesn't make any sense."

"I know. He told me to call the station and speak to Debbie something-or-other. But I'm not sure what good that's going to do."

"You know you won't be able to rest until you have." She knows me so well.

I make the call, but Debbie Martin can't tell me anything new. Basically she repeats everything Skinner told me. She sounds genuinely sympathetic and promises to let me know if any new information comes to her attention. The only thing she does add is that she's pretty sure the caller was a young male. I push for more information but she just apologises and says that's all she's got for me.

"So that's it," I say, throwing my phone onto the table.

Stacy frowns and pushes the dark hair away from her eyes. "I'm sorry."

Before she leaves, Stacy makes me agree to go to Yolanda's for the coffee morning. I know she only wants the best for me, so in the end I relent. That leaves almost an hour to kill, so to take my mind off things I decide to give Joanne a call to see if I can find out what the hell Greg was going on about. Part of me wants to call him and tell him about Harry, just so that he can take on some of the pain. But I can't be that cruel. I will tell him, when I'm not feeling so vindictive. I just don't trust myself today.

I make a coffee, settle into a chair and dial my grandmother's number.

Joanne doesn't sound like a ninety-year-old. Her voice is clear, and there's an almost child-like lilt, hinting at something awfully wicked that she's managed to get away with. "You don't have to concern yourself about it," she says, in answer to my question.

"Gran. I need to know."

"There was a clause in the contract," she says simply.

I feel my forehead crease into a thousand lines. "A clause? What sort of clause?"

"The sort that stops greedy little bastards getting their hands on things they have no right to. The house never belonged to you in the first place. It only becomes yours once I'm dead."

For once I'm speechless. I'm trying to remember back to when we first moved into the house: To the moment Joanne told me this was her wedding gift to us. I seem to recall talking to her about deeds and other such things, but obviously there was so much more going on at the time. I'm a solicitor for God's sake. I don't miss things like that. I can remember discussing it with her at some point, probably several months later, but as far as I was concerned it was all legal and above board. The fact that I never delved any deeper into the finer details about 'my' house probably says more about my ineptitude than it does about Joanne's devious nature.

"I'm sorry," I say, still quite stunned by this revelation. "Exactly what are you telling me? That for all these years we have just been tenants? albeit living rent free."

"I didn't say the clause has always been there," she says, and starts laughing. "Ask no questions..."

What the hell is she talking about? For just a moment I start to believe that my grandmother has finally lost her mind. The thought disappears as quickly as it arrived. But if I've understood what she has just told me correctly, somehow Joanne has persuaded her solicitor to alter an existing document. I can't deal with it right now, not on top of everything else. Besides, this is a conversation that needs to be held face to face, not over the phone. Does she actually realise the ramifications of her actions? I mean, we are talking major fraud.

"Gran, we need to talk about this when I have more time."

"Whatever you say darling. How's my favourite boy?"

Damn. "Fine," I lie. "I'll give you call later in the week to let you know when I'll be over."

I hang up and sit staring into space for several minutes with a vacant expression on my face. Could my grandmother really have persuaded her solicitor to alter a document? It just sounds so unlikely. The fact is, right now I should be sitting here feeling relieved; ecstatic even. If she's telling me the truth, Greg has no rights as far as the house is concerned. That bothers me the most, because he won't let it slide without putting up a fight. Greg will get his solicitor straight on the case - in fact he's almost certainly done so already – and if they do uncover the truth...Bloody hell!!!

Yolanda welcomes me into her home with a warm hug and a sympathetic, "How are you feeling now?"

"Okay." I'm not, but what else can I say.

We pass along her immaculate hallway, with its gleaming wooden flooring and perfectly decorated walls, and enter the lounge. The buzz of conversation dies the moment they see me walk through the door. Five pairs of eyes firmly fixed on the poor woman who is grieving the loss of her dog. And straight away I can see half of them are torn; after all, it was just a pet, their eyes seem to be saying.

They are seated on three, large brown leather sofas which surround a coffee table that probably costs more than most second hand cars. Helen Pierce and Dawn Brown are sitting on the sofa facing the doorway we have just entered. Leah Derby has a double armchair all to herself and there are two faces I don't recognise. No Stacy however, which is strange.

"These are a couple of girls I used to model with," Yolanda announces proudly.

I let the 'girls' part slide. A brunette and a blonde, both at least my age, possibly a little older, it's hard to tell because they're plastered in heavy-duty make up. The blonde has prominent cheek-bones and short hair; the brunette has oversized lips and and long, curly hair.

"Christine and Freya, this is Megan, she's the one we were telling you about." She pats my arm to emphasize the fact I need sympathy. "Harry was such a gorgeous dog too."

The ex-models both smile politely and the skin on their faces fails to comply. I quickly re-assess my original estimate, age wise. Both of them could easily be mid-fifties - at least ten years older than me - but a combination of Botox and plastic surgery makes them appear far younger, from a distance at least.

"We're all sorry to hear about Harry," Helen Pierce says, "He was such a lovely dog. Always friendly, not one of those snappy little beasts," she adds, as if it's important this fact is conveyed to the models.

I really don't want to be here. And bloody Stacy hasn't even turned up. If she hadn't insisted...and right on queue my mobile goes off.

"Excuse me," I say to nobody in-particular. Stacy's number glares at me from the screen. "Where are you?" I ask before she speaks.

"Sorry Meg', I've got a bit of a problem. I don't suppose there's any chance you can get away. I could really do with your help." She sounds worried, and I think I can detect a little bit of anger simmering beneath the surface.

I project my most concerned expression for the watching audience. "Yes, of course," I say. "I'll be there as soon as I can." I slip my phone back into my jacket pocket. "I am so sorry." I force an apologetic smile. "That was Stacy, there's some sort of crisis. I'm going to have to rush off."

"Is everything alright?" Yolanda asks. I know her concern is real, she likes Stacy, we all do.

"I'm not sure. I'll call you later." I wave a hand at the models on the way out of the room. "Nice to meet you."

Yolanda sees me to the front door and grabs me by the arm before opening it. "Call me if it's something I can help with. Oh, and thanks for leaving me with Tinky and Winky," she whispers, a wicked smile twinkling in her eyes. "Promise you'll tell me if I ever start to look like that."

"Oh I will."

Stacy is half way through clearing up her small kitchen. There are fragments of broken crockery on the tiled floor and a broken glass on the draining board. She looks exhausted, and I can tell she's been crying.

"What the hell happened here?"

Stacy puts down the mop she's holding and slumps onto a chair. "Watch your step, there's glass everywhere. I've shut Poppy in the lounge so don't open the door." She lets out a long sigh. "I came back from yours and Liam was here. I'd told him I was going to be out all day helping you look for Harry, which of course we would have been but..." she glances up at me and pushes the damp hair from her eyes. "The little sod must of made out he was going off to school then doubled back as soon as he saw me leave."

I sit down opposite her. "But..." I gesture to the carnage, "all this?"

"He can't have heard me come in because he was sitting here," she taps the table, "with a carrier bag. The moment he heard me coming he tried to hide it. We had a huge row because he wouldn't let me see what was in it. You know what he's like Meg', takes after after his bloody dad with his temper."

Liam is a typical teenager, going through all the emotions teenagers have to endure, but without a father figure to keep him in line. He's almost fifteen, but he's a big lad; almost six feet tall, wiry and muscular. Whenever I've met him he's always been polite – if he can drag his eyes away from his phone screen – but I know he can be a handful from what Stacy's told me. "He didn't hit you, did he?" I only asked because I knew Stacy's history with the father: Apparently he liked to end an argument with a slap or a punch.

Stacy shakes her head vigorously. "No. No he hasn't got to that stage...yet. He takes it out on inanimate objects at the moment," she attempts a half-hearted smile and gestures at the broken glass, "though God knows how long it will be before that changes?"

It's very hard for me to understand her predicament. When I first learned I couldn't have children I was devastated, but at moments like this I can't help thinking that I would never have coped. "I'm sure he's sorry," I say. "Where is he now?"

"He rushed up to his bedroom and crashed around for a while then stormed out of the house." Stacy sits up straight. "I watched him leave. He didn't have the carrier bag with him, so as soon as I was sure he wasn't coming back I went through his things." She shakes her head slowly. "Bloody hell Meg', I virtually tore the room apart looking for it."

"And?"

She gets up, crosses the room and pulls open a drawer. When she turns round there's a thick carrier bag dangling from her hand.

"Where was it?"

"He hid it in the bloody toilet cistern, if you can believe that. I only checked because I heard a clunk of porcelain when he went into the bathroom. I thought he was crashing about, but then I remembered watching a film a few weeks ago, and

99

they'd done the same thing." She slaps the bag – still dripping with water – on the table. "Look," she says.

The plastic is folded over tight at the end, forming a waterproof seal. I gently pull at the edges and spill the contents onto the table. "Jesus! How much is there?" I say, staring at the bundles of notes.

"Almost three-thousand pounds." Stacy wipes away the tears streaming down her cheeks. "What the hell has he gotten into?"

"First thing you have to do is put it back where you found it."

Stacy looks at me as if Ive gone mad. "It's almost three grand, Meg'! It takes me the best part of three months to earn that. There's only a couple of ways a kid his age gets that kind of cash. He's either dealing drugs or he stole it."

They would be the two options I'd come up with as well, but Stacy's not thinking with a clear head at the moment, and if a situation ever called for clarity, it's this one. "You go and put it back and I'll give you a hand clearing up down here. Then we can sit down and discuss it." I'm proud of how calm my voice sounds. Then I realise it's also the first time I haven't thought about Harry the entire day, and immediately feel guilty.

I begin tidying the kitchen whilst Stacy goes upstairs to put the cash back in its hiding place.

It takes less than half-an-hour to clean up. Stacy apologises constantly for having dragged me into her mess, but, although I'm seriously concerned about the situation, I'm quite glad to have something to take my mind off everything else.

As soon as we're sure the floor is clear of glass, Stacy lets Poppy out of the lounge. She scampers straight over and sniffs round my legs, wagging her tail enthusiastically, her head bobbing and twisting, searching for Harry. I try and ignore the lump caught in my throat as I'm stroking her.

Stacy puts the kettle on and I sit down at the table.

"Okay," I say, as soon as Stacy joins me at the table, "as far as Liam is aware you haven't got a clue what was in that carrier bag. He's probably had time to calm down by now, so let him do the talking when he comes home. Don't press him for answers."

"I can't just forget what I saw."

"No, of course not. But if you're going to get to the bottom of it you have to box clever. See what he comes up with. He'll probably try and fob you off with some cock and bull story: So let him. All the time he thinks you're none-the-wiser we have the upper hand."

"But what if..."

"No what if's." I grab her hand, which takes Stacy by surprise as I'm not usually a tactile person. "We don't know anything for certain. Liam is basically a good kid. Right?"

"I thought he was," she corrects me. "The apple doesn't fall far from the tree. That's what they say isn't it? God, if he turns out anything like his father..."

"He won't. You're a good mother," I manoeuvre the subject round to useless ex partners. The conversation is a long one.

By the time we've finished our tea a weak afternoon sun is seeping through the kitchen window, the sky now overcast. I check my watch and try not to think about returning to an empty house. I consider telling Stacy about Greg and the phone call to my grandmother, if only to distract her, but in the end I think better of it. "I'm going to have to get back soon, but the moment Liam gets home, call me." I squeeze her hand a little tighter. "And remember, stay calm."

"Yes. Okay. Whatever you say."

"It'll be fine," I try to sound as reassuring as I can. "Now don't forget, call me."

"I promise, and thanks for today. I feel terrible, dragging you round here."

"No worries," I say, as I leave. "Speak to you later."

I think about my parting words as I walk back towards the village. 'No worries,' what a bloody stupid statement to come out with. Stacy is probably sitting there now, going over every possible scenario in her head. I can't say I blame her, because as hard as I try I just can't come up with a plausible explanation for Liam having that much cash stashed in the house. All my instincts are telling me this can't possibly have a happy outcome.

CHAPTER 15

I haven't been indoors more than five minutes when there's a knock. What now?

I open the door to see Mark standing there with a rather sheepish look on his face. "I hope you don't mind," he says, producing a small bunch of long-stem roses from behind his back. "I heard about your dog. Harry, isn't it? It's not much," he says, offering the flowers to me. "I know how much it hurts to lose a pet."

"Oh, right, thank you," I splutter, rather lost for words.

He smiles and turns to leave.

"Do you want to come in?" I say quickly. Immediately wondering why I asked the question. I mean, I hardly know the man. He's obviously been working because he's wearing a dark pullover that has a slight tear just below the left shoulder - exposing an inch or two of tanned flesh – and faded work jeans. His clothes appear slightly too tight for his frame.

He smiles, squinting in the afternoon sun. "Sorry, I can't stop, I just wanted to give you those. But, if you feel like getting out of the house later, I eat at the pub most nights. If you feel like a chat?"

I watch him walk away from the house, casting a shadow across the gravel, until he finally disappears round the corner.

If this had been any other time...Last week I would have jumped at the chance, who wouldn't? Mark is hot. But today, right now it's all I can do to stop from bursting into tears every time I look at Harry's bowl, or pick up one of his old toys.

I put the flowers in a vase of water and flip open my lap-top to check my new emails. There are fifteen in total, thirteen are work-related, but two of them are from Greg's private email address. I open the first – received at 9.48 this morning – and scan through the message. He's not happy, that's clear, and he doesn't hold back on his opinion of either me or my grandmother, or as he refers to her, 'that vindictive old bitch'. I'm quite impressed with his use of grammar though. The second email sounds like it was obviously sent after he'd given himself time to calm down. He even suggests a meeting, and there's a half-hearted apology for some of the content of the first email. I delete them both and scan through the work-related ones to make sure nothing demands immediate attention.

I've just finished a bowl of tomato soup – which is just about all I can manage to eat right now – when my phone starts bleeping. Stacy, asking if she can pop round in ten. I tap out a reply and spend the time clearing the sink.

Stacy hasn't even got through the door before I ask, "So, how did it go?"

"Is it too early to start this," she says, holding out a bottle of white wine.

"That bad eh?"

We go through to the lounge and I pour out two large glasses. Stacy is standing, fidgeting uncomfortably from one foot to another.

"Come on then," I slump onto the sofa. "What did he say?"

"Oh he said plenty. He was very apologetic about losing his temper. But when I asked him what was in the carrier bag, and why he'd got so angry, he said it was porn magazines and he'd just been embarrassed. I managed to keep calm though, don't worry." She stops, takes a few gulps from her wine glass and finally sits down opposite me. "All day and that's the best he can come up with!"

"To be fair," I try and pick my words carefully, "that's a pretty good explanation if you think about it. It would explain him trying to stop you seeing inside the bag, and his overreaction."

Stacy doesn't look impressed. "Yes, if it wasn't a blatant lie." She takes another gulp of wine. "What the hell am I going to do, Meg'?"

"Where is Liam now?"

"At home, I hope. I told him he has to clean his room and he's grounded for the rest of the week. Little sod even had the audacity to try and haggle with me. He said if he cleaned the whole house and tidied the garden would I let him off being grounded. We settled on two nights in the end."

I couldn't help smiling.

"Don't laugh. It's not funny."

"Sorry, I know. I didn't mean to." To be fair, I was just glad I still had the capacity to see the funny side of things, even if it was completely inappropriate. I take a sip of wine and give myself a moment to think. "Okay, so as far as he's concerned you've accepted his story about the porn magazines?"

"Yes."

"So he won't expect you to be keeping tabs on him then?"

"No more than usual, no."

"Okay, that's what we'll do. Tomorrow night we'll follow him. Whatever he's up to must be happening in the evenings, that's the only spare time he's got unless he's been skipping school."

"No, the school are pretty hot on absence. I had a text from them today." Stacy finishes her glass and helps herself to more wine. "I did have one thought today though, and not a very nice one."

"Go on."

"Well...I don't...no, forget it."

"Stacy, just spit it out." I say, wondering what on earth is coming.

"This spate of dogs going missing," she begins sheepishly, "they fetch good money don't they. I mean, that's why these people do it. For the money I mean.

You don't think Liam has got mixed up in all that..."

The thought hadn't crossed my mind, but then again I hadn't been sitting in the house all day worrying about my fifteen-year-old son. I could see how Stacy might have been imagining every conceivable scenario. Maybe stealing dogs was not the worst option she could think of.

"Really!" I shake my head slowly. "I just can't see it. Whoever is doing that is callous, they'd have to have a really cruel streak, and that just doesn't sound like Liam to me."

Stacy nods. "No, I don't know why I even thought of it."

"Because you're beside yourself with worry, that's why. Any mother would be the same." I pick up the bottle to replenish our glasses, and stop before pouring. "I've just had a brainwave."

"What?"

"I can't believe neither of us thought about it sooner."

Stacy shrugs. "Thought about what?"

"His phone never leaves his side, right? Everything he does, anyone he contacts or speaks to or texts, it's all stored in that little bit of plastic. We don't need to go sneaking round in the dark trying to follow him."

"I already thought about that, but he literally, never puts it down. Besides, I know it'll be locked and there's no way he's going to let me see what he's got stored in there. And let's face it Meg', neither of us are too hot on technology. Even if I could prise it away from him."

"What time does he go to bed?"

"Weekdays about ten-thirty, maybe a little later if he's watching something. Why?"

"Because if you can manage to get his phone for a couple of hours I think I might know a man who can help us. As long as you're okay with delving into your son's private life?"

Stacy sits bolt upright. "If it means I get to find out what he's up to, then bloody hell yes, I'll do whatever it takes."

"Okay," I chew on my bottom lip, trying to work a strategy out in my head. "Right," I say, when at last the sequence of events I need to put in place has been formulated. "You go home, see if you can get your head down for a couple of hours. As soon as you're sure Liam is asleep, text me. If there are any problems I'll call you as soon as I can."

Stacy looks totally bemused. "Problems with what?"

"Don't worry about that, just make sure you can get hold of his phone." I get up, grab the two glasses and half empty bottle and take them out to the kitchen. "I've got to make a phone call," I say, as I'm ushering Stacy out of the door.

Darren Harding answers on the second ring. Just as I thought he would. "Hello. Megan?" There's a reason I didn't give myself too much time to think this through; I didn't want to consider the consequences of making this call. He hasn't, or can't, hide his excitement at my having called him out of office hours. "What can I do for you?"

"My friend has a problem..." Best to get straight to the point, but that sounds so naff. Doctor, my 'friend' has a rash...A 'friend' of mine is drinking too much...I pause, and start again. "I need your help with something."

"Of course. Anything." And I know he isn't exaggerating. Darren is a technological wizard. Our firm have used him numerous times over the years - for various things - and he has never failed to deliver. There are however one or two reasons why me calling him might not be the best idea I've ever had, but I don't want to think about them right now.

"I don't suppose you could spare me an hour or two of your time tonight. I need to hack a phone."

"Yes, no problem," he says, as if this is something he gets asked all the time. He doesn't bother asking whose phone. In fact, he asks nothing except, "What time?"

"Around ten-thirty. I know it's a lot to ask but..."

"That's fine," he says, cutting me off mid-sentence, and I can hear his voice has almost reached falsetto.

I don't want to picture his face, but an image creeps into my head nonetheless: Darren is a big lad, twenty-four stone at least, and when you're only five-foot-seven...well you can imagine. He struggles with several issues, including personal hygiene and a complete lack of interpersonal skills when dealing with members of the opposite sex: Especially if the person in question happens to be me. In short, Darren has a massive crush on me. It's a running joke round the office, and one which I was unaware of until I caught two of the secretaries whispering and giggling by the coffee machine one day.

"Thank you so much. I'll text you my address."

"No need, I've already got it. I'll see you later tonight, Megan." And the sound

108

of my voice rolling off his tongue sends an involuntary tingle down my spine.

What have I done?

I call Stacy to bring her up to speed. I figure if Darren gets to mine at ten-thirty, that will give me time to explain what we need him to do before we head off to Stacy's to implement plan. That leaves me with about three spare hours in my very empty house.

I can't face spending the entire evening alone. I'll just sit here staring at all the things that remind me of Harry, and trying not to cry.

Mark is sitting at a table in the corner of the pub when I arrive. He's almost finished his meal. He looks up when I walk over, and a broad smile lights up his face.

"Are we still on for that chat?" I ask.

He stands, pulls out a chair and gestures me to sit down. "Of course. Can I get you a drink?"

Tonight he's wearing a white v-neck T-shirt. I can't help noticing the material is straining at the shoulders. "Thank you," I say and slide into the chair.

The pub is busy, as always. They have very good reviews in the local paper and people come from miles around to sample their menu. Subtle lighting and a low-beamed ceiling create an atmosphere of intimacy and music seeps from several well placed speakers, although the sound is barely audible above the low hum of chatter from the surrounding tables. I'm happy to see there are no familiar faces in tonight, I really couldn't handle being stared at if any of my friends were to walk in.

I'm already feeling slightly awkward; knowing I was to become this weeks topic of coffee morning gossip wouldn't do much for the butterflies swirling round in the pit of my stomach. Butterflies I might add, that seem to have inexplicably appeared from nowhere and for no apparent reason.

The waitress – a pretty blonde called Emily – is a local girl. She's usually very pleasant and I wonder if it's my imagination, or is she trying to disguise a rather sour expression when she comes to clear the table and Mark orders drinks.

"So what exactly is it you do?" I ask as we wait for the waitress to return with our drinks order.

"Environmental research. Very boring. What about you?"

"I'm a partner in a small firm of solicitors."

"And what do you do when you're not soliciting?" His face cracks into a huge smile. "Sorry, couldn't help myself."

I return the smile to make sure he knows I'm fine with his little joke that I've heard a hundred times before. "Oh, you know, the house, the garden, walking..." an image of Harry pops into my head. "How does your family feel about you working away from home?" I ask, changing the subject and realising immediately the question is far too direct. I might just as well have come straight out and asked him if he was married.

His answer is interrupted when Emily appears with our drinks. She leans over the table further than necessary, and places Mark's glass down with a smile. Nothing says 'I'm available' better than a healthy display of firm cleavage. She puts my glass down without so much as glancing in my direction.

The distraction means my question hangs unanswered far longer than feels comfortable. If Mark has noticed the display, he hides it well, because the moment Emily leaves he says, "I haven't found anyone who would put up with me yet." False modesty? Men who look like Mark must know. They must feel the eyes burning into them when they're standing at a bar, or sitting at a table talking to a middle-aged woman.

We spend the next couple of hours deep in conversation. I can't ever recall feeling so relaxed in the company of a virtual stranger. Mark is a good listener, and when he does speak it's usually to say something derogatory about himself just to try and make me smile, or - on one or two occasions – even laugh. I briefly mention my disastrous marriage, and have to stop myself from going into detail about the current situation with regards to Greg. I do mention that my ex-husband and his child-bride are now expecting a baby.

"Well you have to feel sorry for him," Mark says.

I frown. It's impossible to read his face.

"He's clearly in need of some sort of psychiatric care if he let you get away," he adds quickly. Then he smiles and shakes his head. "God, sorry, that sounded far better in my head."

It's the only corny line he's come out with, so I'm prepared to let it ride. Usually I'd have replied with some witty comment, but I can feel my cheeks burning from this all-too-obvious compliment, so I just smile.

The rest of the evening passes far too quickly. Talking to Mark is like laying in a bath where the water is kept at the perfect temperature: You just want to stay there feeling relaxed, letting all your worries drift away. So when I glance at the clock on the wall above the bar I'm shocked to see it's already gone ten.

"Damn. I didn't realise the time," I say, already rising from my seat. "Sorry, but I'm going to have to shoot off."

"I'll walk you back," he says, starting to get up.

"No, it's fine. I'm literally just the other side of the road." I know Darren will arrive early, he won't be able to help himself. No doubt he'll be hoping I invite him for coffee. In fact he's probably been imagining all kinds of scenarios as he drives through the night. I try not to let this thought spoil my evening. "It really has been nice though. Thank you for taking my mind off of...well, you know."

Mark stands, leans forward and kisses me gently on the cheek. "The pleasure was all mine," he says, "hopefully we can do it again sometime?"

"Definitely." I produce a pen from my jacket pocket and scribble my number on one of the beer mats. "Call me." I like to think he watched me walk away.

It's a chilly night outside and I pull the collar of my jacket tight round my neck as I skip across the village green. The walk back home takes less than two minutes, but it's long enough for me to fight with all the contrasting emotions I'm feeling right now. The ache, buried deep inside me for the loss of Harry hasn't disappeared, but now there's another, lighter feeling, lifting me, promising hope of something better. I want to fight it. I've been here before, let myself get too entangled far too quickly, and before I know what's happening I end up getting hurt. I make a mental note to be on guard, but a little demon is already telling me it's too late for that.

CHAPTER 16

I watch the beams of light bouncing up and down in the darkness as Darren

negotiates the pot-holes in the narrow lane leading up to the house. I'm already

waiting on the doorstep by the time he's turned the car round. Am I selfish for

wanting to keep him out of the house after he's driven all this way? Probably.

He pulls up and applies the handbrake. I rush across to the car before he can cut

the engine. The drivers window is open and he's got his arm crooked over the door,

trying far too hard to look cool. I can imagine his car – a silver Audi A8 – would

widen the eyes of some younger, more impressionable girls. Perhaps he's had

some success, but somehow I just can't see it.

"Thank you so much for this." I smile, trying to make sure I don't overdo it. "Do

you mind if we go straight over to my friend's house?"

He looks disappointed. "No, of course not."

The interior of the car smells of cheap aftershave and extra-strong mints. He's

got the heater turned up full blast and the black plastic trim of the dashboard is

gleaming bright from an earlier clean. He's gone to a lot of trouble.

I slide into the passenger seat. "It's only a couple of minutes away. We might

have to wait outside for a while, if that's okay?"

"Of course it is." His voice is quiet, deeper than usual. The people at work call it

his 'Megan' voice. I usually find that funny, but now I'm sitting next to Darren,

looking at his outer thigh spilling over the edge of his seat and the perspiration glistening on his forehead, I don't find it so amusing. I can see the folds of excess flesh beneath his designer stubble. If he was hoping it would make him look slightly less obese, I'm afraid it hasn't worked.

I text Stacy as we head over. She replies instantly: Liam has just turned his bedroom light off, so now she's waiting until she's sure he's asleep. I text back, 'no problem'.

"So exactly how does it work then?" I ask when Darren cuts the engine. We have parked a few houses down the road from Stacy's. Little spots of rain tap against the windscreen.

Darren smiles confidently. I know from previous experience, he likes to talk about his work. He likes to impress. "Quite simple really, if you know what you're doing," he says, unclipping his seat belt so he can turn to face me.

He starts to explain - in intricate detail - precisely how he plans to 'piggy-back' the information from Liam's phone onto Stacy's. Five seconds into the explanation, I'm completely lost. My brain hasn't managed to fully adjust to modern technology, but even if it had, I don't think I would have a hope of understanding what he's telling me. I'm sure this is something Darren is aware of. There's no doubting his genius, and I nod and smile and try to look impressed when it feels appropriate.

When he's finished, he leans back his in seat looking quite satisfied that his explanation has had the desired impact. If I've understood correctly – as long as he can crack Liam's password – he can install a hidden link which will automatically connect to Stacy's phone. Any messages or calls that Liam receives will appear on Stacy's phone. I didn't need him to tell me this is all highly illegal, a point that he

114

wanted to emphasize just to ensure I understood just how big a favour this is.

"Wow," I say, offering him the look of awe he so obviously craves. "But what if you can't get into Liam's phone?"

"Not likely," he says smugly, and produces a little black box with a short cable from his jacket pocket. "My own invention," he says, swinging the prized possession by the lead as if it were an expensive piece of jewellery. "It's a very quiet village," he says, changing the subject. "What do you do in the evenings?"

Oh God! "Oh there's plenty to do. Work mostly."

"Well if you ever fancy going out for a drink, or maybe dinner..."

"Oh," I cut him short. This was what I was dreading, although if I'm honest I didn't really believe he'd have the balls to be so direct. "That's very nice of you to offer, but, well you're a little young for me to be honest." It's the kindest thing I can think of saying.

"I'm thirty-seven!" he exclaims. "There can't be more than ten years difference? That's nothing."

Eight...eight bloody years you cheeky git. I'm glad it's dark in the car so he can't see the look on my face. Thankfully my phone bleeps with a message: Stacy has got Liam's phone. Talk about being saved by the bell.

We enter the house quietly and go through to the kitchen. Stacy closes the door carefully and lets Poppy in from the back garden, keeping hold of her collar until she's been introduced to Darren. I whisper the introductions and we all sit at the table.

"Thank you for doing this," Stacy says, and offers Darren a perfect smile along

115

with her and Liam's phones.

"My pleasure."

"And here," she produces a small slip of paper, "I found this in his bedside drawer. I think they might be his passwords."

"Oh.." Darren looks genuinely disappointed that he's not going to get the chance to impress us. "I could have done it without them, but this makes it easier." He just had to say it.

It takes Darren less than ten minutes to do whatever it is he has to do. When he's finished he passes Liam's phone back to Stacy. "Done," he says proudly. "Right, this is how it works." He stands up and moves round to where Stacy is sitting, leaning over her whilst scrolling through her screen. "When you want to check his messages use this icon." He taps it with his finger. "Any messages or calls your son receives will automatically be registered here. Times, dates, numbers, everything. I've also installed an invisible tracker."

"God, does this make me a bad mother?" Stacy is staring at the screen, shaking her head. Darren can't help looking down the top of her dressing gown. The tip of his tongue darts out involuntarily and licks his dry lips.

"No," I say, in a slightly louder voice than we've been using. "You're doing what you have to." I cast a glance at Darren and his face flushes red.

"Well thank you so much ," Stacy says, getting up and giving Darren an unexpected hug. I swear, you could fry eggs on his cheeks.

The rain is coming down hard when we leave. The only light comes from two street lamps placed either end of the road; the one in the middle doesn't work.

116

There's no point in racing ahead as I can't get into the car until Darren gets there, and because of his size, he doesn't move very fast. So we pick our way along the narrow pavement in the semi-darkness, trying to avoid the soaking hedges that encroach over the footpath. I'm peering through the rain trying to assess how far we've got to go when I see it. At the far end of the street there's a white van, two wheels up on the curb, sitting at a slight angle. It shouldn't look out of place in a street lined with parked cars, but the silhouette of someone sitting in the drivers seat does. As we get closer the figure slides down in their seat. It's probably nothing, but I can't help feeling a shiver run down my spine.

We drive back to mine in silence. Darren is clearly embarrassed that I caught him ogling Stacy's cleavage and I'm pretty certain he's sitting there trying to think of something appropriate to say, if only to break the silence.

By the time we pull into my narrow lane he still hasn't managed to come up with anything. Under normal circumstances I would of dug him out of his hole and broke the silence, but my mind is elsewhere. I can't shake off the sight of someone lowering themselves down in that van, it's an image that will undoubtedly haunt me tonight, so worrying about Darren's feelings isn't something that's high on my list of priorities right now. The thought that someone could be spying me is really quite unnerving. Of course, there could be a perfectly innocent explanation, but by the time Darren has parked the car I haven't come up with one.

"I am so grateful, Darren. I owe you one." I've already got the car door open and one leg out. "Honestly, you are a star."

He manages an awkward smile. And says, "No problem," but the disappointment is buried deep in his eyes.

I stand under the porch and watch him drive away, wondering if that's the last favour he'll ever do me. Not that I'd blame him. Poor Darren had probably worked himself up into a frenzy on his way over this evening, imagining all kinds of scenarios. Maybe one day he'll meet someone who can love him for his genius and see past the exterior, and the rather pungent odour that somehow managed to claw its way past a layer of cheap aftershave.

I step into the house and bolt the door behind me. The hall light is on, but it seems so dark and empty. So silent. So devoid of life. A tomb, rather than a home. I want to be brave and look to the future. I want to keep thinking about Stacy's problems and about how nice my evening with Mark was, and about anything that won't drag me down into the mire of despair tearing at my insides every time I look at Harry's lead. But I can't. Instead I let the tears come and surrender to the accompanying pain.

It's late and I'm tired. The events of the last couple of days have left me feeling drained. Even so, the chance of me falling asleep straight away are almost zero. I pour some milk into a saucepan, place it on the hob and dig around in the cupboard for a sachet of hot chocolate. If this doesn't help me get to sleep, nothing will. While I'm waiting for the milk to boil I gaze round the kitchen at all the little things that remind me of Harry. His bowl, his blanket, his favourite ball, the list is endless and I know at some point I'm going to have to deal with it all. The thought stabs, far too deep, and I say out loud, "sort yourself out you silly cow."

The bedroom feels colder than usual. The window faces west, taking the brunt of the weather. I slide into bed and sit there sipping my hot chocolate, listening to the rhythmical drum of rain against the window. I haven't felt lonely since Greg walked out. I always had Harry. It didn't matter that he's a dog, I could sit here talking to him if I didn't feel sleepy and he would just lay there listening, soaking up all my worries without offering an opinion. Perhaps everybody needs a Harry. Everybody has little demons lurking beneath the surface: Those little voices that speak to you when you're feeling low, or lacking confidence. Do we all have moments when we ask, why are we even here? I'm sure we do. Those moments are rare, but right now that's all I can think about. I didn't make a choice not to have children, and I have mostly learned to live with the hand I've been dealt, but sitting alone in a cold bedroom tends to poke those demons awake. Right now they are working hard to drag me into a place I really don't want to go. Joanne is constantly telling me, 'life is short, make the most of every moment,' and I do try to heed her advice. But tonight I'm finding it hard.

I don't know how long it took before I drifted off to sleep, but the sound of a chair scraping across the tiles in the kitchen is enough to snap me awake. I sit up, heart thumping far too quickly, one hand on the mattress, the other on the wooden head-board. I slide my legs from the bed, letting my feet hit the floor like a feather drifting to the ground. Now the doubt creeps in. Was it just a dream? That figure in the van has left me feeling jittery. The events of the last few days have left me exhausted. I'm tired that's all. But something doesn't feel right. Yes I'm scared, but it's more than that. The air drifting through the half open door of my bedroom is too cold, too fresh. That could just be the empty house. The next sound cannot be misinterpreted: An item of cutlery hitting the floor, the sound of stainless steel rattling against the tiles. Now I'm certain I'm not alone.

CHAPTER 17

Someone is in the house. The air catches in my lungs for the longest moment, and when at last I do exhale it comes out as an audible gasp. I turn to reach for my phone, realise I've left it downstairs, and my chest tightens. It's funny the things that can enter your head when you're really, really scared. All I can think at this moment is, if I have a heart attack would a burglar call an ambulance or just leave me dying on the bedroom floor. My brain manages to summon up a few other, more horrific scenarios that I try and bat away. Modern technology has shown us all what a dangerous, evil place the world can be. I stopped being surprised by just what some people are capable of a long time ago. Right now none of these thoughts are going to help. Somehow I need to focus on my situation and find a solution.

It has gone silent downstairs. I can imagine whoever's in my house, standing, listening to see if anyone woke when the spoon, fork or knife fell to the floor. Perhaps they will just steal what they want and go? Maybe they've already gone? That thought soon disappears. All my instincts are telling me they're still here.

I grab a pair of jeans from the back of a chair and slip into them without making a sound. It feels important to get dressed. Less exposed. Though what good that will do me? I pull an old sweater over my head and stand by the bed, frozen to the spot. Can I hear breathing? It's hard to tell above the rain battering the window. The window! Maybe that's my way out. I know I can get through the opening, it's just the drop to the ground I'm not sure about. It can't be more than ten feet? I could make it, I know I could. But what then?

The sound of the kitchen door slowly creaking open tells me what I already suspected; they haven't left. I look around for a weapon. You'd think there would be something, anything, that could be adapted to attack an intruder. I pull the top drawer of my bedside cabinet open. Nothing. Unless I want to beat him about the head with my vibrator. Can you imagine the headlines?

I tip-toe across the room and slide open the wardrobe door. Panic is setting in. I grab a wire coat hanger from the rack and twist it until all but the hooked end is gripped in my sweaty palm. If I'm forced to fight, I will, but hopefully that will be a last resort.

I step over to the window and pull it open. As soon as they set foot on the the third tread of the stairs I will know. I'll know because it creaks, it always has. I'm ready to take my chances jumping out of the window rather than remain here, trapped in my bedroom. More front page headlines appear in my mind before I can swat them away: Woman found raped and murdered in quiet country village. The thought makes me feel physically sick. I toy with the idea of screaming from the open window, but nobody would hear. The window looks out across the fields, and what with the wind and rain...

The bedroom door suddenly swings open. I'm half way out the window when I see Harry limp into the room and flop down beside the bed.

A thousand different emotions explode inside me. "Harry!" I scream, rushing towards the wet bundle of fur collapsed on my bedroom floor. Tears are streaming down my face and I'm shaking so violently that I have to grab at him three or four times before I finally lift him into my arms. He's sopping wet and shivering, but his tail is slapping against my leg and he's licking my face furiously.

God knows how long I sat there cradling him in my arms, but it's only when I release my grip slightly that I notice the watery streaks of blood on the carpet and my clothes.

CHAPTER 18

Harry

I thought I was dying, I really did. When I heard the gunshot and felt the sting in my side I knew I'd been shot. Only I hadn't. What really happened was, the pellets had hit the tree and a few splinters of bark had cracked me in the ribs and hind leg. Of course I ran, and I wasn't stopping for anything. Someone was trying to kill me, I wanted to get as far away as possible. That was part of the problem, I ran so far, so fast, that I completely lost my bearings. When I did finally fall to the ground from exhaustion I was lost. I didn't know that at the time, I was just glad I'd managed to escape alive. I lay under a tree panting, watching the red stream trickle from beneath me, fearing the worst. The reality was, the rain made it appear there was a lot of blood and it was only when I started tugging the splinters from my skin with my teeth I discovered the wood had barely grazed my flesh.

I really haven't got a clue how long I lay under that tree. Nibbling little bits of bark from your skin isn't a process that can be rushed. I do know it was cold and wet and very, very dark. By the time the rain stopped I was already soaked through to the skin. My first thought was getting home to Megan, but I was also worried that whoever shot at me was currently stalking through the woods searching for their prey. There was no way I intended going anywhere near the reservoir, so I walked deeper into the forest intending to put as much distance between myself and my attackers as I could. This wasn't a good idea. Apparently I am seriously lacking in navigational skills.

God knows how long I've been gone.

So here I am, happy to be back home, but slightly confused. Megan hasn't let go of me for the last fifteen minutes and she hasn't stopped crying. To be honest I'm shocked by this reaction. The least I was expecting was a severe scolding. I've been gone for ages and I've covered the carpet – not to mention Megan's clothes – in a rather slimy, reddish-brown mixture of mud and blood. Megan is currently running her fingers through my fur searching for the cause.

"Where have you been, boy? What happened to you?" She bombards me with questions and grabs a fluffy white towel from one of the drawers. Then she proceeds to meticulously dry me whilst searching for wounds she probably won't even be able to see. There is no bullet wound, no lead pellets, just a few scratches. They are quite deep though.

Not for the first time, I wish I could speak. Michael Totter is dead, that's what I want to tell her. He's been murdered and buried in a shallow grave in the woods.

Not only that, but I can take a pretty good guess at the culprit. It had to be Mark. That bastard killed Winston, I know it. It was probably him who tried to kill me. I didn't recognise either of the voices I heard shouting in the woods, but then I wouldn't, I was too busy trying to save myself.

"How did you get these?" I can feel her fingers gently parting my fur where the splinters of bark hit me. "Did you get caught in some barbed wire?" she asks, holding my head in both hands, her face so close that my tongue darts out instinctively and I begin licking at her cheeks.

Barbed wire? Perhaps the wounds are worse than I thought. It really does sting.

We stay like this for what seems like an eternity. I can't explain how glad I am to be home and reunited with Megan, and under any other circumstances I'd be more than happy to stay like this forever, but right now all I can think about is food. Also, when we do go down to the kitchen, I can show her the scarf I took when I unearthed the body. As scared as I was, at least I had the foresight to know this will prove important. Once the police realise who the scarf belongs to perhaps they'll start searching.

Eventually Megan leads me back down the stairs to the kitchen. I just can't get over the fact she's being like this. The stair carpet is covered in dark paw-prints and she hasn't said a thing. Maybe I should disappear more often!

We're up early the following morning. Megan let me sleep on the bed all night, which is very rare, usually she ends up pushing me off because 'apparently' I tend to move about a lot. She's one to talk.

124

We have breakfast and Megan spends the following hour making one phone call after another. I have dropped Michael Totters scarf by the kitchen door but Megan hasn't commented yet. I'll bring it to her attention when she's finished making her calls. I'm shocked to learn she actually thought I was dead. Really! No wonder she was so glad to see me. Maybe if I can feign a limp for a few days I can make the most of this. I quickly dismiss the thought. Too wicked. Besides, the way Megan is treating me at the moment I don't see how life could get any better.

"Mark," I hear Megan say and my ears prick up. "Harry isn't dead. No. No he came home last night." She has started crying again. "God knows. He's got a few scratches but apart from that..."

I was shot at! With a proper gun! I could quite easily be dead you know. More to the point, why is she talking to Mark like this? How long have I been gone for Christ's sake?

"I just called to tell you the news and thank you for last night."

What!! What happened last night? And why is she talking in 'that' voice.

"Well I suppose I could, yes. I'm taking Harry to the vets' this morning and I've got something I have to deal with this afternoon, but tonight...yes that would be wonderful."

What would be wonderful? Nothing that man has to do with anything, could possibly be wonderful. This can't be happening. I'm watching her pace the floor, her left hand holding the phone to her ear while she traces lines across the table with the tips of her fingers as she talks. She leans down and picks up the dirty red scarf I left by the back door. She studies it at arms length and wrinkles her nose, then she walks over to the bin and tosses it inside without breaking stride. The evidence I nearly died collecting cast away like a bit of old rubbish.

"Actually, how about you come over to mine. I'll cook something, as a thank you for last night."

Mark. Here!! Over my dead body. I run to the bin and bark, but Megan ushers me away without losing concentration.

"That's great. Shall we say eight? Okay, I'll see you then."

She clicks the phone off and places it on the table, and when she turns round there is a huge, disgusting smile on her face. A smile put there from talking to Mark.

The trip to the vets isn't nearly as bad as I was expecting. We're in and out in less than ten minutes. As soon as we arrive home Megan takes me out for a walk and parades me round the village. It seems I am quite popular after all. People appear from nowhere and lavish me with attention.

"So where have you been then?" Yolanda is out of breath having scurried across the green. She is currently leaning over me massaging my head. "What happened to him? And what was all that rubbish about someone throwing him in the back of a lorry?" she asks, rising to her feet.

"I haven't spoken to Tony yet," Megan says. "I'm planning on calling him later. I suppose whoever called them must have been mistaken."

What's all this about the back of a lorry?

"It's a bit strange though." Yolanda persists.

Megan reaches down and strokes me, as if she needs confirmation that I am really here and it hasn't all been a dream. "To be honest, I'm just glad they were wrong."

"Yes, yes I'm sure." Yolanda places a reassuring hand on Megan's shoulder. "I think we all were. The place wouldn't be the same without you boy," she adds in a soppy voice. "We need to celebrate. How about a girls night? Lance is away for the week so my place is free."

"Tonight?"

"Yes. Bring Harry, I'll call the others."

"I...I can't tonight. Sorry." Megan has a silly grin on her face.

"Oh! Are you going to divulge?"

"I went for a drink with Mark last night. Just to talk."

I was missing - presumed dead - and she was out gallivanting with a total stranger. And if that wasn't bad enough, the man's a killer. He's got Winston's blood on his hands and Megan has been cosying up to him behind my back. I suddenly feel sick.

"What!" Yolanda shrieks excitedly. "Hot Mark? Hot Mark from the pub the other night?"

Megan laughs. "Well I wouldn't quite put it like that but..."

"Well I certainly would. You crafty cow." Yolanda laughs out loud. "Well forget my boring girls night in. You go for it girl. I'll arrange something for tomorrow night instead, and that way we get to hear all the juicy details."

"We've been for one drink," Megan says firmly, but she can't take the smile off her face.

"And?"

"And what?"

"Well he obviously didn't bore you to death did he."

"It was nice. He's a good listener."

Yolanda clasps a hand to her mouth. "Oh you lucky bitch," she says and throws her arms round Megan.

Unbelievable. I'm stunned. If I could speak, I'd be speechless. All I can do now is sink to the ground with a sad look on my face.

"I think Harry needs a rest," Megan says. "I'll call you tomorrow."

"Yes, you make sure you do. Bye Harry."

We walk home slowly, stopping occasionally whenever anyone wants to know what happened to me. Right now I can't be bothered to listen to any of it, I'm too distraught. Megan has betrayed me.

A shocking revelation. It turns out the 'something' Megan has to deal with this afternoon is, Greg. To be precise, it's Greg and his girlfriend, Lucy, who looks like she should still be in high school. Lucy is a pencil-thin blonde, or at least she would be if it wasn't for the huge bump protruding from her stomach.

They arrived mid-afternoon and Megan invited them into the house. Into our house, if you please!! She's made a pot of tea and now they're all sitting at the table in the kitchen. So very polite. So civil. Greg insists on trying to make a fuss of me, and like a fool, I succumb. I want to hate him, but I can't. Perhaps it's different for dogs, but our love is unconditional. If it hadn't been for Greg I would never have found Megan. I can't even begin to comprehend life without her.

Greg hasn't stopped talking since they arrived. I assume this is nerves, Greg is not normally much of a talker. He looks tired. Tired and old. I Assume having a girlfriend half your age and getting her pregnant takes a toll.

"How far gone are you?" Megan asks as she takes her seat at the table.

"Twenty-four weeks," Lucy says, but I notice she glances at Greg before answering.

Megan nods, her face betraying absolutely no emotion whatsoever. "Not long now then?"

Lucy smiles nervously. "No."

"So," Megan says, turning to Greg, "I presume you have come up with a new demand, as you wanted this meeting."

"Come on Meg', I didn't demand anything."

"You wanted me to give you the bloody house."

"We were together a long time. Surely I'm entitled to something..."

"You're entitled to exactly fuck all," Megan jumps in. I'm shocked, Megan almost never says that word.

Greg's cheeks flush red. I can't decide whether he's angry or embarrassed.

"If that's the case," he says angrily, "then why the hell did you agree to this meeting?"

Megan smiles, but it doesn't look like her usual smile. "Maybe I just wanted to see you squirm."

Lucy jumps up. "Come on Greggy'," she says, standing with one hand on the bump and the other grasping the back of the chair for support. "We're wasting our time."

Greggy!! Oh-my-God, that is hysterical. I can't believe Megan has managed to keep a straight face. Greg glares at Lucy, then Megan, then at table. I can almost hear his brain counting down from ten, trying to remain calm. "Whatever stunt that witch of a grandmother of yours thinks she's pulled, it'll backfire. It will. I'll get my solicitor to delve into all the records. I won't let it drop, you know I won't."

"One-hundred-thousand," Megan says.

"What?" Greg is half standing, palms flat on the table.

"You heard me. That is my one and only offer. It's final and I won't be negotiating. Take it or leave it. For that, you walk away and never contact me again. Oh, and I would of course want you to sign a contract just to verify things." She forces a smile. "Because, as we both know, you can't be taken at your word. So you and your little gym-slip girlfriend toddle off and let me know what you decide. The offer expires at midnight tomorrow."

Greg looks stunned, and Lucy has slumped back into her chair.

"Who the fuck do you think you are?" I'm sure there's steam coming out of his ears, but Greg is moving round the table towards Megan in a very threatening manner, and I'm not having that. I crouch down in front of Megan and give my best impression of a vicious growl.

Megan rests her hand on my back. "It's okay Harry."

I must have been impressive because Greg stopped in his tracks and Lucy

130

managed a pathetic squeal as she leapt from her chair. Just to make sure he got the message I curl my top lip back, baring my teeth.

"Jesus!" Greg looks stunned. "What the hell have you done to him?"

Lucy has reached the door. "Let's go," she whimpers. She really does look terrified.

"I think you managed to do that all by yourself." Megan says, and her voice has a hard edge that I can't recall hearing before. "I meant what I said, you've got until midnight tomorrow, after that, all bets are off. It's more than you deserve. Oh, and by the way, I hope you'll be very happy together."

Megan waited until they had left before she threw her cup against the wall.

CHAPTER 19

The house is filled with wonderful aromas. Megan spent most of the afternoon in the kitchen doing all sorts of things that I haven't seen her do since Greg was living here. The oven is on and there are pots steaming on the hob. I tried to sneak a taste of something Megan left on the table but got a tap on the nose for my trouble. I can't see how this is fair, if she was that happy to have me back surely she'd let me taste her cooking?

Right now I'm laying on the bedroom floor watching Megan try on her fourth outfit in the last half-hour. She looks amazing in all of them, but as soon as she stands in front of the full-length mirror she tuts, and starts fishing around in the wardrobe. Finally she settles on a plain black skirt and beige sweater. She looks stunning, as always, but she tried on this ensemble twenty-minutes ago and it wasn't good enough then, so I don't know what's changed.

We eventually head back downstairs to the kitchen. Megan is now wearing her slopping-about-in dressing gown; a blue towelling creation that has seen far better days. She resumes stirring, chopping and preparing her meal, and what's worse she is now humming along to the radio. I'm really not sure if I can get through tonight. If he makes one move out of place I'll be ready.

Megan is busy stirring a boiling pot when there's a knock at the door. I really hope it's Mark calling to cancel.

Unfortunately it's Tony Skinner. "Sorry to come round unannounced," Skinner says, when Megan opens the door. He's wearing his uniform. "I should have spoken to you earlier but I just haven't had the chance." He's hovering, as if he expects to be invited in.

"No problem." Megan says, standing her ground.

"I feel awful. I don't know whether the person who called the station was just mistaken, or malicious. There are some sick people out there."

"Really, it doesn't matter. Harry's home now, and apart from a few scratches he's fine."

I take issue with the 'few scratches' remark. What about the psychological damage? What about malnutrition? Okay, perhaps I'm going a bit far, but I certainly haven't felt myself since getting home. A thought suddenly pops into my head. I quickly disappear into the kitchen leaving them talking on the doorstep. The bin isn't tall, it has one of those plastic lids that flap open whenever you put something in, then closes automatically. I jump up and place my paws on the lid with the intention of dipping my head inside and retrieving the scarf. Unfortunately the bin is only half full and my weight causes it to tumble forward, spilling the contents all over the floor.

"Harry!" I hear Megan shout, but I've already grabbed the scarf - which is now covered in bits of chopped vegetable and a slimy sort of grey cream – and am heading towards the front door with the scarf flapping from my mouth.

Megan's shadow looms before me, blocking my path to the bemused-looking policeman standing open-mouthed on the doorstep. I try to dart round her but she grabs my collar and yanks my head round. "What the hell are you doing, Harry?" she says, and grabs the scarf.

"What's he got there?" Skinner calls from the door.

"God knows. He's been acting weird ever since he got home." Megan wrenches the rag from my teeth, ushers me back into the kitchen and slams the door shut. "Naughty boy," she calls through the door.

Wonderful! Not only have I failed to show the evidence to Skinner, but now I'm in big trouble. I hear the front door close and make a bolt for the flap in the back door.

"Harry, come here, NOW," Megan screams as she throws open the kitchen door.

There's really nowhere to run. I know Megan won't hit me, but it hurts so much just to know she's angry with me. I slink back through the flap, tail between my legs, head down, eyes turned towards her in the most pitiful look I can muster. Megan is standing over me with the scarf in her hand and an angry look on her face. I wait for the inevitable scolding.

"Here you are then," Megan sighs, squatting over me and dropping the scarf at my feet. "If you want it that badly, you may as well have it." She fluffs the top of my head. "Just stay out of the bin," she adds, groaning as she surveys the garbage strewn across the floor.

My earlier reprieve lulls me into a false sense of security and, like a fool, I convince myself that Megan might cancel her evening with Mark and we can spend the night curled up on the sofa in front of the fire instead. My optimism is short lived. Mark arrives at exactly eight o' clock, bearing gifts: A small bouquet of flowers for Megan and a rather tasty smelling bone for me.

"Oh, I wasn't expecting this," Megan says, taking the flowers. "Look Harry," she says and tries to hand me the bone.

I am standing in the hall behind Megan. My hackles are raised and there's a deep, throaty growl emanating from the depths of my chest. Slowly, I start to back away.

Megan looks bemused. She squats and offers the bone with an outstretched hand. "Here boy," she says in a soft voice.

No. I'm not relenting. I know what I know. I start growling a little louder.

"I'm so sorry Mark," Megan says standing upright, the offer of the bone now withdrawn. "Harry, get in your bed now. Please, come in Mark. I really don't know what's got into him."

I'm determined to stand my ground. This man is not welcome.

When Megan turns and sees me standing there she stomps across the floor, grabs my collar and drags me into the lounge. She slams the door shut and I'm left looking through the glass panel as Megan leads Mark past me, through to the kitchen. From here I can see the whole fiasco play out before me. The table is set with cutlery and there's a candle burning in the centre. Megan opened a bottle of red wine about half an hour ago – at least half of which she's already drunk – but as Mark takes his seat she fills his glass.

"Honestly, I'm sure it's nothing to do with you," I hear Megan say.

I'm getting a little bit annoyed at her keep apologising for me. I'm now standing with my face pressed up to the glass. Mark needs to know that I'm watching, and if necessary I'll smash through the glass if he takes a step out of line.

"It's fine." Mark turns in his chair to look at me. "I'm a stranger in his house; he'll come round."

I bloody won't. And you know what you can do with that bone.

For the next two hours I'm forced to watch from behind the door. I can hear every word they're saying, and it's torture. Mark keeps making her laugh, and every time he does I want to sink my teeth into his leg. It seems like Megan is hanging on his every word, her fingers playfully twirling her hair like one of those teenage girls who get off the school bus and skip across the village green. It's disgusting. Sickening. Surely she should have learnt her lesson after all these years?

The evening passes painfully slowly, and at some point a second bottle of wine miraculously appears on the table. Megan's laugh has got increasingly louder as the night wears on. I know what he's doing, he's getting her drunk before he launches his attack. I'm just about to start scratching at the door when it happens.

I watch it play out as if in slow motion. Megan reaches round to grab something from the worktop, turning her eyes away from him for probably the first time tonight. The moment her head is turned, Mark flicks a hand at her wine glass and the contents spill all over her skirt and top.

"Oh shit! God, I'm so sorry," Mark says and leaps to his feet.

I start to growl.

"It's okay," Megan says, giggling. She stands up, grabs a tea towel and starts dabbing at the wine which is already soaked into her clothes. "Harry be quiet," she calls.

Mark is playing his part perfectly. "Bloody hell, I've soaked you. What an idiot."

"It's nothing. Stop worrying. I'll nip upstairs and throw on something else. I won't be a minute."

Megan passes me on her way to the stairs and doesn't even bother glancing in my direction. The ultimate snub. No sooner do I hear her feet on the stairs than I see Mark move across the kitchen to a small stack of papers Megan keeps on a wooden shelf. He spreads the papers out and starts snapping away with his phone camera.

I start barking and continue scratching at the door.

"Harry, will you be quiet," Megan bellows from the bedroom.

None of this appears to phase Mark. He has moved on to a small black book that Megan uses to make various notes – mostly work related – flipping through the pages one at a time, clicking away with his phone. It all looks very professional,

I'm guessing this isn't the first time he's done this sort of thing.

Footsteps on the stairs. I'm on hind legs now, frantic. Mark quickly flips the note-pad closed and returns to his chair, tucking his phone back in his pocket.

"Harry, get down," Megan says as she passes the lounge door. She's wearing a large, blue and white striped men's shirt that is three sizes too big for her and barely covers her bottom. Her legs are bare and her face is flushed red. She's trying hard not to shout, but her eyes are wide and angry. "Go and lay down on your rug. Go on."

I refuse to obey.

Mark stands and approaches Megan. "I think this might be a good time for me to make a move."

Megan can't hide her disappointment. I put that down to the amount of alcohol she's consumed. "Really," she says, placing the palm of her hand on his chest. "I thought maybe we could move through to the lounge. I'll put Harry in the kitchen."

Oh will you? She might as well be purring. Honestly, the way she is offering herself to him is embarrassing.

"Another time," he says, gently removing her hand. "I've got a really early start tomorrow." He leans in to give her a kiss on the cheek, and Megan – quite clearly far worse for wear – goes for a full blown lip-to-lip smacker. I am beside myself with fury. If I scratch any harder at the door I'm going to put a paw through the glass. To my surprise, Mark turns his head away and grabs Megan by the shoulders. "I'm not sure that would be a good idea," he says, holding her at arms length.

Megan looks mortified. Her face a mixture of disbelief and shock.

"Oh...err...yes...sorry..." Megan mumbles, her face glowing red.

If only she knew the truth. Whatever it is he's up to, Mark has managed to get what he came for. The photos are now stored safely in his phone.

I hear the front door close and sit quietly on the floor, not quite knowing what to expect. When Megan does eventually open the lounge door, instead of shouting at me she just flops on the sofa and lets out the saddest sigh I've ever heard.

CHAPTER 20

Megan fell asleep on the sofa. I'm guessing she would have stayed there until morning if it hadn't been for her phone ringing. She reaches out an arm and grabs at fresh air as she searches the floor with her fingers. When she can't find it she rolls over and crashes onto the floor with a thud.

"Fuck's sake," she says, and slaps the palm of her hand to her forehead.

I've moved out of the way. She doesn't look happy.

Eventually she finds the phone and holds it out in front of her, squinting in the semi-darkness. "Stacy!" Megan says, placing the phone to her ear, "It's two-thirty in the morning!"

I can hear Stacy's voice on the other end of the line. "I know. I'm so sorry Meg', I just don't know what to do. Liam has disappeared. I got up for a pee half-an-hour ago and noticed his door ajar. He was asleep when I went to bed. I checked his messages on the app on my phone, he got a text an hour ago but I didn't see it

138

come through because I was asleep."

Megan shakes her head, trying to snap herself fully awake. "What did the text say?"

"It just says we need to meet. Now. Usual place."

"Is there a number? A name?"

"Number withheld. God Meg', what the hell is he into?"

Megan has dragged herself onto the edge of the sofa. She runs a hand through her hair and tries to shake herself awake. "It could be a girl," she says, but there's no conviction in her words.

"I wish. No, this has got to be connected to the cash I found."

"Is the tracker device Darren fitted working?"

"First thing I checked. I've got a location. At least I have for his phone. Oh God, it's so late. I'm so so sorry."

"Stop apologising. I'm going to head over to yours."

"You don't have to..."

"I'm coming. Ten minutes. No arguments."

Megan clicks her phone and throws it onto the table. I follow her up the stairs and wait while she slips into jeans and a jumper.

Five minutes later we're heading out of the house. I'm surprised she's taking me with her, I was convinced I was still in the dog house, but it's cold and dark outside and Megan is not stupid enough to get behind the wheel of her car while still clearly under the influence, so I guess having me tag along makes her feel safer than walking on her own at this hour of the morning.

The village is deathly quiet, everyone fast asleep, just as they should be. There aren't many street lamps in a country village, and as we make our way past the pub and start the climb up the hill it seems like the dark is closing in on us. It can feel very claustrophobic, and I can easily understand why Megan wouldn't want to make the journey alone. Considering she's still feeling the effects of her evening she's moving surprisingly fast. We stick to the path until we reach the first few houses of the estate, then Megan leads us into the road because of all the cars parked half way across the pavement. We are a third of the way down the street - nearing Stacy's house – when I pick up the scent. It's the same smell I had to put up with all evening: Mark's aftershave. I stop abruptly and feel the lead tug at my collar. Then I start to growl.

"Harry. Come on." Megan pulls my lead harder. She looks at me for a few seconds, sees my hackles raised and her expression changes. "What is it boy?" I can hear the nervous edge in her voice.

There's a gentle, south-westerly breeze coming from the far end of the street. It's too dark to see if there's anyone lurking in the shadows, but I don't need to see, I know he's there.

Megan's phone goes off, making her jump. "Stacy!" she says, nervously looking around her.

"Where are you?" I hear Stacy say.

"Nearly at yours. But..."

"What?"

"Harry's stopped half way along the road. I think...I think there's someone out

140

here." Megan has lowered her voice to barely a whisper. "Shit, I've got bloody goose-bumps." Megan looks at me, looks down the street at Stacy's house, then yanks my lead and says, "come on Harry, run."

I'm not sure I had a lot of choice, Megan was already bolting and if I hadn't followed she would have ripped my head clean off my shoulders. The scent gets stronger as we hurtle down the middle of the road. I know he's here, but I just can't see him. I try and stay ahead of Megan so if he pounces out of the shadows I can take a chunk out of him before he gets anywhere near her.

Stacy is standing in the open doorway when we reach the top of her path, the light from her hallway spilling out of the house. Megan grabs hold of the gate post and leans forward, greedily sucking in oxygen. "Remind...me...why...we're friends," she manages between breaths.

Stacy has closed the door and is halfway up the path. "Because you love me," she says as she reaches us. "Come on, we'll take my car."

I'm not really focussed on their conversation, my attention is directed towards the far end of the road, where the scent appears to be coming from. The street lamp that should be showering the area in a pale light isn't working, so it's almost completely black.

"What?" Megan says, managing to straighten upright. "Where are we going?"

Stacy is half way across the road. "To find the little sod." She clicks her key and the indicator lights flash on her battered Ford Focus. "He hasn't moved since I called you."

Megan starts to follow, dragging me with her. The car door lock clicks open, but

I'm not looking at the car, I'm staring at a line of conifer trees at the far end of the road and the branches that appear to be parting on their own.

Megan has the back door open. "Harry!" she snatches at my lead.

Another second, that's all I would have needed, but I'm being unceremoniously thrust onto the back seat of the car. The engine starts, and we pull onto the road with a bump. I'm staring out of the back window at the figure now having fully emerged from his hiding place. The figure stands like a an ebony statue and watches us drive away. I let out a sharp warning bark and Megan tells me to shut up.

"So, where are we heading?" Megan asks as we drive through the night.

"Here." Stacy passes her phone to Megan. "It looks like an isolated farmhouse from what I could gather looking at Google maps. It's about two miles from the coast."

"What the hell is he doing there?"

Stacy shakes her head. "I don't want to think about that. God knows how he got there. There has to be someone else with him. Someone who drives."

Megan scans the screen of Stacy's phone. "Do you think maybe it's time you got the police involved. I mean, come on Stacy, we could be walking into anything."

"I know, I know, and to be honest I did think about calling them. But...what if it is drugs, or something equally bad."

"Even more reason to call the police. I know it's hard Stacy, but there are some seriously dangerous people out there. Liam is just a kid after all. The police aren't going to throw the book at him."

142

"Yes, I know all that and I've been over it a thousand times in my head, but that's not the way he'll see it. All Liam will see is me, his mother, dobbing him into the cops without having even discussed it with him first. I blame his fucking father for all of this."

We are making steady progress. The roads are deserted at this hour of the night. The sat-nav takes us along the main road, heading south for seven miles, before diverting us off down a winding country lane. We've gone less than a mile down the narrow lane when an arrow appears on the phone screen, informing us we need to turn right onto what looks like a dirt track. If it's possible, it seems to have got even darker. The rain is falling like mist, the skies overhead a dark blanket, devoid of even the merest glimmer of light.

Stacy brings the car to a halt. "That's where it's saying to go," she says, looking at Megan for reassurance.

"Bloody hell Stace', I'm not sure about this."

"We've come this far..." she doesn't sound convinced.

"How far does it say we've got to go?"

Stacy scrutinizes the small screen. "Less than half-a-mile."

We sit there with the engine idling for what seems like an eternity. Megan and Stacy exchange several nervous glances without speaking and I sit on the back seat waiting for one of them to make a decision.

Finally Megan says, "Okay, drive half way with the side lights on. If you go slow enough we should be able to see the track. There must be somewhere to leave the car along here, and we can walk the last few hundred yards. That way, at least if there is anyone here they won't see us coming."

It sounds like a pretty flimsy plan to me. Neither of them have a clue what we could be walking into, but I suppose a mother's instinct to protect her off-spring far outweighs any fear for her own safety. She's just lucky enough to have a friend like Megan, who's willing to put her neck on the line alongside her.

Stacy cuts the headlights and sticks the car into first gear. Even at ten miles-an-hour, the ride isn't a smooth one. The car lurches from one side to another, the sound of water splashing against the chassis as the wheels sink in and out of deep pot-holes.

"I can't see a bloody thing," Stacy says as the side of the car brushes up against the overhanging hedge.

"Okay, pull over there." Megan points at a gate at the side of the track. The road is wider here, presumably where the tractors turn into the fields.

Stacy pulls over and cuts the engine. We exit the car and begin to carefully pick our way along the track, side-stepping the worst of the puddles.

We've only been walking for a few minutes when we see the building standing alone in the darkness. It's hard to see any defining features. The walls are large and windowless; a blank screen of timber slats rising towards a pitched roof that disappears into the abyss of the black, night sky.

Stacy has hold of Megan's left hand, Megan's other hand is holding tightly onto my lead. I'm assuming she doesn't trust me enough to let me loose; either that or they just need me to show them the way.

"Okay, what now?" Megan whispers.

We are crouched down by pile of logs about twenty yards from the building.

"I can't see any cars." Stacy checks her phone. "He's still here. Hasn't moved."

Megan sighs. "Okay, well come on then." She stands up. "Don't you make a sound, Harry," she warns.

We pick our way round the exterior of the barn, Stacy using the torch on her phone, pointing it straight at the ground ahead of us. The place appears to be derelict. Long, wispy grass and tangled brambles have found their way between some of the missing slats in the barn. There are parts of machinery and old tyres stacked in various heaps, and the smell of oil hangs in the air. No signs of life. Not to a human anyway, but I have picked up a scent that seems quite out of place in this remote spot.

I gently tug on the lead. Megan doesn't put up a fight, she seems happy for me to show them the way. We skirt round the side of the barn until we reach what looks like a large, broken door. The door is hanging lop-sided from rusted hinges. There is a triangular gap in the bottom right hand corner, just large enough for me to poke my head through.

"Well?" Stacy asks, looking at Megan for guidance.

"I don't think there's anyone here." Megan whispers her reply.

I shove my head through the hole. It's black inside, the stench of rotting timber and stale straw is overpowering. The lead is tight, Megan reluctant to release her grip. I make a choking sound, knowing full well she'll loosen her hold. She obliges and I make my move. One quick pull and the lead slips from her hand.

"Harry!" I hear her call in a hushed voice, but I'm already making my way through the building, nose to the floor. Somewhere behind me I can hear creaking

timbers as Megan and Stacy try and force the door open wide enough to climb

through. I'm not concentrating on them however, I've picked up a strong scent. The

sound of rats scampering along the rafters overhead can't distract me.

The interior of the barn is a cavernous, black space, strewn with bits of old

machinery. An old tractor sitting on concrete blocks along the wall to my left is

missing its wheels and engine. A few yards further a stack of old tyres have been

heaped unceremoniously in pile in the centre of the floor.

I hear the scraping of footsteps behind me, and Megan anxiously calling my

name in a hushed voice as she and Stacy pick their way across the ground. I can't

believe they've followed me in here. I would wait, but I don't want them dragging

me out before I've found what I'm looking for.

I make my way past the stack of tyres towards the back of the barn. Here, the

building appears to be empty. It's only when I look up that I see it. Megan and

Stacy must have been closer to me than I thought, because the scream that echoes

throughout the building comes almost at once. The sound bounces off the walls,

filling the blackness with all the pain a mother can unleash.

CHAPTER 21

I know it's Liam hanging from the rope. The rope is tied to one of the low rafters,

his feet dangling a few inches from the floor. A small wooden crate close by still

bears Liam's muddy footprints. His hands are tied behind his back.

Megan rushes past me, grabs Liam's legs and tries to lift him into the air. "Stacey!" she screams, teetering unsteadily as she desperately struggles to support the weight. "STACY!" So much louder this time. "Call for an ambulance."

Stacy is on her knees, hands clasped to her face. I bark, loud as I can, and this seems to snap her back to reality. She fumbles with the digits on her phone, jumps up, rushes over and throws her arms around her son's legs. Her phone falls to the floor and I can hear a voice saying, "What service do you require?"

"Ambulance. I need an ambulance. My son..."

A calm voice replies, "Try and remain...." and then the phone goes dead.

"NO!! Fuck no..." Stacy grabs the phone from the floor, but even from where I'm standing I can see the screen is cracked top to bottom.

"Forget it." Megan says. "Just grab his legs. Try and lift him." Stacy obeys and Megan reaches up and begins pulling at the rope round Liam's neck. It seems like it takes an eternity, but eventually Megan pulls the rope over his head and they all collapse to the ground in a heap.

"No! Please no," Stacy flings herself on the limp figure now sprawled in the dirt. She grabs his shoulders and pulls him into her chest. Megan removes the thin rope from his wrists. Stacy's arms fold round her son and she sits there rocking him to and fro, tears streaming down her face as she wails incoherently.

Then, to my surprise, Megan shoves Stacy out of the way and pushes Liam backwards onto the ground. Ignoring Stacey's protestations, she leans over his lifeless body, puts her mouth to his, pinches his nose between her fingers and begins puffing air into his lungs. "Push his chest," Megan shouts between breaths.

147

"NOW!"

Eventually Stacy snaps out of her hysteria and does as she's been told. Together they blow and push and push and blow. The sound of Stacy's uncontrolled sobbing fills every inch of the cavernous barn. Tears stream down her face, falling like warm, salty rain onto the chest of her prostrate son.

They tried their hardest, I'll give them that, but minutes later there is still no sign of life from the boy.

Megan finally stops blowing. She's on her knees, her back arching as she throws her head backwards and turns her eyes towards the heavens. She reaches out a hand and gently rests it on her friend's shoulder. "Stacy," she whispers. "It's too late." Her fingers close round the top of Stacy's arm.

"No! No! Come on baby." She pushes Megan's hand away and starts pounding his chest with both fists, screaming at him to wake up.

I sit, taking in the scene, saddened that there's nothing I can do to help. I can literally feel her pain. It's like a cold, dark fog, sucking all the goodness out of any living creature who is unlucky enough to witness such agony. And just when I think all hope is gone, Liam's mouth opens wide and there is a long, wheezing gasp as his lungs fill with air.

"Oh baby!" Stacy cries, leaning over her son, stroking his forehead.

Megan slumps back onto her behind, her eyes wide in disbelief.

"Mu...I..." Liam's strangled voice is nothing more than a rasping whisper, the words he's trying to spit out sticking deep in his throat.

"Don't try to talk." Stacy is cradling him like she must have done a thousand

148

times when he was a child: The man-boy still a baby to his doting mother. "Thank God. I thought I'd lost you." She rocks him gently back and forth, stroking his hair, planting hundreds of tiny kisses on his forehead.

Megan struggles to her feet. "We need to get him to a hospital. Liam, do you think you can walk?"

He shakes his head, and even this small movement causes him to flinch with pain. "N...no...yo...you...can't." He gently pulls away from his mother's grasp and rubs his throat with the palm of his hand. "If they....if ...they know I'm alive...they'll come...after all of us." The words choke out between coughs and croaks.

Stacy looks at him, horrified. "Who? Who will come after us?"

"The people who did this to me."

"Jesus Liam! We have to call the police."

"No!" He reaches out a hand and pushes Stacy away so he is now staring right into her eyes. "I mean it mum, they'll kill all of us. You can't..." choke, cough, "let anyone know."

"What the hell have you got yourself into?"

Liam hangs his head, turns his eyes away from his mother and says, "I'm sorry."

"Sorry!" Stacy pushes him in the chest. "I thought you were dead, and all you can say is you're sorry." She bursts into tears.

While they are sitting in the dirt arguing, it occurs to me that none of them seem to have considered the possibility that whoever strung Liam up might be coming back, if not right away, then at some point. I have picked up several scents, most of which I don't recognize. Some of the smells are probably days old, but there are a couple of fresh scents which seem vaguely familiar, although I cannot immediately recall where I recognize them from. It will come to me.

It is Megan who finally decides to act. "We need to get him out of here," she says, "we can decide what we're going to do later."

They help Liam to his feet.

"How did you find me?" Liam asks, as the two women support an arm each.

"I tracked your phone."

Liam stares at his mother. "How?"

"It doesn't matter." Stacy reaches on the floor and picks up her own, broken phone. "Fucking hell," she says, inspecting the cracked screen. "Where is your phone anyway, Liam?"

"I threw it over there when they were dragging me in here." He points at a small stack of straw bales dumped lopsidedly against the wall to our left.

"Why?"

"Because I knew it was my only chance of someone finding me. I just wasn't expecting it to be you."

Stacy's eyes widen and she spins him round to face her. "Then who? Who did you think was going to come looking for you?"

Before Liam can answer I start barking. The sound is only just audible to me, it will be several minutes before their ears detect it, and by that time it will be too late.

"What is it Harry?" Megan crouches down and places her hand on my head.

150

Finally, someone wants to listen to me. I head across the floor, back towards the front of the barn. I don't hang about, I know they'll be following me.

I can see the beams of light dancing across the blackened sky the moment I step out of the door. Stacy and Liam stumble through the opening just behind me, Megan catches up a few seconds later having first retrieved Liam's phone from the floor of the barn.

"Shit!" Stacy says, craning her neck to look in the direction the lights are coming from. She eases Liam against the side of the barn, now supporting him by one arm. "Who the hell are they?"

Liam looks truly terrified. "I don't know."

"More to the point," Megan says, "why are they coming back?"

"I don't fucking know, alright." Liam pushes his mother's arm away.

Before Stacy can argue, Megan intervenes. "Okay, forget all that for now. We need to get out of here before they find us. Come on." She grabs Liam's hand. "Are you alright to walk?"

He rubs his neck. "Sure."

The lights are getting closer. Too close. I can hear the splash of tyres as the vehicle heads down the track. The only good thing is, it doesn't appear to be moving fast. Whoever is heading our way doesn't appear to be in a hurry.

"Harry. Here boy." Megan slaps her thigh.

I know what she wants, and I know I should do as she asks, but right now I think I'm their best option of getting out of here. Instead of obeying her command I run towards a thick Blackthorne hedge about forty feet from the barn. I know

Megan can't risk shouting, I've just gotta hope she decides to follow me. It takes a moment, but in the end they don't really have a choice. They can't risk me barking and giving them away. Not that I'd ever do that. I wait while all three of them stumble across the mud in the darkness. A second before they reach me I disappear through a gap in the hedge I spotted on the way in. The opening is just wide enough for them to squeeze through, one at a time, and once we're on the other side at least we're hidden from whoever is coming down the track.

Two beams of light dance across the sky, the crashing and splashing of water now louder than ever as the vehicle reaches the end of its journey. The headlights sweep overhead as the driver brings the vehicle to a halt in front of the barn.

Megan grabs my lead and pulls me in close as she crouches in the mud. I'm not sure if she needed prompting, but I start tugging anyway. If we stay close to the hedge we can make our way back to the car without anyone seeing us. If we are really lucky they might spend a good while searching the barn; hopefully it will give us enough time to make our escape.

The lead tightens as I claw at the ground, but I pull hard enough that Megan has to follow or fall flat on her face. I sneak a glance to make sure Liam and Stacy are still with us. They are, but Liam is struggling. Stacy is trying to support him, but he's obviously far too heavy for her, so reluctantly I stop and wait for Megan to do the only sensible thing. Eventually she makes her decision and lets go of the lead. When I don't run off she breathes a sigh of relief and goes to help her friend.

Somewhere in the darkness behind us a car door slams shut. I guess we have no more than a couple of minutes before they discover Liam is gone. What then? I

152

suppose that depends on what these people want. Liam's insistence on not calling the police suggests – even if someone has come to help him - they are not law-abiding citizens. The silly boy is obviously way out of his depth.

"How much further?" Stacy whispers, grabbing Megan's arm.

Megan stops, stands on tip-toes and cranes her neck. "Not far now. How's he doing?"

"I'm okay," Liam says, although he looks very much not okay.

Despite the mud, rain and total darkness, not to mention the fact that Liam is obviously struggling, we make good progress. It's amazing how much energy one can gain when fear is causing an adrenalin surge throughout your body.

Behind us there's a crash of timber and the sound of shouting. I assume they've made the discovery.

"Shit!" Stacy sounds terrified.

"Keep going. We're nearly there. As long as we keep down they can't see us through the hedge. If we can make it back to the car, hopefully we can get the hell out of here while they're rushing about looking for Liam."

I can hear the fear in Megan's voice, but I feel quite proud of her. I never would have believed she could stay so calm in a situation like this. We are on the run from God-knows-who and yet my owner seems to be taking control of the situation. I wonder if she can tell I'm smiling right now?

We reach the car faster than any of us were expecting. Stacy flings open the rear door and pushes Liam onto the back seat. Megan shoves me unceremoniously onto the floor in the back of the car and the next thing I know the engine is screaming and we are moving. The car lurches from side to side, water, mud and stones crunch against the chassis as we hurtle along the track. I can't see a thing from the floor so I scramble up onto the back seat beside Liam. Well, okay, maybe not quite beside him, more on top of him, but if he finds it uncomfortable he doesn't protest. I poke my head in the space between the two front seats just in time to see the solid tarmac surface of the lane rushing towards us. Stacy hits the brakes, but it's too late. The back end of the car swings left, then right. Stacy is desperately tugging at the steering wheel trying to control half a ton of metal that is moving far too fast to be approaching the end of a lane where there is only two options; left or right, and we aren't going to manage either of them.

We slide sideways across the tarmac until the wheels collide with the grass verge the other side of the lane. There is a loud crash – or so I assume – because as I'm hurtling across the back of the car towards the rear passenger window I'm not really thinking about anything except how much this is going to hurt.

Yep, I was right, it did hurt. OUCH!! I yelp and the sound comes out as a pathetic cross between a whimper and a yap. It certainly doesn't convey the full enormity of my pain.

"Is everyone alright?" Megan's voice echoes round the inside of the car.

Her voice is the only sound now. The car has managed to stay upright – somehow – but the engine isn't running and the lights have gone out, so it's deathly black. I'm in the rear foot-well in the back of the car, all four paws pointing skyward.

"Yeah," Liam says, struggling into a sitting position."

"Shit! Only just." Stacy gasps.

I'm trying to scramble into an upright position. An image of a turtle laying on its back, legs flailing, springs into my head and I scratch at the back seat with increasing vigour as panic begins to set in.

"Harry! What are you doing down there? Liam, help him up will you." If Megan is concerned about me she manages to keep the anxiety out of her voice. She does sound nervous however, and for good reason. The night sky explodes into light outside the car just as Liam drags me onto the back seat by my collar.

"Start." Stacy shouts as she turns the ignition key. "Oh please start."

I can hear the engine whirring, but it doesn't seem to want to spring into life, no matter how hard Stacy turns the key. The lights – which were a vague beam way overhead – now glare through the side windows of our car, drawing ever closer.

"Start, you fucking piece of shit!!" Stacy screams, and smashes her left hand against the dashboard.

Perhaps her car is fitted with an onboard computer, one of those new high-tec gadgets that are activated by voice command, because no sooner has she screamed at it than it fires into life. The engine roars, the tyres spin and we have lift off, leaving a trail of wet mud and exhaust smoke in our wake.

"Oh...my...God!" Megan sounds rather less scared than she did a few seconds ago. "Well done Stace'." She twists round in her seat to look behind us. "I can't see any lights yet."

I'm also looking out of the rear window, and almost before Megan has stopped speaking two beams of light appear as our pursuers reach the end of the track and turn onto the lane. They are probably no more than a quarter of a mile behind us, and judging by the way the headlights are bouncing around I think it's safe to assume they are moving very fast: Certainly faster than Stacy's old heap can go.

"Shit!" Megan cries, unable to hide the fear.

"Yes, I saw them," Stacy says, and thrusts the gear stick into a different position. The engine growls its disapproval and the rear of the car slides left, then right as our driver struggles desperately to keep control on the wet road.

The lane has a lot of twisting bends, I remember that much from our drive here. It is not the sort of road you can negotiate at high speed, even if you are being chased. The lights behind us are drawing increasingly closer. The car lurches to the right as we hit a sharp bend, and the following lights disappear for an instant.

"Turn off the headlights," Megan shouts.

"What! I can barely see the road as it is."

"We can see enough. It's our only chance, we can't outrun them. Go on, do it."

Stacy hesitates a moment, then flicks the light switch.

The road instantly disappears and Stacy takes her foot off the accelerator. The sky overhead is illuminated by the lights of the car giving chase and just as I'm beginning to think this is one of the worst ideas Megan has ever had, she grabs the steering wheel and tugs. Stacy gasps, Liam shouts something incoherent and the car jumps about a foot in the air as we leave the road.

It feels as if we are hurtling through the darkness for an eternity, the tyres no longer connected to the ground; an airborne vehicle heading into a black abyss. I have no idea what this feeling is rising from the pit of my stomach, but I don't like it, not one little bit. At this moment however I'm more concerned about the other three occupants who are screaming extremely loudly.

Our brief transformation from car to plane ends abruptly when we hit the ground with a deafening crunch. To my amazement we are still upright. Even more amazing is the fact that none of us appear to have sustained any injuries. The screams subside almost immediately, replaced instead with a lot of groaning. Now, the only sound is rain hitting the roof and the roar of an engine as the car that was following us rushes past on the road some forty feet away.

"What the hell...?" Stacy says.

"I saw the opening to the field," Megan cuts in, "it was the only chance we had. Sorry. Is everyone okay?"

A deathly silence consumes the interior of the car. It's not easy to see the faces of my fellow occupants, but I'm pretty sure none of them are smiling.

Stacy finally snaps her head round. "Are you okay?" she asks, looking at Liam.

"Yeah."

"So what do you suggest now?" This time Stacy is glaring at the woman sitting in the seat beside her. "There's no way this car is moving anywhere. I need to get him to a hospital to get him checked out, and it's only a matter of time before whoever was chasing us realise what's happened and double back. And then what?" Stacy breathes in loudly and suddenly whirls round to face her son. "Who the hell are they?" she screams.

"I don't know," comes the reply with an open-handed display to emphasize the point, but his voice is too loud, the gesture way over-the-top. He's lying. I know it and I think both his mum and Megan know it too.

"Try the engine again." Megan says. "We can't just sit here and wait. Go on Stace'."

Stacy turns the key and the engine splutters into life. Next thing I know the car's skidding sideways across the wet field, like a snake trying to navigate a well-oiled pane of glass. Moments later – amazingly – the tyres connect with the solid tarmac surface and we are off and running, heading back in the direction we've just come.

"YES!" Stacy shrieks as we gain speed, and before the sound has stopped reverberating round the inside of the car, the engine explodes and a thick, black plume of smoke spews from beneath the bonnet. "Oh FUCK!" are the next words to come out of her mouth. Her despair is truly palpable.

Before anyone can say anything else, the beams from two distant headlights briefly illuminate the sky overhead.

Even for a canine, this is too much. Megan drags me from the car and we all run like rats deserting a sinking ship. We get less than a hundred yards when we come across a wooden gate leading into the field. The mud is deep, and wet. Very wet. Of course, none of us are giving the terrain too much consideration because by now we can hear the screaming engine of the car that belongs to the headlights that are heading our way.

I suppose fear must do strange things to the body – even humans – because none of them appear to be labouring as we trudge along the edge of the field keeping close to the tall hedge, which is all that now separates us from from our pursuers. We are heading towards the cover of a very dark copse of trees, and for my part we can't get there soon enough.

Somewhere behind us there's a skid of tyres and the opening of a car door. I can hear voices; two men, and they are not best pleased by the sound of it. One is shouting, the other just seems pissed off. I'm pretty sure the others can't hear anything except for the wind and rain and the heavy breathing that inevitably accompanies having to wade through ankle deep mud in the middle of the night.

We reach the sanctity of the trees just in time. A narrow beam of torch-light appears in the distance, sweeping over the barren fields in search of our group. If the idiot had half a brain he'd point it towards the ground and find our footprints. Oops.

"They came through here." I hear him call to his accomplice. "Grab the gun."

What?!! The noise of the wind through the branches overhead means none of them are aware of what I just heard. I know they can hear distant voices, but none of the words will be clear enough to understand. Luckily Megan has already decided this isn't a time to stop and rest.

"We need to keep moving," she gasps between breaths. "It doesn't look like they're going to give up."

Stacy is bent forward, hands on her knees. It looks like it takes all her energy to raise her head. "I...I don't know if I can."

"We can't stay here," Megan says, and grabs Stacy's arm, dragging her upright. "We don't have a choice. Liam, help your mother, we need to keep moving, they won't be able to follow us very far. What tracks don't get covered by falling leaves, the rain will wash away. Come on."

My mistress appears to have taken on the persona of superwoman. She's standing there like some ancient, female warrior, wet hair flailing round her face and water dripping from the tip of her nose. Not for the first time, I feel an enormous sense of pride.

Before we can start our trek deep into the black abyss of the trees, another set of headlights appear in the distance. Another vehicle, heading our way. We all stop and stare. The sound of the engine I heard a moment ago, finally reaches human ears. The lights twist and turn and dip out of sight momentarily as the vehicle negotiates the narrow, winding lane. Thirty seconds later the car reaches the point in the road where our engine died. The sound of tyres struggling on the wet surface is followed almost instantly by angry shouting. A door slams shut. More shouting, louder this time. And then, a gunshot.

The scream that emanates from beyond the hedge fills the night: A piercing, shrill cry that could belong to man or woman.

"Jesus!" Stacy stares at Megan, who now looks terrified.

Before any more words can be exchanged between the two women, another shot rings out. Then, it would appear, chaos ensues. Shouting, doors slamming, the sound of an engine firing into life and tyres angrily tearing at the wet tarmac. The headlights pass our position at a rate of knots, the tail lights disappearing into the distance before anyone can catch a breath. The silence that follows this commotion is deafening. It doesn't last long.

"Aaaaaaargh....."

"They've shot someone!" Megan says, eyes wide. "Come on." She grabs Stacy.

"But what if they come back?"

"We can't leave them there."

The screaming is now accompanied by words, but it's impossible to make out what he is saying. Yes, I can now tell the victim is male.

By the time we reach the scene the screams have turned into a mixture of sobbing and begging. Megan, Stacy and Liam scramble over the gate. I nip between the slats, eager to put a face to the victim. The man is lying half out of the driver's door, blood seeping from a wound in his leg, which he is clutching with both hands whilst rocking to and fro and sobbing like a baby.

"Darren!!" Megan says, having reached us. "What the hell are you doing here?"

Darren!! Who the hell is Darren? And how does Megan know him? Even if Darren wanted to answer, I don't think he could. The colour is visibly draining from his plump cheeks.

"Get him into the back." Megan barks out the order to her companions.

I have to take a backward step at this point and watch the drama unfold. Darren is a very big man, and I think he just passed out, so even with all three of them on the task, hauling his limp frame from the front of the car to the back takes a monumental effort. I assume – because he is such a large man – he must have much more blood than an average person, which is quite good because otherwise at the rate it's seeping from his wound, in a few minutes he wouldn't have much left.

Once again I'm bundled into the back of a car and forced to wedge myself between Liam and the stricken Darren. Megan jumps into the drivers seat, Stacy beside her, and with one turn of the ignition key we are heading through the night in our newly acquired vehicle, the owner of which is currently bleeding all over me and the back seat. I don't think we've gone more than a mile when I realise where the bullet from the second gunshot ended up. I assumed it was water at first, but I soon realise the liquid soaking into my fur is too warm for water. No wonder Darren passed out, the second shot hit him in the stomach. I assume the only reason none of us noticed was because he didn't make a fuss about it. I suppose a bullet hitting a bone in the leg must hurt much more than one to the stomach.

"Here," Megan fishes in her jacket pocket and throws her phone to Stacy. "You need to call the police right now."

"NO!" Liam shouts.

Megan shouts back. "You need to listen to me now, Liam. Whatever it is you're mixed up in has just got him shot," she gestures at Darren with her eyes. "So we no longer have the option of keeping things to ourselves. You are going to have to deal with it."

"They'll kill me. They'll kill you and mum too if you go to the copper's."

Stacy spins round. "Megan's right, we don't have a choice. I know about the money. I know you're mixed up in something dangerous. Whatever it is, we can deal with it."

I can feel Liam shaking against me. His bottom lip is quivering. Just for a moment I feel sorry for him, but when I think about what he's put us through the sympathy soon dissipates. Stacy makes the call as I sit there watching the darkness flash past the window.

The police are already waiting at the hospital when we arrive. Unfortunately nobody seems to care about me as the paramedics haul Darren from the back of his car and the police close in from all sides.

It's at least half an hour before Megan finally leads me away from the vehicle. To my surprise, Mel is waiting, leaning against the front wing of her parked car, arms folded tight across her chest.

"Thank you so much," Megan says, handing my lead to Mel who still appears to be half asleep. "I'll explain everything to you tomorrow."

Ray is sitting in the driver's seat of the car. I can see him staring out of the rain spattered windscreen as we approach. As we draw closer he winds down his side window and snaps, "You're not putting him on the back seat, look at the state of him. Stick him in the boot."

Luckily for me, Mel refuses, so at least I wasn't locked in the boot all the way home.

CHAPTER 22

It's not home, but at least the surroundings are vaguely familiar. Mel slept downstairs with me because – and I'm slightly ashamed to admit this – I couldn't stop whining. I heard her and Ray arguing before she brought a duvet down and slept beside me on the sofa. It wasn't like having Megan there, but it was enough to calm me down.

The following morning Mel fed me and took me for a quick walk whilst Ray bumbled about the place moaning about all the bloody dog hairs and feeling tired because he hadn't managed to get a wink of sleep all night. It didn't sound like that when he was snoring at four-thirty this morning.

Mel's phone rang several times while we were walking. She ignored the first two calls, but the third time it rang, she answered. My ears pricked up when I heard Megan's voice.

"How is he?"

We were walking along the edge of the field. Mel stopped, leaned down and gently stroked her hand along my back. "Yeah he's fine. How are you doing?"

"Oh God, it's been a nightmare, Mel. Darren – that's the guy who was shot – is off the critical list, so that's good news. Anyway, I just called to thank you again and say I should be home by lunchtime. I'll fill you in then. Say hi to Harry for me."

I felt much happier knowing that before long Megan would be home.

It is almost two-thirty by the time Megan finally comes for me. She looks clean, has changed clothes and smells of the scented soap she pours in her bath.

"Thank you so much Mel. I don't know what I'd have done without you," Megan says, pulling her friend in close for a long hug.

Apparently I am well down the pecking order. Not only has she been home for a bath and change of clothes, but when she does finally deign to come and fetch me I have to wait in line for any attention. I let all of this slide when she finally folds her arms round my neck.

Mel makes tea and the two of them sit at the kitchen table. I sidle up close to Megan and lay on the floor at her feet.

"So, what the hell happened then?" Mel asks.

Megan offers up a very brief account of the previous night's events. Somehow she manages to do this without revealing too many details.

For the most part, Mel just sits there open-mouthed. When it appears Megan has finished her summary, Mel begins firing questions at her. "So where are Stacy and Liam now? Have they caught the men? What the hell is Liam mixed up in? Oh, and who is this, Darren?"

"Stacy has sent Liam to stay with his father for a while. I think she's done the right thing. If nothing else, it gets him away from this place while the police carry out their investigation. Hopefully they'll catch them sooner rather than later and we can all get back to normal." Megan pauses to sip her tea. "I'm pretty sure I've mentioned Darren before. He's the tech' wizard from work."

"Fat Darren? The one with the hygiene problem?"

Megan blushes. "Yes, although if he hadn't turned up last night..."

"So how the hell did he know where you were?"

"This goes no further," Megan says seriously.

Mel nods. "Of course not."

"Stacy has been worried about Liam for a while, so I came up with the genius idea of asking Darren to put a tracker on his phone, so that Stacy would know exactly where he is. It looks like Darren installed the same tracking system into

Stacy's phone, without her knowing of course. Not only that, but the police reckon the same system was placed into my phone several months ago."

Mel holds a hand to her mouth. "Oh, that's creepy. You mean he's been sitting at home watching your every move?"

"Well, not quite, but something like that, yes," Megan says. I can't help noticing she's definitely not telling Mel the full story.

By the time we leave for home it is getting dark. It's a short, five minute stroll back to our cottage, yet 'miraculously' it just so happens that we bump into Mark at the entrance to our lane.

"Hey, how are you?" he asks, as if the meeting is pure coincidence.

I resist the urge to display any negative behaviour towards him. After being locked in the lounge for being aggressive when he was at our place I realise it won't do me any good. Instead I sit by Megan's feet trying to ignore the odious man.

"Oh, hi Mark." Megan's voice has taken on 'that' tone again, the one she reserves exclusively for him. She brushes the hair from over her eyes and tilts her head to one side, flaunting herself unashamedly. I manage to choke back the feeling of nausea. To be honest, I'm embarrassed for her, he's already rejected her drunken advances once, short of carrying round a sign that says 'I'm not interested' I'm not sure what else he can do. It also occurs to me that whatever documents he photographed last night can't have been what he was looking for otherwise he wouldn't be wasting his time now.

"I tried calling you a couple of times this morning," Mark continues. "Haven't done anything to upset you have I? I really did have an early start," he adds, and makes it sound like an apology.

"No, no, not at all." Megan flushes ever-so-slightly. "I err, well to be honest with you I was involved in a bit of a drama last night."

"Oh!"

"Yeah....but I'm not sure..."

Mark holds up open palms. "That's okay, I don't want to pry."

Really!! You seemed to be alright prying around our home last night snapping away with your bloody phone. He's a good liar, I'll give him that.

"No, it's not that." Megan reaches out and grabs his arm. "Look, why don't you pop round later tonight. I want to tell you, really, but I'm shattered and need to grab a couple of hours sleep or I'll go insane."

"Well, if you're sure?"

"Yes, honestly. So, I'll see you later then? Around eight? It looks like Harry has finally come round anyway," Megan adds, finally releasing her hold on Mark's arm to pat me on the head.

I bloody haven't. I'm just being sensible. One wrong move and I'll gladly sink my teeth into his leg. So, not content with making a fool of herself once, my mistress is going for a double whammy. What the hell has gotten into her? Surely I should be more than enough? I sulk all the way home; the prospect of spending another night stuck in the lounge watching Megan make a fool of herself has made me feel really depressed.

167

CHAPTER 23

Megan

I promised myself I wouldn't get emotionally involved with another man unless I was absolutely certain they wouldn't let me down. What a bloody stupid thing to promise yourself. I was certain about Vince Hillier when I let him take my virginity on his parents bed two weeks after my sixteenth birthday. I was even more certain about Ade Thompson, who I dated for almost a year before I discovered the reason he could only see me three nights a week was because the other four nights he was shagging a little slut called Nancy Bauemont. And then there was Greg. Greg was my forever man. Greg would never let me down, or hurt me. Only he did, and in the worst way imaginable, and I don't think I will ever truly forgive him. It's been eighteen months since I discovered the affair. Sometimes the pain still stings as if it were yesterday. I really don't want to get emotionally entangled with anyone. But life doesn't work that way does it? Last month, last week even, I was quite content; I had my little house and Harry, and work was going great. And then Mark happened. Jesus, I feel like slapping myself for even feeling like this. I mean, it's ridiculous, I'm old enough to know better. Been there, done that, should be etched into whatever organ in my body has allowed me to lower my defences.

I manage to grab a couple of hours sleep when we get home. I should of given Harry a bath first, but I was just too tired. So when I finally wake up I have to drag Harry into the bathroom – no easy task as he really doesn't like baths - and scrub

168

him down before I can give the house a quick once-over with the hoover.

It's well past seven-thirty before I slump onto a kitchen chair and pour a glass of wine. If Mark wants to eat I'll grab a pizza out of the freezer. I just can't think about cooking at the moment. All I really want is a quiet night snuggled up on the sofa; some soft music and good conversation would be a bonus, but after the way Mark shot off last time I won't be counting my chickens.

My phone rings ten minutes before Mark is due to arrive. "Hi Stace'," I answer automatically when her name flashes up on the screen.

"If you want to see your friend alive again, keep your mouth shut and listen."

If I wasn't sitting down my legs would have buckled. The voice sounds like something out of a horror movie; deep, semi-automated and sinister. Without even realising I'm doing it, I begin trolling through my memory, searching for a face to put to the sound. But none comes.

"Reef Forest, northern parking area," the voice continues. "You've got twenty minutes. If you call the police, she dies. If you try alerting anyone, she dies. If you're not alone, she dies."

I'm shaking and nervous as hell, but from somewhere I manage to summon up enough courage to blurt out, "How do I know you have her?" I realise almost immediately that I'm probably just repeating something I've heard people say on the television, but there's a little part of me that feels immensely proud that I managed to spit the words out.

Silence. It lasts just long enough to make me wonder if I've crossed a line. Then a sharp squeal and muffled sobbing. "M..Meg...Megan," the unmistakable sound

169

of Stacy's voice. "Please, do as they ask." I don't want to, but I can picture the scene; a hand, holding the phone close to her mouth. I can hear her breathing coming in short, frightened bursts. "Whatever you do, don't let Tony know. You'll have to sneak out of...."

"Eighteen minutes," the voice that snatched the phone away says, and the call is ended.

Don't let Tony Know!!! I'm proud that my friend is thinking so clearly; trying to make them believe Tony is my partner with the 'sneaking out' remark. Obviously she means Tony Skinner. A random notion stabs at a part of my brain before I can stop it: I've had a gut feeling for some time that Stacy might be seeing someone on the quiet. I didn't want to press her, I thought she'd tell me when she was ready. Of course I knew that Stacy had a bit of a crush on our local bobby - hence my constant little digs – but I thought the fact that he's married would deter her from getting involved. I never considered Stacy to be 'one of those women'. Maybe I'm wrong. I do hope so.

I quickly snap myself back to the moment. Stacy wants me to alert him, that much is obvious, but what if I call him and they discover I've disobeyed them? I suddenly realise I'm shaking and finding it hard to breathe. This can't be happening. Things like this only happen on T.V. or in the movies. I slap that thought away before it's had time to set up home. Last night I rushed Darren to hospital when he was shot for trying to help us. As much as I want someone to shake me out of this nightmare, I have to face up to the fact that's not going to happen.

I grab the car keys, throw on my jacket and head out of the door. Before I can stop him, Harry rushes past me and sits himself down by the passenger door of the car.

"Harry, no. Back inside. Come on." When I go to grab his collar he jumps out of the way. "You have to stay here." I can hear my voice quavering, and that scares me even more. Harry is having none of it though. It's almost as if he can sense I'm scared and doesn't want to leave me.

When it becomes clear he's not about to relent, I give in and open the passenger door.

I know the northern parking area to Reef Forest very well. It's about a ten minute drive at this time of night. I also know it's secluded. The parking area is an expanse of compacted gravel - big enough to take about twenty cars at a push – you turn into it directly off of the B road. A lot of people go there to walk their dogs, but not at this time of night, at this time of year. The place will be empty. The thought causes an involuntary shudder.

I start the engine, because at least then I have taken some positive action. But as I'm sitting there listening to the engine softly purring as it warms I realise the reason I haven't already called Tony Skinner, or started to drive, is that I'm hoping against hope that by some miracle Mark will come strolling up the driveway: my knight in shining armour. I will explain everything to him and he will know exactly what to do.

Two minutes later I'm still sitting there, and I can feel the seconds ticking away. I thrust the car into gear and press the number for Tony Skinner stored in my phone. The phone rings and rings and I'm already heading up the hill out of the village when the answer phone cuts in. "Sorry I can't take your call at the moment, but if you would care to leave your name and...."

I end the call, hitting the screen harder than intended as the sense of fear and foreboding slowly begins to seep from every pore of my skin. A cold sweat, they call it don't they? I'm not sure I've ever really understood what that meant until now. Before I have time to consider the ramifications of my action I scroll through my recent numbers. I tap Marks name highlighted on the screen. I'm on speaker and the sound of his phone ringing out fills the dark void in my car. I let it keep ringing, knowing that at any moment he will pick up.

I've driven past the church before I end the un-answered call with a string of expletives borne out of frustration. Harry pricks his ears and leans a little closer. Silly, I know, but I'm sure he'd give me a hug if he could.

The silence that ensues is claustrophobic. I'm out of my depth, terrified, not only for Stacy, but also myself, and right at this moment I feel very, very alone. But I can't let Stacy down.

When the entrance to the northern parking area of Reef forest appears in the distance, my chest tightens. The sound of my tyres crackles over the gravel and Harry jumps up excitedly. He knows where we are. I push him down onto the seat with my left hand as the right steers us towards the lone vehicle – a white, Ford Transit van I think - parked beneath a canopy of overhanging branches at the far end of the parking area.

I was right, aside from the van the place is deserted. Little specs of rain dripping from the overhanging branches of the surrounding trees dapple the windscreen.

172

The beam from my headlights feels too bright as they wash over the lone van. I have slowed to a crawl. Everything seems to be happening in slow motion. The passenger door of the van swings open as I draw closer. The figure is tall and wiry, dressed all in black. The peak of a loose- hooded jacket almost reaches his brow. He's wearing a scarf, wrapped round the lower part of his face, leaving a tiny slit for his eyes.

Harry growls and I force his head against the seat. "Harry, please be quiet." The noise that comes out of my mouth doesn't sound like me.

I bring the car to a stop without cutting the engine.

Less than six feet away, the man opens a side door and drags Stacy from the back of the vehicle. She stumbles to the ground, landing on her knees. Her hands are fastened behind her back and she looks terrified. There is a smear of blood on her cheek and a slight swelling over her left eye.

"Get out of the fucking car." Not a voice I recognize.

Harry growls and tries to snatch his head away from me.

"Move. Now," the man says, holding Stacy upright, his hand cupped under her chin, long bony fingers reaching almost completely round her throat.

I'm torn. I know I have to get out of the car, but if I let go of Harry...

The man grabs Stacy's hair and jerks her head to one side, causing her to emit a sharp squeal. "I said, get out of the fucking car. If I have to ask again she loses an eye." He slips his free hand inside his jacket and produces a short-bladed knife, the tip of which he presses into the soft flesh below Stacy's left eye.

Without waiting, I force Harry into the passenger foot well, and while he's trying to struggle out of the space I quickly leap from the car, slamming the door shut behind me. The door has barely closed when I hear his nails slapping at the window, barking, snarling, all bared teeth and curled upper lip, desperate to come to our aid.

"You need to shut that fucking thing up before I kill it."

I'm thinking 'you dare touch my dog and...' but instead I spin round and hiss, "Harry, lay down. NOW." By some miracle, eventually he stops barking. I stare into his eyes, his face pressed up against the glass, a deep, guttural growl rumbling from somewhere deep inside him.

"Where is it?" the man asks as I turn to face him.

"Wh...where is what?"

"I told you, we don't know anything about your drugs," Stacy says, as the tears stream down her face.

"Drugs!!" I'm genuinely shocked. So this is what it's all about. It had crossed my mind – if only for a split second – when Stacy told me about the cash she'd found that Liam had hidden, that there was the smallest possibility Liam might be involved in something like that, but I'd dismissed the idea in an instant. Liam is just a boy. Sure, he's a teenage boy, but he would never be so stupid as to get involved with drugs. Not Liam.

"She's telling the truth," I blurt out.

It's impossible to know what he's thinking right now. Maybe he's deciding whether or not to kill us. I try to push the thought away. I can't see inside the cab of the van as it's facing away from me, but I do hear the voice - barely a whisper -

174

coming from inside. The man drags Stacy a step backwards and reaches a hand inside the cab. After a very brief exchange of words with whoever is sitting in the drivers seat, he produces a phone and drags Stacy over to where I'm standing rooted to the spot. "Maybe this will jog your memories," he says, holding the screen up so we can both see it.

It looks like the video is a live feed, the footage bobbing around in the hand of whoever is holding the phone the other end. The room is gloomy, I can just make out faded white paint peeling from the brick walls. The dirty concrete floor is dappled with small pools of water and there is green mould on the walls. The camera pans to a solitary figure sitting on a chair. As the image slowly comes into focus, Stacy gasps.

The man who is filming, reaches out a hand, grabs Liam by the hair and raises his head so he is staring directly into the lens. His eyes look empty; devoid of all hope. There is dried blood smeared across his face and what appears to be fresh blood seeping from the corner of his mouth. The hand releases its grip and Liam's head falls forward without a sound. Then the screen goes blank.

Stacy is trying hard to fight the sobs, but I can hear her choking back the tears. Harry is scratching at the window, his snarling getting increasingly louder.

"You've got twenty-four hours," our captor says, and shoves Stacy into me. "If we haven't got our goods back by then, the boy dies."

We stand there clinging to each other as we watch the Transit drive away.

CHAPTER 24

How do you possibly console someone when they've just witnessed their child badly beaten, tied to a chair with the threat of death hanging over them? I wait until we're back at Stacy's before I state the obvious. "We have to call the police," I say, shoving a steaming mug of tea across the table.

Stacy raises her head slowly. In the bright light of her kitchen I can see the damage those thugs have inflicted on her far more clearly. The bruising round her swollen eye looks far worse than it did in the comparative darkness standing in the shadows of the trees. There are grazes and cuts I hadn't noticed before, and bruising to her upper arms. "I can't," she says, shaking her head.

"They didn't..." I'm trying to pick my words as carefully as I can. "They didn't...do anything else to you did they?"

Stacy shakes her head slowly. "No." She pauses, sips her tea, and then says, "I was sure he wanted to, but I got the impression whoever was driving the van was in charge. Maybe if he'd been on his own..." she doesn't manage to spit the rest of the sentence out before floods of tears begin streaming down her face. "I just want my son back, Meg'."

"That's why we have to call the police. Stacy, we are so far out of our depth. Christ, we don't even know what they're after, let alone where it is. I mean, are we talking weed? cocaine? heroin? And how much? It has to be a hell of a lot for them to go to these lengths."

"I can't take the chance. I need to speak to Tony."

"How long have you been seeing him?" The words pour out of my mouth before I've really had the chance to think about what I'm saying.

Stacy wipes the back of her hand across her face, and stares at me with a blank expression. I can almost hear the cogs turning. Eventually she says, "A few months. How did you know?"

"I didn't. Lucky guess."

Poppy is nuzzling Harry on the floor, but he's showing absolutely no interest whatsoever. Instead he's just sitting there, looking at us as if he can understand every word. I gesture to him with my hand hanging limply by my side. He skips across the floor and starts nuzzling his head against my leg.

"Tony will know what to do," Stacy says, without conviction. "I wanted to tell you but...what with him being married, he didn't..."

"You don't need to explain." I quickly change the subject. "How the hell did they get to Liam anyway? I thought he'd gone to spend some time with his dad."

"So did I. Joe called me this afternoon asking where Liam had gotten to. When I called Liam's phone...I should have known something was wrong. He sounded scared, but I just thought it was because of everything we'd gone through last night. He asked me to come and pick him up from some back street house near the train station. He said it was a mate's house. Of course when I got there, there was no Liam."

While I'm sitting listening to my friend blurt all this out, it suddenly dawns on me that neither Tony Skinner or Mark have tried calling me back. Tony, I suppose I can understand. If he's on duty he could be dealing with a dozen things. But Mark, Mark is a different proposition. He was meant to be at my house over an hour ago. He must have seen my missed call on his phone. The thought angers me more than I feel it should, then I get annoyed for feeling angry. Vicious circle.

Stacy lifts her phone from her pocket and stares at the screen as if she's just read my mind. "Ten missed calls from Joe," she says sadly. "What the hell do I tell him?"

"Which is exactly why we don't have any other option. Stacy, we cannot possibly try and do this on our own. We don't a choice, we have got to call the police." Even I'm getting sick of hearing me say it.

"Maybe there is another way."

I know my friend is grasping at straws, but I go along for the ride. I raise my eyebrows and gesticulate for her to elaborate.

"Liam's phone. If Darren can get into it and trace every number..."

"Stace'," I say, throwing my hands aloft. "Firstly, how the hell are you going to get hold of his phone? And second, Darren is laying in a hospital bed with gunshot wounds, I very much doubt he's going to feel like helping us out after all we've put him through."

"That's the thing, see," she says, her face full of hope. "I was convinced the police would keep hold of Liam's phone, or at least want to go through it at some point. So I swapped it for his old phone which can only make calls and receive text messages. And as for Darren, we didn't ask him to come running to our rescue."

She's going through hell, so I forgive her apparent lack of empathy for Darren.

"And Liam didn't protest? When you swapped phones I mean."

"No. I suppose he thought the same as me."

I let my head drop into my hands and just sit there staring at the table for what seems like an eternity. The whole thing is ludicrous. "Have you tried calling Tony yet?" I ask at last.

Stacy shakes her head. "No. I'm not sure what to say. I'm not sure what he's going to say."

"He's going to tell you the same as I have."

Harry suddenly pulls away from me, the hairs on his back bristling. Poppy is up off the floor, racing towards the front door, yapping, that sharp, snappy little bark that goes right through your head.

"Harry," I shout, but I can see he has no intention of obeying me. When the doorbell rings, they both go berserk.

Tony Skinner isn't in uniform. He looks surprised when he sees me standing there as I pull the front door open. "Oh, Megan. Err...is Stacy here?"

I lead him through to the kitchen. The dogs – who have now calmed down – escort us along the hallway, sniffing at Tony's ankles.

Stacy is sitting at the table with her face buried in her hands.

"I just thought I'd pop in to see how things..." Tony stops as Stacy slowly raises her head, an audible gasp halting his diatribe. He clears his throat before saying, "What the hell happened to you?" He spins round to look at me. "Is this why you tried calling me?"

"No, well not how you mean." I think about my next words before adding, "I know. About you two I mean."

He stares, first at me, then Stacy, his face a blank canvass betraying absolutely no emotion whatsoever.

"She guessed," Stacy says. "I didn't tell her."

I'm slightly concerned that my friend feels she needs to explain herself, but I say nothing. Instead I just stand there waiting for Tony to begin some long, complicated explanation about how his marriage is a sham and he's intending to leave his wife as soon as the time is right, blah de blah. Instead, he surprises me by stooping down and placing an arm round Stacy's shoulder. "What happened?" he asks, not bothering to disguise his anger.

Stacy throws me a glance. "I'll leave you to it," I say. "Make sure you call me as soon as...well just make sure you call me." I gather Harry and head out of the house, already knowing where I'm going.

The hospital car park is busy, even at this hour of night. I dropped Harry back home after leaving Stacy's – he wasn't at all happy – and headed straight here. I tried calling Mark twice while I was driving, but he's still not answering. To be honest, I am now getting quite worried. Obviously with all that's been happening I could be overreacting, but there's this horrible feeling niggling away inside my head, like an annoying itch that I just can't get rid of.

"I'm sorry, visiting hours finished at eight-thirty." The young Asian nurse has a pretty smile. She can't be more than twenty-four or five, even so, it appears she has sole charge of this ward tonight.

"I know," I say, trying as hard as I can to force a tear from the corner of my eye. "But I was in London and I've literally rushed straight back as soon as I heard what happened. The police haven't told me anything except my fiancée' has been shot, and that he's in a stable condition." I place a hand over my face and shake my head slowly.

"I do appreciate that but..." the young nurse glances over her shoulder, "look, let me speak to Mr Harding. Wait here," she adds, before scurrying along the ward.

She returns two minutes later. "Five minutes," she says, holding the ward door open for me to enter.

Darren is in a small, single room at the far end of the ward. He's sitting up in bed when I walk in, and I have to be honest – apart from the tubes poking out of his arm – he looks better than I've seen him in a while. He tries to force a smile when I enter, but it just looks like he has constipation.

"How are you doing?" My opening salvo sounds pathetically predictable when I hear the words out loud.

Darren shuffles his immense bulk into a comfier position. "Yeah, just great. They took two bullets out of me, but apart from that.." Sarcasm doesn't suit Darren.

"Sorry, silly question."

He smiles and leans his head forward just enough to form several chins beneath his jaw. "Have they caught anyone yet?"

"No." I intend to give away as little information as possible.

"Was it Liam they were after?"

"Yes."

"Why?"

At least I can be honest. "Truthfully, we're not entirely sure." It's time for the elephant in the room to be mentioned. "My turn to ask a question," I say. "What the hell were you doing there?"

Darren lowers his eyes as his cheeks begin to colour. "I err..."

"I know about the tracker on my phone," I say, trying to make it sound like a statement rather than an accusation. "We can talk about that another time. Right now I need your help."

He looks relieved, and a little surprised, which was my intention. "My...my help. I don't think I'm going to be a lot of help to anyone for a while," he says sadly. This is clearly an attempt at playing the sympathy card.

"I need you to give me the names or numbers of everyone Liam has been in contact with recently. Is that possible?"

"Not if the police have his phone, they will..."

"They don't."

"Well then, yes, it's possible. I would need Liam's phone, of course." His expression suddenly changes. "Given the circumstances, I'm assuming this is all highly illegal."

"Almost definitely," I say, already rising from my seat as I see the young nurse pull open the door.

"I'm afraid that's enough for now," the nurse says.

I lean over the bed and plant a kiss on Darren's cheek, just for effect. "I'll drop those things off to you in the morning darling," I say, already having pangs of guilt at the possibility that - given Darren's apparent infatuation with me – such a gesture could quite easily push him over the edge. I can only hope he realises it's all part of the charade.

I know something is wrong the moment I open the front door. No Harry. Before I left for the hospital I let him out into the garden so he could have a wee, and I made sure I fastened the flap when he came back in. Harry should be here. Panic sets in almost immediately. I race through to the kitchen, check the lock on the flap - which is still bolted – and try to stop myself from hyperventilating without success. My nerve endings are shredded because of the events that have occurred over the last couple of days, and this is just too much. Panic stations. Full alert. My heart rate skips to a hundred and just as I think I'm about to collapse, I hear a whine coming from one of the bedrooms above me. I take the stairs two at a time, stumble onto the first floor landing, claw my way upright and head for the second bedroom where the wardrobe door is now almost coming off its hinges.

When I pull the door open, Harry leaps out and jumps up at me, licking and frantically wagging his tail. It is a moment before I notice the little drops of blood on the faded cream carpet just outside the wardrobe.

CHAPTER 26

Harry

Megan hadn't been gone more than fifteen minutes when I heard someone approaching the house from the driveway. The sound of footsteps on gravel carries a long way. I can usually hear them long before they get anywhere near the house. It has got to the point where I can tell who it is long before they arrive: The postman has a long stride; Stacy, short quick steps; Yolanda is slow, and heavier...and so on.

These steps were slow and considered; someone didn't want to be heard. I started barking long before they reached the front door. It didn't stop them. He must have had a key because it seemed that no sooner had I started barking than the front door was opening, forcing me backwards across the wooden floor as I frantically tried to gain a purchase with my claws. The sight of my bared teeth and raised hackles didn't appear to bother him. I was scared, don't get me wrong, but there was no way I was letting him into our house without a fight. When I leapt at him he grabbed me by the collar, almost lifting me off my feet. He'd come prepared. He wore a pair of thick, black leather gloves and he'd wrapped some sort of cloth round the lower part of his right arm so my bite wouldn't break the skin.

There can't be any worse feeling in the world than being completely helpless when you are meant to protect the home you love. That was exactly how I felt as he dragged me up the stairs by my collar. I scratched and snarled and tried twisting from his grasp, but the harder I struggled the more my collar choked me. When we got to the top of the stairs, he stumbled on the last step. It was his only mistake, but it was enough. As he pitched forward and groped at the wall with his free hand I felt his grip on my collar slacken, ever-so-slightly, but enough. I twisted my head and sank my teeth into his ankle. I know it must of hurt because he shouted, "Shit", before he managed to regain his feet. Unfortunately he still had hold of my collar and he wasn't looking at all pleased. If I'm completely honest I thought this was it. I was expecting him to hang me over the bannister until I choked to death, or perhaps lift me off the floor and snap my neck like a twig. I had visions of Megan coming home and finding me dead, and the thought of how she would feel bothered me far more than the prospect of my own demise.

Amazingly, none of that happened. Instead he dragged me unceremoniously into the back bedroom and shoved me into the half empty wardrobe. I did try to bark, but my throat was so sore hardly anything came out. I tried clawing at the door, but it soon became apparent that nothing I could do was going to open it. So in the end I just had to sit there listening to him rummaging through our house. And all the time I'm dreading Megan coming home and this...this man...a man who Megan invited into our home, a man I know Megan has feelings for, is still there, waiting to attack her.

I can't describe the sense of relief I felt when I heard Mark close the door on the way out of the house some fifteen minutes later.

CHAPTER 27

Megan

Why? Why would someone break into my house and lock Harry in the wardrobe? As far as I can tell, nothing is missing. In fact, if it wasn't for the fact they'd locked Harry away I wouldn't have had the first idea anyone had been here.

The first thing I do is check Harry for injuries. I spend at least five minutes sitting on the floor, raking through his fur with my fingers, but there isn't a scratch on him. The intruder has made a big mistake. The drops of blood are from whoever broke in. Their DNA is spattered across my carpet. I don't want to get too far ahead of myself, but it doesn't take a genius to come to the conclusion that the men who took Stacy and are holding Liam, are responsible; and if it wasn't them, it must be one of their cohorts.

As soon as I'm sure Harry is okay I grab a cotton bud from the bathroom cabinet and dab a drop of blood from the bedroom floor. Then I wrap it in cling-film. Once the evidence is safely stashed in the fridge I begin checking my paperwork. Most of my files are kept in the top drawer of my dresser in the kitchen. Nothing appears to have been taken. There's no money in the house to speak of, and the only things of value are my lap-top, the TV and a sound system that's as old as the hills, and they haven't taken any of those.

It's almost midnight when I finally make the call.

"Meg'," Stacy answers almost immediately. " I was just about to call you. How did it go at the hospital?"

"Fine. Is Tony still there?"

"No, he left about ten minutes ago. Why?"

"Someone broke into my house. Well...actually that's not strictly true; someone has been in my house, while I was at the hospital. Whoever it was locked Harry in the wardrobe in the spare bedroom."

"Christ Megan! What the hell?"

"I know. It has to be the men who have Liam."

"Did they take anything?"

"No. There isn't a thing out of place. But they did leave something."

There's a short pause, as if she doesn't really want to ask. "What?" she says at last, the word edged with trepidation.

"Blood. They left some of their blood on the carpet. As soon as I've finished talking to you I'll call Tony and he can come and collect it. With any luck these bastards will be on some sort of data base..."

"No, don't call him." The pause isn't quite long enough for me to ask why not. "I'm coming over to you. I need to bring you up to date."

"What, now?" I glance at the clock. "You haven't got a car, remember."

"I'll be ten minutes," she says and hangs up.

It actually takes Stacy twelve minutes to make it to my front door.

"I would of come and picked you up," I say as she falls through the door, clearly exhausted at having run most of the way.

We go through to the kitchen and I wait impatiently while she recovers her breath.

"I told Tony everything," she says at last.

I can feel my eyes widen. "And?"

"Once he got over the shock, he was amazing. Oh God Meg', I just wish I'd told him about finding the money at the time..." she places a palm flat against her face as if she's trying to punish herself. "How could I have been so bloody stupid? If anything happens to Liam..."

"Don't. None of this is your fault. You did what you thought was best." I grab her hand - because this feels like a hand-grabbing kind of moment – and give it a little squeeze. "So what did Tony say? What is he going to do?"

"I told him what they said, about what would happen if we go to the police, and how scared I was, for Liam I mean. Tony says there's a protocol for just this type of situation. He has gone straight to the station. The moment he knows what's happening he'll let me know." Stacy blurts the words out as if she'd been holding a breath for the last minute or so. Her face a picture of relief.

"And in the meantime?"

"We sit tight."

The thought of doing absolutely nothing just seems wrong. Sitting tight might be fine if someone hadn't been in my house tonight, but I feel violated; I need someone to be held accountable. I think the initial shock has begun to wane; what started out as anger - and of course relief when I knew they hadn't hurt Harry or taken anything from the house – has slowly evaporated. Suddenly I find the thought of being here with just Harry for company just a little bit scary.

I glance at the clock. "Look, it's late now. Why don't you stay the night? I'll drive you back to yours to pick up Poppy..."

There's a vague expression on her face and I know she's thinking 'why on earth would she want to drive me back to mine only for us to come straight back here', but at some point the penny drops and she says, "Yeah, let's do that."

By the time I finally fall into bed it's almost 2am. I should be exhausted, and maybe I am, but I still don't feel like sleeping. I have the comfort of knowing

Stacy is just a few feet away in the spare room, but Mark still hasn't called. What

the hell is going on with him? I feel angry, but the anger is tinged with fear. I pick

up my phone and tap his number to give him one last chance before I try and grab

some much needed sleep. The phone rings out, as it has done every other time I've

tried calling him. I slam my own phone down hard on the bedside table. At some

point I finally drift off to sleep.

I wake to the sound of Stacy moving around in the bedroom next door. The house

is old, nearly every floorboard creaks, you can't move without someone hearing. I

can tell from the sound Stacy is pacing whilst talking quietly to someone on her

phone. There's no light seeping through the curtains so it must be early. I glance at

my phone for confirmation. Almost 5.30am.

Harry is by the bedroom door, ears pricked.

Quietly, I slip out of bed and put on my dressing gown. There's a little part of

me that feels I shouldn't really be sneaking about in my own home eavesdropping

on my best friend's conversation, but that little part of me isn't winning the

argument right now. I'm in too deep to be kept in the dark.

"Are you sure?" It's the first words I hear Stacy whisper as I reach my bedroom

door. She sounds scared.

Harry wags his tail and looks up at me with appealing eyes. I touch his head,

gently running my fingers through his fur, as much for my own reassurance as his.

"And what about Liam's phone?" she continues, totally unaware that I'm standing just a few feet away. "Surely it's worth a try?" She waits for the answer before saying, "Okay, well if that's what they are saying," she replies, in a tone that sounds just about as uncertain as it is humanly possible for anyone to sound. "Right, I'll wait to hear from you later."

I give her a moment before making out I've just woken up and got out of bed. "Did I hear you on the phone?" I say, stretching my arms wide and faking a yawn as I reach her bedroom door.

Stacy turns, startled. "Yes. That was Tony. They don't want us to do anything. I told him what we discussed, about getting Darren to try and track some of the numbers from Liam's phone, but he said it wasn't a good idea, we should just leave it to the police."

"That's hardly surprising is it?" I note the look on her face and move into the room, place an arm round her shoulders and gently ease her onto the bed. "We have to trust them Stace'. The best chance of getting Liam back safely, is the police. They know what they're doing."

"But he's not their son," she replies stubbornly.

I don't have an answer to that. Instead I say the only thing that comes into my head. "I'm making coffee. Do you want some?"

We sit at the kitchen table sipping coffee and trying oh so hard to not make it obvious we are both avoiding the one subject we should be talking about. I think that by now it has become evident - even to Stacy - that her son is into something far more serious than we could ever have imagined. Just how deep, neither of us know. Deep enough to end up in this predicament that's for sure.

I wait until we're on our third cup of coffee before I summon up the courage to ask the question I should have done days ago. "Do you think there's any chance Joe is involved in this?" I spit the sentence out quickly, as if it will reach her ears with slightly less of a sting.

The moment she looks at me I realise it's crossed her mind. "I've thought about it," she says, "but no, I'm sure not even Joe would sink that low."

Stacy had spilled her life out to me on several occasions in the past - usually when she'd had too much to drink – and the period when she was with Joe didn't make for easy listening. Joe liked to drink, a lot. Joe liked to experiment with drugs. Joe liked to use Stacy as a punch-bag when it all became too much for him. When Liam was born things got worse. It was only after Joe finally 'came out' that it became obvious he'd been fighting the demons in the only way he knew how. It sounded like she was trying to make excuses for him the first time Stacy said that to me, but on reflection I think she was just trying to search for some redemption for herself for putting up with him so long.

"Sorry, but I had to ask," I say, and before she can reply, my phone rings. I don't recognise the number and just for a moment I feel my heart beat a little faster. It's barely six-thirty, who hell is calling me at this hour? I hesitate just long enough for Stacy to throw me a wide-eyed look before I hit the answer button.

"Good morning. Am I speaking to Megan Harris?" The man's voice is soft, and there's a hint of a European accent buried somewhere beneath the hesitancy.

"Yes."

"My name is doctor Gonzalez. Megan, I'm so sorry to call you at this hour, but it's your grandmother."

I ignore the involuntary shudder that surges up my spine and manage to say, "What is it?"

A pause. Too long.

Stacy is looking at me, mouthing, "who is it?" her eyes wide with concern.

Doctor Gonzalez finally gathers himself. "I'm afraid she's had a fall... She's sustained some very serious injuries...I, err..."

I want to scream, "spit it out man," but instead I wait for him to come out and say the words I already know must be coming. Instead he surprises me and says, "Your grandmother is in hospital." Before I've had time to enjoy the moment of relief, he adds quickly, "I would suggest you make your way there as soon as you're able."

His words hang over my head like a thick black cloud. It takes a moment for the realisation of what he's trying to tell me to finally sink in, and when it does, the cloud explodes and the deluge hits me. I sit, bolted to the chair as he reels off an address in a voice that oozes compassion that is wasted on me at this moment.

When he's finished I say "thank you", for no other reason than it feels like the right thing to say.

"What is it?" Stacy asks in a voice that is barely a whisper.

I raise my head and fight back the tears. "My grandmother's had a fall. It sounds serious." The words are spilling out as if I'm on autopilot. "I'm sorry Stace', I need to go to the hospital."

"Of course." Stacy says, but buried deep within her eyes, hidden behind the compassion, I can see the fear. Fear that today of all days, when she needs me the most and with everything that's going on, I'm about to leave her to cope on her own.

I'm showered and dressed in half an hour. "I'll call you as soon as I know anything," I say on the way out the door. I don't wait for the reply.

The drive takes an hour and a half because of the early morning traffic. The problem with being stuck in traffic is, it gives you time to think. Too much time to let your imagination run away with you. Is it just bad timing? Or is that too much of a coincidence? The thought's been running around inside my head trying to find willing participants, and now they've managed to form a team and they're kicking the ideas around so fast my brain can't keep up. Joanne is old, I know that, but she doesn't fall. She's not a 'falling' kind of person. Joanne has never rushed anywhere, even when she was younger. In a race with a tortoise she'd come out second best. Careless people fall, people like my grandmother get pushed. I try and force the idea out of my head because it sounds absurd. I try and tell myself I'm only thinking like this because of everything that's been happening over the last few days. I must be paranoid. My imagination really needs a reality check. Even so, by the time I arrive at the hospital I still haven't managed to shift the image of a hand on my grandmother's shoulder, and the scream as she tumbles to the floor.

Reception have been for-warned that I'm coming, because as soon as I mention who I'm here to see, a young male nurse appears and escorts me along the maze of corridors. I feel like I should be asking him questions, but instead we walk in silence.

Joanne is in the critical care ward, first bed on the right as we enter. The curtains are drawn round her bed. "The consultant will be along any minute," the nurse offers as he pulls the curtain aside.

At first I can't see past all the tubes and wires poking out of my grandmother. The monitor beside her bed bleeps, the little peeks appear far too shallow, and I notice the letters DNR scribbled on the notes hanging at the end of her bed. Joanne is laying on her back, the pristine white sheet pulled up just above her chest. Her eyes are closed but her mouth is turned into a half smile that makes her appear at peace with the world.

I pull up a chair and sit at the side of the bed. When I take her hand it feels cold as my fingers close around her thin flesh. I can feel the frail bones and want to hold her tighter, knowing I can't. I want her eyes to open and see me. I want her to know I'm here, caring, loving, willing her to wake up and flash that wicked smile in my direction one last time. A smile that doesn't come from any turning of the mouth, but from the eyes; eyes that still sparkle as brightly as when she was a child. A single tear escapes from the corner of my eye and drips onto the white sheet, staining it grey as the liquid soaks into the cotton.

The curtain makes a swish behind me. "Mrs Finch?"

I wipe my eyes and stand to face the consultant. "Yes."

We shake hands formerly and he adjusts his spectacles with his free hand. "I'm not sure how much information you have been told about your grandmother's condition," he says, and his voice takes on a sombre tone.

194

I stare at my grandmother. "Only that she had a fall."

"Oh, I see." Those three words slap me round the face. His expression speaks volumes. "Your grandmother fractured her hip and sustained quite severe fractures to several ribs when she fell. She also sustained............."

At some point I stop listening. I don't need to know every detail to realise what he's telling me. The only thing stopping Joanne from screaming in pain is the drugs they're pumping into her, and her heart isn't strong enough to cope with that amount of morphine for long.

The consultant disappears. I wait, holding onto my grandmother's hand, selfishly wishing I had someone to comfort me so I wasn't going through all this alone. I think about Mark. I think about sitting on my grandmother's knee as a child. I remember all the little things that seem so insignificant at the time but now those memories are all there is to cling to. Mark would know what to say right now. I remember her laughing when we were at the beach and I stumbled into the water when we were paddling. Her picking me up, drying me off and buying an extra large ice cream to console me. But most of all, I remember how much her eyes shone with love whenever I walked into the room: A love so intense you could almost feel the physical warmth as it wrapped round your shoulders like a thick duvet on a cold winter's day.

At 9:56am Joanne's eyes flickered open for the briefest of moments, and I could swear she smiled at me. That same bright, loving smile I had seen a million times before. I felt her fingers squeeze mine a little tighter, and the machine began it's relentless, monotone drone.

CHAPTER 28

My grandmother's bungalow doesn't feel empty. I step over the threshold half
expecting Joanne to appear from one of the doorways. The air is filled with the
pungent aroma of a fresh spring morning emanating from the numerous scented
candles that fill the house.

I've been told she fell in the kitchen: slipped on the wet floor tiles. I felt
compelled to come straight here from the hospital to see for myself. I head towards
the offending room expecting to see evidence, but there is none. There's a plate on
the drainer beside the sink and a single tea cup in the bowl waiting to be washed.
Someone has wiped the floor dry, the smears are still visible on the dark tiles.

I take a seat at the kitchen table and let the warm Autumnal sun seeping through
the patio doors wash over me. And that is where I let the demons in. Was Joanne
alone? Did whoever broke into my house last night find her address and pay her a
visit. If so, why? What would be the point? The answer is simple, there would be
no point whatsoever. Joanne was in her nineties, she was a frail old woman who
slipped on a wet floor. So why can't I leave it at that.

When I check my phone I find a message from Stacy. She wants to know how
my grandmother is. Can I call her as soon as possible. It's the only message. Still
no word from Mark. I don't want to think about him right now, but I can't stop
myself.

The doorbell sounds and snaps me back to the moment.

196

Clifford Bignal cuts a lonely figure standing on the doorstep in his grey, pinstripe suit. His pale skin is creased into a million fine lines where he's squinting in the morning sun. "Hello Megan," he says sadly, and opens his arms. He was the only person I called when Joanne died. I felt I owed him that.

I accept the offer and we stand there in a silent embrace for what seems like an eternity. I think we both need to feel the comfort of someone who understands our pain. Clifford had been my grandmother's solicitor for as long as I can remember. When I decided to go into practice, it was Clifford who encouraged me. I know from how Joanne talked about him that she considered him one of her closest friends. When he finally took a backward step from his practice, he kept on a few 'special' clients: one of those was my grandmother.

"I'm so sorry," he says when we are seated in the kitchen. "Your grandmother was a wonderful woman."

"Thank you." I clutch his hand and feel the same cold, thin flesh that I did when I took hold of my grandmother's hand such a short time ago. "Do you know who found her?" I ask.

"I believe it was one of the neighbours."

"Was there..." I stumble, searching for the right words, "was there any sign of a break-in. I mean, it was just an accident?"

He nods his head slowly. "I believe so, yes. The police were called of course, but there wasn't anything suspicious to report as far as I'm aware. If there was anything untoward I'm sure you would have heard something by now."

I feel guilty having even asked the question. I'm pretty sure if this had happened a month ago, two weeks ago even, the thought wouldn't have crossed my mind. "Sorry," I say, and wave a hand dismissively.

Clifford stares at me blankly. "What made you ask?"

I shake my head. "Just my mind working overtime. Looking for someone to blame."

Clifford forces the faintest of smiles. "Joanne was old," he says, "she'd had a great life. Unfortunately these things happen." But before he's finished speaking I see a glimmer of doubt suddenly sweep across his face.

"What?"

He frowns, shakes his head, pushes a hand beneath his chin. "Oh it's nothing," he says. "I shouldn't even be thinking about it, let alone telling you."

"Telling me what?"

He pauses and lowers his eyes, staring at the grain on the surface of the wooden table as if it's the most interesting pattern he's ever seen. "I know you're aware of the favour I did your grandmother recently," he says, and puts more emphasis into the word 'favour'.

"Yes, she told me what she'd done. Or rather intimated."

"Well..." he pauses, removes his spectacles and massages his temples with long, bony fingers. "Greg called me a few days ago," he finally manages to spit out. "He was furious. Kept ranting on about ethics and how he wouldn't let this go without a fight. He called Joanne a devious fucking bitch - excuse my French - and said he'd make us all suffer."

"And you think...?"

"No, no," he waves his hand dismissively, "I don't think anything. Like I said, I really shouldn't have mentioned it."

"But you did. So, had it crossed your mind? That Greg could possibly have something to do with her death I mean?"

"Not until you asked me about an intruder, no." He grabs my hands, and folds his fingers round mine. "I really don't know where all that came from. I mean, it's ridiculous. Greg maybe many things, but he wouldn't hurt anyone."

"And you're sure about that?"

"Perhaps you should talk with the neighbours," he says, and finally releases my hands. "If you're still unsure when you've spoken to them, well then maybe you should think about calling the police."

Long after Clifford has said his goodbye's I remain sitting on the chair, staring blindly at the kitchen floor where my grandmother lay in pain until some kindly neighbour came to her aid. I feel a stab of guilt. Joanne was alone. How long did she lay on that hard floor writhing in agony? How bad a grand-daughter must I be to let something like that happen?

If my phone hadn't pinged and snapped me back to reality I think I would have sat there brooding half the day. I slide a finger across the screen and Stacy's message appears in bold letters HOW'S IT GOING. CALL ME WHEN YOU GET THE CHANCE.

I know all my focus should be on Stacy, and Liam, but it isn't. There's something I need to be sure about, if only to put my mind at rest.

CHAPTER 29

Harry

I knew there was something wrong long before Megan ran upstairs, got changed and rushed out of the house without even saying goodbye to me. I could sense her pain. Poppy came over and snuggled up beside me in the basket, which took my mind off things for a while, but the feeling of comfort didn't last long. The whole house is filled with bad vibrations. Stacy is a nervous wreck. She keeps checking her phone every five minutes, pacing the floor and chewing her bottom lip. Poppy can sense it too, she stopped trying to play with me an hour ago and now she's just following Stacy around the house like a shadow.

When Stacy's phone does eventually ring, she almost jumps out of her skin.

"Tony." She sounds relieved. "Where are you? What's happening?"

I can hear his voice clearly. "Calm down sweetheart. It's all in hand. I need you to meet me so I can go over the details. I don't want to take the chance doing it over the phone. You need to make sure you're not followed. Make out you're taking Poppy for a walk."

"Don't forget, I'm at Megan's." Stacy informs him. "Where do you want to meet?"

"Is Megan with you?"

"No, her grandmother had an accident. Megan rushed off first thing this morning. I've been trying to get hold of you for the last couple of hours. Megan hasn't answered my text, so I haven't got a clue what's happening." She slumps onto a kitchen chair and pushes a hand through her hair.

"Okay," he replies in a soft, steady voice. "I know it's hard, but please, try not to worry. I promise you, everything is going to be just fine. I won't let anything happen to you or Liam."

"I wish you were here," Stacy whispers.

"Me too." He pauses, obviously thinking something through. "Do you remember when Poppy ran off and I came to help you find her? You remember where we took shelter when the storm came in?"

Stacy nods. "Yes, of course."

"Don't say it over the phone. Meet me there in half an hour. Try to make sure you're not followed."

"What!! You think someone might be...."

"Just a precaution. We have to be careful. If they're watching you it's important they don't realise the police are involved."

"Yes. Yes of course." Stacy shakes her head and rolls her eyes.

As soon as Stacy is dressed we head out of the house.

We're heading North out of the village, towards the church. The skies are dark this morning, sort of raining but not quite. October has arrived, and with it, the sombre reality of another English winter.

We haven't even reached the outskirts of the village when we bump into Helen Pierce and Dorothy Barnstaple.

"Morning Stacy. Megan's got you looking after Harry today has she?" Dorothy Barnstaple squats down with a sigh and ruffles the top of my head. Poppy nudges her hand and the attention immediately diverts to her.

"Morning," Stacy says vacantly. "Err, yes, she's had to shoot off. Her grandmother's had a fall," She's tugging at our leads as she speaks, clearly eager to move on.

"Oh no," Helen Pierce says, in that horrible, high-pitched squeal that stings my sensitive ears. "Is there anything we can do to help?"

"No, err, I don't know. Sorry," Stacy starts walking, pulling me and Poppy after her, leaving Dorothy Barnstaple still squatting, her head turned in our direction, mouth slightly gaping at the snub.

"What was all that about?" I hear Helen Pierce say before we're out of earshot.

If Stacy hears it, she doesn't react, instead she picks up her pace, leaning into the early-morning breeze as if she's in a race with an unseen competitor.

We continue at speed, heading along the narrow, overgrown footpath up the hill out of the village. Every time a car roars past us heading into the village, Stacy ducks her head and tries to shield her face with her free hand. I'm not entirely sure what she's frightened of, but something is scaring her.

We stop when we're only half way up the hill. The large wooden gate leads into a long, narrow driveway that takes you all the way up to the old Mortimer house. The Mortimer's moved out about a year ago and the house has been empty ever since. Occasionally Megan brings me up this way when she doesn't want to walk too far. Before you get to the Mortimer house there's a footpath that cuts to the right alongside one of the fields, it brings you out on an bumpy old track the other side of the valley and you can head back down into the village from there.

We don't cut down the footpath though. Instead Stacy unclips my lead, then Poppy's, and seems quite content to let us run ahead. Or so it's seems until she calls us back with a sharp whistle. When I turn round, Stacy is heading towards the old Mortimer barn; a ramshackle timber clad building set back some twenty yards or so from the main track. She's standing by the door waiting for us to reach her when I see the arm appear from inside the barn and grab her round the neck.

CHAPTER 30

Megan

I should reply to Stacy's text, but I don't. I do check my phone though, searching for a message I know isn't there: The teenager in me forlornly hoping for a crumb of comfort that lets me know I haven't been cast aside without a second thought. I search through texts, emails and voice messages, but there's still nothing from Mark, and as hard as I'm trying to not let that annoy me, it really does. If he's not laying dead in a ditch somewhere, there really is no excuse. I instantly chastise myself for allowing those sort of thoughts to creep up on me. That's the trouble with letting someone into your life; before you know what's happening they're messing with your emotions and you find yourself thinking all sorts of weird things.

I know what I should be doing right now, I should be jumping into my car and heading back home at a rate of knots. My best friend is in bits. Her world has been torn apart and right now the thing she needs more than anything is support. But I don't do that. Instead I walk across the road and press the doorbell of the small bungalow opposite.

A rather plump, elderly gentleman, with thin grey hair and an impressive moustache greets me with a sympathetic smile. "Hello my dear," he says as if he was expecting me.

"I'm sorry to bother you...." I begin, and don't get any further before he's joined at the door by an equally plump woman of similar age.

"Frank," the woman snaps, "don't leave her standing on the doorstep."She elbows poor Frank to one side, grabs my hand, and all but drags me into her home. "How is poor Joanne doing?" she says, leading me into a rather chintzy front room that is far too hot to feel comfortable. She pulls out a chair and gestures to me to take a seat. "Frank, go and put the kettle on."

I reply before Frank has had a chance to leave the room. "I'm so sorry," I say, bracing myself for the words that are about to spill out of my mouth. "My grand-mother died this morning."

They both appear suitably shocked. Frank slumps into a chair and the old woman collapses into the one opposite him. "Oh no!" She clasps a hand to her mouth and instinctively reaches out with her other hand for the comforting touch of her husband.

A morbid, uncomfortable silence that seems to last for an eternity, engulfs the room. After what seems like a very brief period of mourning, Frank struggles out of the chair and says, "I'll make tea."

"I'm so sorry for your loss," the old woman says as Frank wanders aimlessly out of the room. "I'm Alice, Alice Watson. Frank and I are...were, good friends with your grand-mother. Such a lovely woman. Always so friendly. Do anything for anybody. Never a cross word in thirty years."

Hmm, that's not exactly how I'd describe my gran. Yes she was friendly when she had to be, but she was also extremely introverted. My grandmother liked her own company, didn't suffer fools gladly and was always ready to stand her ground if she believed she was in the right; which – almost without exception – she was. "That's very kind of you," I say, offering Alice Watson a sad smile. "Do you know who found her?"

"Oh yes, didn't you know? I thought that's why you were here. It was Frank who found her."

Frank wanders back into the room carrying a tray of cups and saucers.

"I was just telling...Megan, isn't it?"

"Yes."

"I was just telling Megan, it was you who found Joanne."

Frank places the tray on the table and nods in the affirmative. "Yes," he says, shaking his head as if he is just remembering it all too clearly. "I stayed with her until the ambulance arrived."

"Did she say anything?"

"Well, she was in a lot of pain..."

"Frank!" Alice snaps, glancing at me, "I'm sure poor Megan doesn't want to know..."

"No, that's fine," I say. I don't want to picture my grand-mother writhing in agony on her kitchen floor, but at the same time I have to find out what happened, and if that means I have to listen to some uncomfortable truths, so be it.

"Well, no, she didn't say much at all," Frank continues. "I made her as comfortable as I could, and asked if she wanted me to call anyone - other than the ambulance of course - but she wasn't really making much sense."

"How do you mean?"

Well..." Frank casts a glance at his wife, as if he's seeking her approval to proceed. When she doesn't say anything, he continues. "She was mumbling, you understand, so I can't be certain, but it sounded very much like she was saying 'get that man out of my house'. At first I thought she was talking about me, but she kept trying to turn her head as if she was looking for someone." Frank lets out a long, pitiful sigh. "I just wish I'd gone over sooner."

"I'll make the tea shall I?" Alice says, and gets up from the table.

"Why did you go over?" I try my hardest not to make it sound accusatory.

Frank fixes me with a long stare. His eyes are all red and puffy, and he's clearly fighting hard against unleashing any further display of emotion. "The back bedroom light wasn't on this morning. Joanne always puts the light on first thing." He glances surreptitiously at the doorway. "We were quite good friends you know," his voice not much more than a whisper now. "Nothing more than that you understand," he adds quickly. "I used to pop over and do bits in the garden and then we'd sit and talk...for hours sometimes. She was a remarkable woman your grand-mother." He manages a pitiful smile and pretends to rub his forehead, but I notice his thumb brush a tear from the corner of his left eye.

206

"And you didn't see anything untoward? Anything that would suggest someone had been in the house."

He shakes his head. "No, there wasn't any sign of a break-in and the doors were all locked when I arrived."

"How did you get in?"

"I've got a key. Joanne has one for our house as well. It's a very friendly neighbourhood."

Alice appears in the doorway carrying a tea pot; a little spiral of steam coming from the spout. "What about that car last night?" she says, catching the last part of our conversation.

"What car?" I ask, interest suitably peaked.

Frank rolls his eyes. "They're always parking there. The people who live down the road have a small driveway and they're always entertaining, so some of their guests have to park up the road. It was a blue Audi, I think. But like I said..."

"A blue Audi?" The image springs into my head instantly. The last time Greg came over, when he brought 'her' with him, I'm sure he was driving a flashy blue car. I remember thinking at the time it was more suited to a much younger man: boy racer's, I believe they're referred to.

"Yes, at least I think it was." Frank continues. "Little sporty thing with low profile tyres. But like I said, people are always using this part of the road for parking."

"It was gone before we went to bed." Alice says absently on her way out of the room.

"So what time did it arrive?"

"Oh," Frank ruffles his moustache and scratches his head. "About seven-thirty, maybe a little after that."

"And it had gone by...?"

"Sometime before eight-thirty."

I can feel him staring at me, and I know what he's thinking. He's thinking I'm clutching at straws, searching for someone to blame, because then I won't have to feel so guilty for not being here when my grand-mother needed me the most. Or at least that's how I interpret it.

"And you didn't hear anything else?"

"If I had, I would have gone straight over." His forehead creases into a thousand fine lines and he adds, "Is there any particular reason you're asking me this?"

I force a smile. "No, not really."

"The police would have noticed if there was anything suspicious: They don't miss a thing these days. But if you're still concerned it might be worth calling on the Green's. They live half way down the road and they've got one of those security cameras because they had a break-in a few years back. I'm sure their camera picks up all the vehicles that come up and down the road."

Alice ambles back into the room and takes a seat next to her husband. I sit at the table listening to the Watson's reminisce about my grand-mother, while my mind is racing off in the distance.

The rain has finally cleared by the time I leave Frank and Alice still sitting in their overly hot living room sipping tea. A thick blanket of clouds blot out the sun, causing everything to appear grey and sombre. I stroll the hundred yards down the road to the Green's house. Maybe it's my imagination, but I'm sure I can see curtains twitching as the sound of my feet crunching against the shingle echoes between the buildings . I know from what my grandmother told me, this is a very close knit community; prying eyes and ears lurk behind every window. I hope that is the case.

I pass four houses before I reach The Willows, Alice having given me the name before I left. The house itself is unremarkable, set back a short distance from the road, it's a square brick construction and reminds me of something a five-year-old would draw. On my way up the short driveway I spot the surveillance camera bolted to the front wall, just above the garage door. The camera faces straight onto the road, which is good, but there are two large Willow trees in the front garden, which is bad because the branches may well block the view of the road.

The doorbell sounds inside the house when I press it, knocking out a sickeningly jolly little tune.

The door swings open a moment later to reveal a thin, balding man wearing a rather too short, blue towelling dressing gown and a pained expression. The stench of stale cigarettes and alcohol hits me even before he speaks. "Yes," he says, not bothering to hide his agitation at being disturbed after what was clearly a heavy night.

"I'm sorry to bother you - my name's Megan by the way – my grandmother lives a few doors up the road, The Gables." I pause, feel the next words catching in my throat.

"Joanne, yes," he says, not quite managing to stifle a disinterested yawn.

"Oh, you knew her?"

His eyes widen and he suddenly looks very alert. "Knew her?" he repeats, an unexpected look of concern registers in his eyes.

"I'm afraid she passed away this morning." Somehow the use of words doesn't sting as much as I was expecting. "Yes. She had a fall sometime in the night. Mr Watson discovered her this morning."

"We heard the ambulance," he says vaguely. "I'm so sorry." The sympathy appears genuine and he shakes his head slowly as if to emphasize his grief.

I cut to the chase. "Does your security camera work?"

He glances upwards and sideways. "Sorry, no. It stopped working a few months back and I haven't gotten round to getting it fixed yet." His expression quickly changes. "Why? She wasn't broken into was she?"

And now, for the first time, I wonder if this is an avenue I should be heading down. The police would surely follow up if there was the slightest chance anything untoward had occurred. "No, I don't think so. I just want to..." I start to turn, shaking my head, apologising again for having disturbed him.

"There was something," he says before I've got more than a couple of paces. "It's probably nothing but..."

"Go on," I urge when he pauses.

"When I took the bins out a car was coming down the road. It was doing a fair lick."

"Did you see the make?"

"Blue Audi I think. Low profile tyres."

"I don't suppose you got a look at the driver?"

He shoves his hand under his chin. "Just a glimpse. Chap was about my age, light brown greying hair. I remember thinking the car didn't fit the driver. Mid-life-crisis car we'd say in the office."

His description sums Greg up perfectly.

CHAPTER 31

Maybe I should have called the police straight away, and perhaps if my mind wasn't in turmoil that's exactly what I would have done. Instead I end up taking an hour's detour to the house where Greg now lives with his pregnant, child-bride. Okay, maybe 'child bride' is a slight exaggeration, but not by a mile. The house is a little brick box in the middle of an estate surrounded by a thousand identical boxes. How the mighty have fallen. If the situation wasn't quite so serious maybe I'd have felt a glimmer of satisfaction as I sat in my car staring out of the window on that bleak afternoon.

There's no blue Audi on the single car driveway, but there is light spewing from the front, downstairs window. I sit, staring out of the driver's window at the little box where Greg has set up home with his pregnant lover, wondering if the decline in circumstances would be enough to push him to take such drastic action. And to what end? Or was it just a moment of rage? Did Greg have that in him? The more I thought about it the more it just didn't make sense. Greg maybe many things, but he's not capable of killing. Or is he? There was a time I would have sworn he wouldn't ever leave me: I was as certain as it's possible to be about anything, and yet here I am, sitting outside his love-nest watching the shadow of his pregnant girlfriend pace the floor through faded net curtains. I suppose I'm just angry enough, because the next minute I find myself standing on the doorstep knocking on the front door.

I watch the vague shape waddle along the hallways towards me through the frosted glass panel, not knowing quite what I'm about to say.

"Oh!!" she exclaims as she pulls the door wide, her face a true picture of surprise. There's no doubt I was the last person she was expecting to see. It's hard to look past the huge tits and tummy, but once I do all I can see is a tired, scared little girl.

"Is Greg in?" There's no time for pleasantries. I don't bother disguising my agitation.

"No, he's at work." She shakes her head but the lank hair is too greasy to move. "What do you want Megan?"

"Where was he last night?"

"What?"

"Last night. Where...was... Greg..." I repeat, mouthing the words slowly as if I'm talking to a deaf person.

"Yes," she snaps back, cutting my dialogue short. She pushes a few loose strands of hair from her face with one hand while the other instinctively caresses her swollen stomach. "I heard what you said, I just wonder what the hell you think you're doing turning up on our doorstep like this?"

She sounds angry, but she looks scared, and that makes me feel guilty: A child trapped in a woman's body with a baby growing inside her. Perhaps she didn't want any of this, perhaps she did, but there's no doubt she feels out of her depth right now. "I just need to know if Greg was home last night," I say, lowering my voice, trying to take the threat out of the words.

"Yes, of course he was, but what the hell's that got to do with you?"

She's lying. I'm certain. "All night?"

A flicker of doubt registers in her eyes. "What are you trying to tell me?" An unwanted frown wrinkles her forehead, enough pain in her eyes for me to realise she's just made two plus two add up to five. "Are you saying...."

"No." I stop her before she can get the words out. "Nothing like that."

She bites her bottom lip and drags the back of her hand across her eyes leaving a smear of yesterday's mascara on her cheek. I know the insecurity is probably down to raging hormones, unless she has other reasons for doubting Greg's fidelity. That wouldn't surprise me. "Then...then why are you here?" she finally blurts out.

I force an unwanted smile. "It's very important," I say softly, "that you tell me the truth. If Greg went out last night, I need to know."

"Why?"

"So he did go out?"

The pause is just long enough. "For an hour, yes."

"An hour?"

"Maybe a couple of hours. Look, just tell me what the hell this is about."

213

"What time?"

"Sorry!!" The frown increases.

"What time did he go out?"

"I don't know. Half six maybe. He had to pop into the office."

No sooner had the words left her mouth than I felt a shudder run up and down my spine. On the drive over here I'd questioned myself over and over again. Greg was an arsehole; is an arsehole, of that there is no question. But a killer!! Never in a million years would I have believed that the man I spent so many wonderful years with would be capable of that. But the timing was just too perfect to be a coincidence. The car, too much of a coincidence. The motive...it goes on and on, and even though I'm angry and hurt there really is only one conclusion that makes sense.

Part of me, a very large part, wants to blurt out what I think I know. Deep inside me, swirling in the depths of my stomach; my empty, barren stomach, there's something evil that wants to tear her world apart. Just like she tore mine apart when she fluttered her eyelashes at my husband, wiggled her perfectly formed arse in front of him or leaned in a little closer as they talked, offering him a glimpse of her firm, twenty-something-year-old cleavage, until the temptation finally became too much to bear and he succumbed. Maybe there was a time when I could imagine that scenario, but now I knew better. Greg didn't need coaxing.

Tempting as it is, I like to think I'm better than that. If I'm right, her world is about to be shattered soon enough without me standing here gloating about it.

"So what is all this about then? What's he supposed to have done?" Her tone now defensive.

"I'll let him explain." And before she can reply, my phone pings.

MEGAN, CALL ME NOW!!

The text is from Stacy and I'm immediately filled with guilt because I can't even begin to imagine what she's going through at the moment.

"You can't just turn up here out of the blue and start..."

I'm already half way down the path when I turn back and say, "Just tell Greg I called. He'll know what it's about." I don't hang around to hear her reply, but I can imagine her mouth gaping open wide as she watches me get into my car and drive off down the road.

CHAPTER 32

Harry

I'm tearing towards the barn as fast as I can go, but Poppy passes me before I've got half way there. She must have seen it too and now her hackles are up and she's snapping and snarling, her paws barely touching the ground as she races to protect her mistress. I watch her disappear round the corner, cutting through the overgrown nettles as if they weren't there. I'm going as fast as I can but I'm a couple of seconds behind. Neither of us have a clue what awaits us when we reach the barn, but I don't think we care, the only thing that matters is protecting Stacy from her attacker.

I'm forty feet behind her when Poppy disappears through the open doorway. I hear a snarl, a bark and then Stacy screaming, "No!!"

By the time I arrive, Poppy is laying on her back. Tony Skinner is squatting, rubbing her upturned belly. "Good girl," he says, as Poppy wags her tail furiously. He sees me and says, "Hello Harry," reaching out to stroke my back. I notice the muddy paw prints on his trousers and wonder how the hell Poppy can get away with that.

The attention only lasts a moment.

"You weren't followed?" Tony says, standing, folding his arms round Stacy, pulling her in close.

"I don't think so." She falls into his arms as if it's the safest place in the world.

Tony pulls away, holding her at arms length by her shoulders. "Okay, well we don't have much time. If they haven't contacted you yet, they will soon. When they do, you have to play along. You have to make it convincing. They're going to ask you if you've got the package. Tell them you have, but you want to speak to Liam." He pulls Stacy closer. "That's important Stacy. If they think you're lying they'll kill Liam and you'll never see them again."

Stacy gasps, tears appear in her eyes. "Oh Christ..."

"Sorry, but I need to make sure you understand just how important it is that they believe you're telling the truth. Any doubts, any slip-ups..."

"Yes, I get the picture, "Stacy snaps, the tears now streaming down her cheeks.

"Oh darling, I'm sorry," Tony pulls her close, folding his arms right round her, "but these are seriously dangerous people, and we are only going to get one chance." He pulls back, plants a kiss on her lips and then clutches her to him once again. "Don't agree to anything unless they let you speak to Liam first," he repeats. "Once you've spoken to Liam they'll probably tell you where you're meant to make the drop. It doesn't matter where it is, try and get them to change it. They're probably going to pick an isolated destination; somewhere out in the countryside where there aren't many people. Tell them you don't trust them. You don't feel safe. Tell them you want to meet somewhere there are other people: A pub car park, something like that. They won't agree to it, but it'll seem more convincing."

"What if they ask me about the package?"

"They won't."

"But what if they do? I haven't got a clue what I'm meant to be taking them." Stacy begins nervously wringing her hands.

"I'm sure they won't, but if they do ask anything that you're not sure how to answer just make out someone has walked into the room and you've got to get off the phone." Tony pauses and plants a gentle kiss on her lips. "We have an entire unit on stand-by." he whispers. "I'm not going to let anything happen to you. You know that don't you?"

Stacy lowers her head, staring at the dirt floor. Poppy has run off into the depths of the barn in search of rats, but I can't stop listening to this conversation. I don't need to hear Tony say it to know these are dangerous people. Megan put her neck on the line last night when she went to collect Stacy. I know my mistress, she won't let Stacy go through this on her own, and that worries the hell out of me.

Tony cups his hand beneath Stacy's chin and gently raises her head until she is looking directly into his eyes. "There are going to be a dozen armed officers

217

already in place before you arrive. They are the best, Stacy. As soon as we're sure Liam has been delivered safely to you, we'll move in." He smiles, plants another kiss on her lips and then pulls her in closer than ever. "It will all be fine," he says, and I can't tell from his tone whether he's trying to convince Stacy or himself.

Back in the depths of the barn, Poppy is growling. The back of the barn is filled with old furniture, stacked from floor to ceiling, left over from when they cleared the house out. It sounds like Poppy is doing her best to move some of the offending items in her desperation to reach her prey. Neither Stacy nor Tony pay any attention.

"I'm going to have to go," Tony says.

"Already?"

Tony leans in and kisses Stacy on the forehead. "No point in taking any more chances than we have to, besides, we have to finalise the operation. Just try not to worry."

"Huh, how can I not worry?"

"Okay, stupid thing to say." Tony forces a smile. "Well, try not to worry too much. Just remember, I will be there. A whole team will be there. Nothing bad is going to happen."

"Okay,yes."

"And the moment you know where and when the drop is you need to text me. As soon as I receive the message we can start making arrangements." He hugs her one last time. "I do love you Stacey." He kisses her tenderly and turns to leave.

"Give me a five-minute head start before you leave. I'm going to head up the hill towards the church, you go straight back to the village. I'll see you later."

I move to Stacy's side because right now she looks like she could do with a friend.

Behind us a piece of furniture crashes to the ground and Poppy starts barking. Stacy turns as if she's going to see what the commotion is about and before she's taken a step, her phone rings. She pulls her phone from her pocket and stares at the screen, eyes wide, hands shaking. "Tony," she calls out, louder than I'm sure she intended.

Tony had only got a couple of paces from the door, and he appears in an instant. "Is it them?"

Stacy nods. "I think so. Number withheld."

"Okay, breathe. They'll expect you to be nervous, but try and stay focussed." He raises a finger, waits until the fourth ring, and then gestures for Stacy to answer.

"Hello!!"

A short pause from the speaker, and then, "Have you got it?"

"Yes."

A longer pause this time, but I can hear a muffled conversation at his end. "I'm going to call you later with the details. You and that bitch who came to get you last night..."

"I want to speak to Liam!" Stacy suddenly blurts out.

"I don't care what you fucking want."

Tony gives her a nod of approval, urging her to stand her ground.

"If I don't speak to Liam, forget it." Stacy barely manages to spit the words out before she has to cover the mouthpiece so they can't hear her choking back the sobs.

Silence. It seems to last an eternity. When he speaks again he almost sounds impressed. "Okay," he says, "just make sure this isn't the last time you ever get to speak to your son."

The next voice we hear is Liam. "Mum?"

"Oh baby, are you okay?" Stacy splutters.

"Yeah, I guess so. Just do what they say. I'm so sorr..." You don't need to be there to picture the phone being snatched away.

"Satisfied?" The voice is harsher now, almost teasing. "If you want him to stay that way just make sure you don't do anything stupid. If we even think you're not being straight with us, the boy dies. Do I make myself clear?"

Stacy takes a deep breath and says, "Yes."

"Good. I'll call you later and give you instructions where and when to make the exchange." He pauses, and I can hear him drawing on a cigarette. "You could of saved yourself a lot of heartache if you hadn't got greedy and taken something that doesn't belong to you. Make sure there are no more mistakes." There is a very sinister edge to his voice now. "I'll very much look forward to seeing you later." The phone goes dead and Stacy falls into Tony's waiting arms.

"You did great, darling," he whispers. "The moment he calls you, let me know and I'll set the wheels in motion." He takes her head in his hands and holds her face a few inches from his, staring into her eyes. "Everything is going to be fine: you just keep telling yourself that." They stand there, locked in each other's arms

220

for an eternity, before Tony finally tears himself away.

As soon as Tony has left, Stacy takes out her phone and taps out a text message. "Come on Megan," she whispers through gritted teeth as her finger taps the screen, "please get back to me."

We've only been here a few minutes and yet it has grown increasingly dark. Through the half open doorway I can see the sky has turned a thunderous shade of grey, and somewhere in the distance I hear the low rumble of thunder. Then, from the back of the barn it sounds like an avalanche of chairs and tables have just crashed to the floor. The noise is immediately followed by a loud whimper from Poppy. I tear in the direction of the sound, Stacy a couple of paces behind me.

CHAPTER 33

Megan

I've tried calling Stacy half-a-dozen times but I can't get through. So far I've managed to stave off full panic mode, but I can feel the first stirrings of discomfort begin to swirl inside me. Her message sounded urgent. Was urgent. So why not answer her phone? The sensible part of me knows there could be any number of reasons she's not answering, but given the events of the last few days it's hardly surprising I ignore the obvious. Trouble is, once I open that particular box there's no escaping from the images that have decided to crawl inside my head: Stacy, laying on the ground, blood seeping from her chest, Liam beside her, eyes wide and lifeless. I push the thoughts away and mumble, "get a grip," under my breath, before turning my attention back to driving.

I pull onto the main road, hit the accelerator and then have to brake almost instantly. It's started to rain and the afternoon traffic has slowed accordingly. The prospect of crawling home at this rate only heightens my state of agitation. I need a friend right now, more than I have ever done. But most of all I need Harry. I need to feel his warmth and unconditional love. I also need to talk to someone about what I now suspect although, even given all the evidence I still can't quite convince myself that Greg is capable of murder. If this had happened any other day I would have gone straight to the police, of that I have no doubt. But Stacy's dilemma trumps mine. I have no idea how it's all going to pan out with regards to Liam, but I do know I can't let my friend down when she needs me the most.

I'm almost half way home when my phone rings. I press the hands-free, hoping rather than expecting to hear Stacy's voice. Instead it's Greg.

"What the hell were you doing at my house?" he's shouting. His voice echoes round inside the car which probably makes it sound louder than it actually is.

I don't answer immediately, I can't. Is this some elaborate ploy to throw me off the scent? It would be just like Greg, when cornered to go on the offensive. How fucking dare he? "I watched my grandmother die this morning," I scream back. " A neighbour found her lying on the kitchen floor. You were at her house last night, weren't you?"

Silence.

"Come on then, deny it. Tell me I'm wrong."

Nothing. I'm sure, buried behind the drone of the traffic and rain spattering the windscreen, the sound of Greg's nervous breathing is seeping from the speaker but

222

the noise isn't reaching my ears. Is he sitting there trying to concoct some elaborate lie? Is he truly stunned by my revelation?

"Oh God Meg', I'm so, so sorry."

"Were you there?"

"No!!" He answers far too fast. He's lying.

"You were seen." I fire back a semi-lie of my own.

This time the pause says more than words ever could. "What?" he finally manages to spit out.

"Why did you go there, Greg? Were you hoping to talk her into changing her mind? Or did you go there with the intention of threatening her and it all got out of hand? Which one was it, Greg?"

"Okay, I did go and see her..."

"You bastard. How the hell could you..."

"I didn't touch her, I swear. Please Meg', you have to believe me. When I left she was fine."

"Tell it to the police," I scream into the speaker and the driver in the car next to me throws me a rather worried glance.

"Please Megan, I promise you on the life of my unborn child, I never touched a hair on her head. I wouldn't. You know me better than that."

His words make me flinch. Whether intentional or not, bringing the life of his unborn child into the conversation, the child we could never have, stabs far deeper than I would ever have thought possible. But I know Greg, I know how good a liar he can be when he's cornered. I know the depths he will sink to try and extricate himself from any given situation. I learned that to my cost. So now, when he's faced with something as serious as this, there's no doubt in my mind that he would say anything to slither his way out.

Somehow I manage to blurt out, "Fuck off Greg," before I hit the button and cut him off.

CHAPTER 34

Harry

Poppy is limping towards me. A ramshackle pile of old tables and chairs scattered across the floor in the far corner of the barn is obviously the result of the noise we heard. Poppy must have been scrabbling about in the pile when it all came crashing down.

"Come here girl," Stacy says, reaching down to inspect Poppy's paw. "What have you been up to?" She lifts Poppy into her arms and begins gently patting at her legs in an attempt to assess the damage.

Poppy looks fine to me, she's probably just after a bit of attention. A thorough examination from Stacy confirms my diagnosis, and miraculously, Poppy now appears to be able to walk without so much as a hint of a limp. I've seen her do this a thousand times before. The pile of old furniture that came crashing to the floor probably just scared her and she was after a bit of comforting. The problem is – having been delayed by several minutes - the heavens have now opened. The storm I heard rumbling in the distance when we first arrived has finally reached us.

All three of us stand in the doorway staring at the torrential downpour. It's dark outside, and even darker within the barn, but I don't think any of us fancy the idea of walking home in this. Stacy pulls out her phone, flicks through her numbers, and presses the call button. No sooner has she done this than the phone emits a short bleep, and the light goes out.

"No!" Stacy holds her phone at arms length, desperately pressing all the buttons. "Shit! Shit! Shit," she repeats over and over again, before finally giving up and shoving her phone back into her pocket.

We stand there for a while, staring at the rain, and I'm wondering just how long it will be before Stacy eventually makes the only decision available. As it happens, not long. "Sod this," she mutters, pulling her jacket tight round her neck and fastening the buttons. "Come on then," she says, and we head out into the storm.

It seems to take an eternity to make it home. Stacy can't stop shaking as she fumbles in her pocket for the key to our house. She's soaked through to the skin and shivering with cold. Both myself and Poppy shake most of the rain from our coats as we're standing under the cover of the porch.

The house feels warm when we finally make it inside. I can't help looking at the muddy wet paw prints leading up the hall and thinking how mad Megan is going to be when she gets home and sees the mess. Stacy has already begun ripping her clothes off before the door closes behind us. We follow her into the kitchen and wait patiently as she strips down to her underwear. I notice she's wearing a black bra and blue knickers, which seems very peculiar because Megan always makes sure her underwear is matching colours; I thought it was some sort of rule that women had to adhere to.

"You two wait here," she says, disappearing up the stairs at a canter.

We do as instructed. I think we both realise now would not be a good time to test Stacy's patience.

Half an hour later, having bathed and thrown on a pair of loose jogging bottoms and a jumper, Stacy finally slumps into a kitchen chair. She's stopped shivering, but the skin on her hands is all wrinkly and shrivelled. The entire kitchen is spattered with water where myself and Poppy felt the need to keep shaking off any excess water clinging to our fur. We are now snuggled together on my rug, but I don't feel happy. The kitchen is a mess, and all I can think about is how furious Megan will be when she walks in and sees the state of the place. And just as I'm laying there with all these thoughts running round inside my head, I hear the crackle of tyres coming up the driveway.

Normally I would be standing in front of the door waiting to greet Megan with a brisk wag of the tail and looking overly excited – because I know she loves that - but not today. I decide the best option at this moment is to remain as inconspicuous as possible.

The front door clicks open and Megan calls out, "Stacy!"

I wait for the tirade which will undoubtedly follow. Instead, Megan clips slowly down the hall without saying a word. When she appears in the doorway, instead of looking angry she just appears sad; sad and confused.

"Don't ask." Stacy says, shaking her head slowly. "How's your gran?"

226

Megan takes a seat opposite Stacy. "I tried calling you," she says, and her voice has a tremor.

"I forgot to bring my charger with me, the bloody phone ran out of battery and then we got caught in the storm and it was quicker to come back to your place than mine. Sorry about all the mess. So, how is she?"

"Gran died this morning," Megan says, and wipes a hand across her eyes.

I'm at her side in a moment, nuzzling my head against her leg, rolling back my eyes so she knows I feel her pain.

Stacy is round the table in an instant, throwing her arms round Megan, holding her tight. "Oh God Megan, I'm so sorry."

Megan pats Stacy's arm and says, "Thank you," which always seems like a rather weird thing to say at a moment like this. "If that kettle's boiled I could really do with a cup of tea."

"Yes, yes of course."

"Your hands are freezing by the way. And where the hell did you find those clothes?" she adds.

"Yeah, sorry, I had to rummage through your drawers and find something to wear. My clothes are saturated. I hope you don't mind."

"Of course not." Megan is stroking my neck, and I can feel the tension coming through the tips of her fingers. She's in pain. I so want to take that pain away, but all I can do is sit at her side and accept her loving caress.

"Do you want to talk about it?" Stacy asks as she makes the tea. "I mean..."

"It's okay, I know what you mean. Maybe later. Let's just concentrate on your problems for now. Have you heard anything yet?"

Stacy places two steaming mugs on the table and takes a seat next to Megan. "Yes, that's why I had to go out." She proceeds to explain the events of our morning to Megan, as briefly as possible but without leaving anything out. "So now, all we can do is wait," she finishes, taking a sip of her tea, clasping both hands round the mug as if it's the most precious thing in the world. "I don't expect you to come with me," she adds nervously. "This is my problem. You have enough troubles of your own without..."

Megan reaches out and clutches Stacy's hand. "There is no way I'm letting you do this on your own. Bloody hell Stace', what sort of friend do you think I am?"

"I know...I just..." she can't quite get the words out because she's started to cry. I've noticed some women tend to do this a lot, and at the most inappropriate moments. I mean, her best friend has just offered to put herself in danger for her, and she starts crying. Surely that should be a reason to be happy. It just doesn't make sense.

"It'll be fine," Megan persists. "The police aren't going to let you put yourself in any real danger, are they? And from what you tell me, Tony definitely wouldn't let anything happen to you." She pauses, swallows a mouth-full of tea and adds, "I don't suppose he's said anything about...about his wife? I don't mean to pry, but..."

"He's told me he loves me."

"And do you feel the same?"

"Yes, I think I do. I never intended it to develop into anything. I think we both just wanted a bit of fun to begin with. I was lonely, and Tony, well to be honest I

228

think to start with Tony was just after sex. God, that makes me sound like a right little tart, doesn't it?"

"We all need someone to want us."

"You can never be sure of these things, but the way he is with me, the things he says, well, I believe him. And to be honest, when you manage to turn your husband gay, it does rather shake your confidence." she laughs nervously and Megan hugs her.

"As long as you're happy," Megan says, but I can tell from her tone she has her doubts.

"I'll need to go back to mine and get a change of clothes," Stacy says, pulling at the loose material on the leg of the jogging bottoms. "I borrowed one of your leads, my phone should be charged enough by now. I'll finish my tea and head back. As soon as I hear anything I'll let you know. I'll give you a hand to clear up first." She casts her eyes round the room, in particular the floor which is smeared with dirty paw prints.

"I'll drive you. You can't walk home dressed like that, they'll nail you to a pole and stick you in the middle of a field."

"Cheeky cow," Stacy says, and they both manage a smile.

"Seriously though, it's still raining hard, you'll be soaked before you reach the end of the driveway. They were saying on the radio in the car the storm is going to get worse. Apparently they're expecting really high winds."

Stacy rolls her eyes. "Great!"

Megan, Stacy and Poppy head off a few minutes later. I'm left at home - which I find completely inappropriate under the circumstances – considering the last time I was indoors on my own I was man-handled into an upstairs wardrobe by that twat, Mark. Apparently my welfare is not that important. I deal with the situation in the only way I know how, I sulk.

CHAPTER 35

An hour passes, and I'm getting hungry. I'm also in dire need of a pee. I can't slip out through the flap in the door because it's bolted shut, and there's not a morsel of food left in my bowl from this morning. I have also become very bored of sulking, especially as there's nobody here to appreciate it. If it wasn't for the fact that Megan is grieving and Stacy is in turmoil I would be getting quite angry at the situation right now. There was a time when I would have ripped up a pair of slippers or scratched at a piece of furniture, but not today. All I can do is wait. Wait and starve.

As it turns out, I don't have to wait much longer. The sound of Megan's car coming up the driveway gets me far too excited and instead of staying on my bed, which was my original intention, I find myself hurtling towards the front door to greet her.

"Good boy Harry," Megan says, although she pushes me away when I try and jump up. Not quite the ultimate snub, but not far off.

Stacy follows Megan into the house. She has changed into more suitable attire: a pair of faded blue jeans, thick woollen jumper and a rather bulky black overcoat.

Poppy is noticeable by her absence.

I follow them through to the kitchen and settle onto my rug.

"Have you spoken to Tony since this morning?" Megan asks.

"No. I'm meant to let him know as soon as they contact me and tell me where they want me to make the drop. What time is it now?"

"Almost five-thirty."

"They're leaving it late. What if something's happened?"

"Just try and stay calm. Sorry, I didn't mean it to come out like that." Megan is fussing around with some paperwork stacked randomly on the work surface. She tends to do this a lot when she's trying to distract herself. "I've tried getting hold of Mark, but he's ignoring me," Megan suddenly blurts out. She picks up a small pile of unopened letters and slaps them down onto a much larger stack. "Sorry. I don't know what made me come out with that." And her cheeks turn slightly red.

"Erm...okay, I'm not sure what I'm supposed to say..." Stacy throws Megan an awkward glance. "Is there something you haven't told me?"

"Oh, it's nothing. I don't know why I mentioned it." Megan waves her hand dismissively.

"You can't just launch that into the conversation and expect me to let it go. Have you...have you been seeing him?"

"No! Well, not in the sense you mean." Megan sits down and pushes the hair back from her forehead. "We've talked a few times, and he came round the other night."

"Oh yes."

"Nothing happened. And now, well now he isn't answering my calls or messages." Megan lets out a long, exasperated sigh. "Sorry. I shouldn't have said anything. I don't know what I was thinking of?"

Stacy smiles and shakes her head slowly. "I think you do. And yes, it is a distraction, so thank you." And before the conversation can progress, Stacy's phone starts to ring. "Shit!!" Stacy stares at the screen, wide-eyed. "I think it's them," she says, nervously pressing her bottom lip with her finger.

Megan moves to her side and rests her head on Stacy's shoulder. "Go on then," she urges gently, "answer it."

Stacy taps the screen. "Hello."

"Have you talked to the coppers?" It's the same voice we heard this morning. The man who threatened us last night. I can picture his face, and the hairs along my spine bristle with rage.

"No. You told me not to." Stacy looks terrified, but somehow she manages to sound convincing.

"Well done. Maybe little Liam will make it through the night after all." His tone is menacing, as if he's revelling in the threat his words pose. "Drive along Packman's lane until you reach the reservoir. The gates will be open. Take the right hand fork in the driveway and park outside the timber hut near the jetty. Be there at eight-thirty and stay in the car until we contact you. Can you manage that?"

"That's isolated. Can't we meet somewhere..."

"Do you want to see your son again, or not?"

"Okay, Sorry. Yes. Eight-thirty. And wait in the car." Stacy repeats.

"Good girl. Liam is looking forward to coming home, so let's try and make sure he comes back in one piece shall we?"

Megan is leaning in close, listening to every word. She gives Stacy's shoulder a reassuring squeeze.

"Please, don't hurt him." Stacy says. Her voice has a tremor, but she is managing to fight back the tears.

"Just do what you're told and you'll get him back safe and sound."

The caller hangs up and Megan folds her arms round her friend. They sit there in a silent embrace until Stacy finally says, "I have to let Tony know."

"There's only one way into Packman's lane," Megan says rising to her feet. "It's about as remote as you can possibly get."

"I know." Stacy agrees, the apprehension displayed on her face in deep worry lines, her phone pressed hard to her ear. "He's not picking up. I'll have to text." She begins tapping out a message on her phone. "But we won't be alone, will we?" She presses send, gets up and takes hold of Megan's hand. "There, it's done. Like you said earlier, the police won't take any chances. They won't let anything happen to us."

I tend to agree with everything she's said, but I'm still not happy about the situation. It will be pitch dark and there's not a house within a mile of the Packman's lane entrance to the reservoir. If the police have any problems getting access, Megan and Stacy will be on their own. Two vulnerable women at the mercy of these ruthless thugs. I can't let that happen.

Stacy's phone pings. "Okay," she says, scrutinizing the responding text that has now appeared on her screen. "Tony says they're putting the wheels into motion now." She reads the last part of the message without repeating its content, but a little smile has curled her mouth at the corners.

Although I can't be certain, I would bet Megan has plans on making sure I don't get to go along with them. I only got to go with her last night because I forced the issue and she was in such a rush. There's not a cat-in-hell's chance she'll make that mistake again, which means I have to be one step ahead.

It's almost seven-thirty and I still haven't managed to think of a way round my predicament. Megan let me out in the garden a couple of hours ago and I checked the side gate: It was bolted. Megan stood in the doorway watching me like a hawk, so even if I wasn't certain before, now I'm convinced I will be spending the evening locked in the house if she has her way. It will take me the best part of an hour to reach the reservoir, so time is of the essence. Eventually I formulate a plan of sorts, albeit rather crude, but it's my only hope.

I wait until Megan goes upstairs to use the toilet. Stacy is sitting at the kitchen table twiddling her thumbs, looking extremely nervous. I can imagine her going over every possible scenario in her head and coming up with varying outcomes each time. But all this means she's distracted, which is good for me.

Suddenly I leap up from my blanket and hurtle towards the front door, barking for all I'm worth.

"Harry!!" Megan screams from the floor above. "Is there someone at the door

Stacy?" she shouts, and adds quickly, "Harry, stop."

I can hear Stacy tracking down the hallway towards me. "I'm not sure," she shouts back, and clips the safety chain into place. I'm still barking, although not quite as aggressively. Stacy runs her hand along my spine. "Okay Harry, that's enough." Slowly, she turns the lock and edges the door open a crack. The wind is gusting, driving cold rain into the hallway, spattering the wall and floor. I stop barking and edge closer. Stacy, now secure in the knowledge an intruder isn't lurking on the doorstep, unclips the chain and eases the door open a little further. She has both hands on the inside of the door, ready to slam it shut if anyone should appear from the shadows round the corner of the house.

But of course that doesn't happen, instead, when the gap is wide enough, I make my move. Before Stacy has a chance to react I'm out of the door and off down the driveway. I can hear Stacy screaming my name, panic etched in every word, but within seconds the sound of her voice is swallowed up by the wind and rain as I disappear into the darkness.

The most direct route to the reservoir is across the fields, but I know that won't be the quickest way tonight. The ground will be like a quagmire in places, making running almost impossible. Instead I head across the village green and take the road past the estate, keeping to the footpath as best I can. It's still early and there are more cars on the road than I'd like, there are also one or two brave souls foolhardy or desperate enough to venture out on a night like this. I avoid any pedestrians by crossing to the other side of the road, staying in the shadows as best I can, remaining inconspicuous is a little easier when your coat is jet black.

I quickly race past the two roads that lead in and out of the estate and push on up the hill away from all signs of human life. By the the time I reach the top of the hill I'm drenched. The one small thing in my favour is the wind is coming from behind me. I turn briefly and look back towards the little brick boxes, accepting the stinging rain now driving directly into my face. Light seeps from the windows of the houses and I try not to think about the occupants tucked up in the comfort of their homes, safe from the onslaught of the storm. But there's no time for self-pity, I'm past the point of no return. What I need to do now is draw on all my courage and push on into through the darkness.

Within half-a-mile the road quickly narrows: long, wet grass encroaching over the tarmac, wind howling through the trees, causing the branches to flail around like skeletal limbs, reaching out as if they are trying to grab me. It's hard not to be scared, but I know I won't succumb to fear because the thought of not being there for Megan if she needs me by far outweighs any reticence of my own.

A mile further and the road forks into three, narrow lanes. Straight ahead, the winding, overgrown sliver of tarmac slices it's way downhill, between rolling green pastures of Sussex countryside, finally coming to a dead end at the reservoir. Only two cars have passed me in the last half-an-hour, and I have no idea in which direction they went upon reaching the fork. Any cars that pass me now can only be going to one place.

Heading downhill gives my aching legs some respite, it's also a chance to recover my breath. The further down I go, the narrower the lane becomes. On my left, an impenetrable Blackthorne hedge of at least seven or eight feet in height, rises into the night sky. To my right, a two feet wide ditch, gushing and gurgling with the torrent of water feeding down from the surrounding hills is overflowing onto the tarmac. The other side of the ditch, the bank is a vertical wall of wet mud and tangled clumps of grass. The gap between the rock and the hard place is just about wide enough for a family saloon, without an inch to spare. And that is what I'm thinking about when I see the beams of a cars headlights appear in the distance, heading my way fast.

Somehow I find the energy to put in one final sprint. I try not to think about the burning sensation coursing through my body or the feeling that my lungs are about to collapse, instead I focus on the glinting rails of the steel farm gate in the distance: Too far away to offer more than a glimmer of hope, but close enough that I can almost persuade myself it's possible to reach it.

The headlights slowly fall from the sky as the car reaches the summit of the hill and begins it's decent. A second later, the snaking black road explodes into light and the roar from a ton of metal hurtling my way thunders in my ears. It's at this moment I realise I have no chance of reaching the sanctuary of the entrance to the field. Every stride sends shock-waves coursing up through my legs as my soft pads tear into the gritty, rock-hard tarmac. I'm now so far past the point of exhaustion that even if I leap into the ditch, the torrent of icy water would suck me under; I wouldn't have the strength to swim or scramble my way out of it. Death by drowning or ending up as road kill: Not much of an option. The road ahead begins to blur, my head starts flopping from side to side as exhaustion overwhelms me. And then finally, my legs refuse to comply with the urgent messages sent from my brain. A moment before I collapse I hear the screaming engine that is about to send me to my death. I don't feel any pain when the metal strikes me; the final thought that goes through my head is that I've let Megan down: That, and how much I'm gong to miss her.

CHAPTER 36

Megan

The last thing I needed right at that moment was for Harry to run off. I rushed downstairs to find Stacy standing with the door open, screaming "Harry," at the top of her voice.

"What happened?" It was all I could manage at the time, because I knew exactly what had happened. Harry had seen a cat, a squirrel or some other form of wildlife and taken off after it. His timing couldn't have been worse.

Stacy, bless her, was beside herself. She apologised relentlessly until I finally insisted she had to stop. We ended up spending too many precious minutes running round the village shouting for the little sod; in the end there was nothing for it but to give up. The decision was made a little easier because I could see Stacy becoming increasingly anxious.

"Okay, that's it," I said reluctantly as we made our way back up through the village having checked in pretty much every front garden on our way. To make matters worse, it seemed like half the village had come out to assist.

Yolanda was the first to hear me shouting. "What's the matter?" she called from her doorway. I quickly explained the situation and she appeared five minutes later dressed in a bright yellow oilskin jacket. Several other people, Mel included, joined our meagre search party. Even Daniel came out to assist, but it all proved fruitless. We spent too many precious minutes searching for Harry, and when I finally told everyone to go home, that I was certain Harry would turn up eventually, I had to fend off some very awkward questions from the party. I'm not sure any of them really believed I was willing to give up that easily, not when there had been so many instances of dogs going missing in recent weeks, and after Harry's disappearance the other day, but I was way past caring by then. Mel and Yolanda were the only ones who pressed me.

"So what's wrong?" Mel asked. Four of us were standing huddled under the canvas canopy in front of Mel's tea room front window: Stacy, myself, Mel and Yolanda.

"Nothing." And as soon as I said it I knew I'd blurted the word out far too quickly.

Yolanda grabbed my hand. "There is, isn't there. What is it?"

I glanced at Stacy, but by this time I think she was in a sort of daze. I couldn't even begin to imagine how painful it was for her, standing here in the rain having a conversation when time was rapidly running out.

"Honestly, it's nothing. We're all wet and cold and Harry will come back when he's ready," I insisted, but neither of them were going to accept that, especially when Mel saw the look I gave Stacy.

"For God's sake, just tell us," Mel blurted out. "It's pretty obvious something's wrong. Maybe we can help...." and she would have carried on if it wasn't for Stacy having a complete breakdown.

"Okay, that's enough," Stacy suddenly screamed, and burst into floods of tears. She then proceeded to quickly explain our predicament while Mel and Yolanda stood open-mouthed waiting for the punchline. When none was forthcoming they both threw their arms round Stacy in a display of sisterly unity.

"I'm coming with you," Yolanda said defiantly, stepping out of the huddle.

"No!" Stacy's eyes blazed wide, clearly terrified that she had just blown any chance of getting her son back alive. She regained her composure in a moment. "No, sorry but you can't."

I proceeded to explain – in the briefest details possible – exactly what the situation was. When I told them about the police operation it did appear to ease their concerns, a little. I made it quite clear that neither of them could mention a word about what Stacy had just told them to anyone. Eventually I had to drag Stacy towards home, first having promised that we would call them when it was all over.

So now we are in my car, heading towards the reservoir with the windscreen wipers working flat out in a futile effort to keep the glass clear of rain, leaves and any other flying debris. Time is rapidly running out, but I can't drive any faster than crawling speed because it's almost impossible to see more than a couple of car lengths in front of me. Neither of us have said a word since we set off, we are both bolted to our seats, soaking wet, cold and too terrified of what we are walking

240

into to be able to speak.

CHAPTER 37

Harry

The last thing I remember is trying to summon up any remaining energy, and leap. I was mid-air when the van clipped me and sent me hurtling into a muddy wet puddle at the entrance to the field. The only sore part of me – apart from my pads which are stinging and probably bleeding – is my rear end, which bounced off the puddle and crashed into the lowest two rails of the gate. I'm bruised and battered but very much alive, and having taken a few minutes to recover, I'm now ready for the final assault.

I managed to raise my head just in time to see the big white van turn off about two hundred yards down the road. So that is where I am now heading, keeping to the narrow verge as best I can as every step is blindingly painful.

When I get to the entrance of the reservoir, the gate is open. The driveway is made up of a mixture of gravel and slightly larger stones, most of which seem to have washed out into the road. Luckily there's a large area of grass separating the driveway from the vast lake of water about fifty yards to my right. At this end of the reservoir a massive concrete damn rises a few feet above the water and stretches along the front of the water towards the forest in the distance. I can only see about half away, then the grey monstrosity disappears into the darkness. I wonder if the police are secreted somewhere along the damn, anxiously waiting to leap into action.

I pick my way through the wet grass, heading towards the bailiff's hut, located at the far end of the parking area. A set of three steps, created from old railway sleepers, leads from the gravel parking area up to the hut. The jetty is barely twenty feet away: A long, precariously narrow structure that is intended to float on the water, thus enabling anglers to walk out to whichever row boat they have been allocated that particular day. I can hear the row boats jumping around on the waves, battering against the jetty, most of which is pretty much submerged. I know from previous visits, there should be ten boats tethered to the jetty, but I can only count six and I wonder if maybe the police are using the missing boats as a way to access the area. It seems like a rather drastic measure given the stormy conditions, but I can't see how else they are going to get here without alerting the kidnappers. Perhaps, where the driveway forks into two, they have taken the left hand lane, followed the track round the back, and secreted themselves amongst the tall pine trees.

The white van that hit me earlier is parked close to the hut, at the bottom of the bank. There is a small window in this side of the hut, facing out over the jetty, emitting a very dim light from within. Even though I am now very close, I can't hear any voices coming from inside the building, but that's probably because any voices will be drowned out by the wind howling through the trees and heavy rain drumming on the roof of the van.

I shake some of the water from my coat and creep towards the van, keeping low to the ground. I'm very aware that although I can't see them, there will be police marksmen hidden somewhere nearby, and I don't fancy the idea of some nervous novice getting jittery and taking a pot shot at the first thing he sees move. Slowly, I crawl from the cover of grass and head towards the rear of the van. I know the rain has probably washed any scent away, but there's no harm in trying. I sniff the back doors, moving back and forth along the metal foot plate. My ears are pricked, listening out for any signs of movement: A creaking door or foot slapping the wet ground. The last thing I want now is to get caught at the last minute.

I'm just about to concede defeat when I pick up the faintest of scents. The rain has washed away most of the smell, but a tiny fragment still remains, lingering on the handle of the rear door. Liam is here. But also, mixed among the diluted plethora of barely detectable odours, is one I know only too well: Mark, just as I knew he would be. Even as cold and tired as I am, I feel my hackles rise.

I take the steps one at a time, crawl across the path, and nestle up against the dry timber boards of the hut. It feels good to finally get some respite from the wind and rain. Now I'm close enough to hear voices coming from inside; two, maybe three people, talking quietly. It's impossible to interpret what they're saying, but at least one of them sounds extremely agitated.

Keeping tight to the building, I make my way round the hut. When I get round the corner, the rain hits me again, driving against my face like stinging little pellets of ice. It hurts, but I have to get close to the door if I'm going to have any chance of gaining entry before Megan and Stacy arrive. Then, for the first time tonight, my luck changes. Half way along the rear flank of the hut, about a foot from the ground, there is a small hole where the timber has rotted away. The gap isn't quite big enough for me to squeeze through, but the wood is so rotten that with a bit of

243

gentle persuasion I'm sure I can tear enough of a hole to force my way through. The roof of the hut is made of corrugated steel, and the sound of rain thundering against the thin sheets will hopefully drown out any noise might I make.

I grab a piece of board between my teeth, and pull. A six inch wide section of timber tears away, revealing a faint sliver of light from within. I bite again, and again, and in a matter of seconds I have managed to create a hole just wide enough to force my way through. I think I recall - from the times Greg brought me here - the interior layout of the hut. If I'm right I should be entering the building behind a large wooden counter; the bailiff sits behind it to take payment and check the anglers licenses are valid. The other side of the counter is a large wooden table with about four or five steel framed chairs where the fishermen all sit around and brag about the ones that got away. As long as anyone inside the hut isn't this side of the counter they won't be able see me.

A moment before I force my head through the opening, two beams of light explode over the surrounding area, and the low rumble of a car engine stumbles up the driveway. Megan is here. Torn between wanting to race to her side or keep to the plan, I make a quick decision. Any fragments of timber still jutting out on the inside of my newly formed entrance splinter away easily as I wriggle my way in. I claw at the wooden floor, dragging the rest of my body inside, grateful for the deafening sound of the rain hammering against the roof. And then, just when I'm feeling pleased with myself, I look up and see the one face I didn't want to see staring back at me.

CHAPTER 38

Megan

The journey seems to have taken forever, but finally the entrance to the the reservoir hones into view. I've been a bag of nerves all the way here, but that was nothing compared to the uncomfortable feeling of nausea swirling in the pit of my stomach as I drive up the slope towards the white van, parked at the foot of a bank. It's the same white van I saw last night, the one that horrible man dragged Stacy out of. I'm terrified, but I suppose I must be thinking clearly because I reverse park, just in case we have to make a quick getaway. I turn off the headlights, but I'm reluctant to do the same with the engine.

"Where do you think the police are?" I almost have to shout make myself heard. It really is the most awful night.

Stacy looks like she's struggling to breathe. When she turns to face me her eyes are wider than ever. "I don't know," she says, "they'll be here somewhere though. Won't they?"

"Yes, yes of course," I assure her, staring out the rain spattered side window, hoping to catch even the merest glimpse of someone in uniform hiding in the shadows of the trees. "They'll be here," I say, but I think we both realise any confidence in my voice is fake. There's nothing to see out there but darkness.

"I have to make the call." Stacy glares at her phone as if it's the most diabolical piece of technology ever created.

I nod and force a half smile that is intended to put her at ease. I know it didn't work because she struggles to find the number. Her hands are shaking too much.

After several failed attempts she eventually manages to hit the right button.

"You'll hear better if you put it on speaker phone," I suggest, and Stacy shoots me a glance that either says, 'I'd already thought of that' or 'mind your own business'.

The rhythmical sound of the dial tone fills the car. It rings once, twice, three times before he answers. "Cut your engine," the voice commands.

I do as requested and immediately feel far more vulnerable.

"Have you got it?"

Stacy shoots a sideways glance at me, and we both stare at the carrier bag on the back seat of the car stuffed with two of Harry's old towels. It was all we could come up with at the last minute. Of course, neither of us have a clue what the item we are supposed to be delivering is meant to look like: I wouldn't have the remotest idea how large a stash of drugs is meant to be, even if I knew what type of drug, or value. Our best hope is that they don't get to take a close look at the bag before the police arrive. That's if they ever put in an appearance. Where the hell are they? I try hard not to let any negative thoughts winkle their way in, but it seems the harder I try, the more I become convinced that we have been left high and dry.

"Yes." Stacy finally answers. "Is Liam here?"

"Bring it to the hut in front of you," the voice says, ignoring her question.

To her credit, and my amazement, Stacy stands her ground. "I need to know my son is here."

The silence is long enough for me to conjure up an image in my head that I didn't really want to visualize: The thug on the other end of the phone staring at it with contempt, thinking, 'who the hell does she think she is?'

After what seems like an eternity, he says, "Yes he's here. As soon as we have our goods you can take him and get the hell out of here. Now, do I have to make him scream for his mum, or are you coming in?"

Stacy grabs the bag off the back seat, shoots a nervous glance in my direction, and we get out of the car. The wind, sweeping across the vast expanse of water, seems stronger than ever; the rain harder. Along the edge of the water the forest of tall pine trees bend left and right, dancing to the tune of the storm. Stacy takes my hand and we make our way across the gravel towards a short flight of steps. Everything is happening far too quickly. Where are the bloody police? They should be here by now. The whole area should be surrounded. How much closer are they going to let us get before they intervene?

We edge round the perimeter of the structure, hand in hand, stealing apprehensive glances at one another in the forlorn hope that one of us will come up with a plan to get us out of this mess. I can't speak for Stacy, but as we reach the side of the building where the door is situated, I have given up all hope. Any moment now we are going to step through the door and offer these men a bag of dirty towels: I can't see how that is possibly going to end well.

The front of the cabin faces west towards the woods. A narrow strip of drive dappled with pot holes passes close to the building where we're now standing. The track seems to disappear into the black abyss of the forest, but I know it must lead somewhere. Perhaps the police are waiting just round the corner. But what are they waiting for? Surely Tony wouldn't let them use Stacy as bait?

As we edge closer, Stacy grips my hand so tight that it feels like she's trying to crush it. There's a small wooden porch jutting out over the entrance, and four wooden steps rising up to the door. We take each step like it's our last: Slow, purposeful, praying for divine intervention. The door opens as we reach the top step, showering us in light. The same man we encountered the previous evening is standing in the entrance, his left shoulder pressed against the door, holding it open. I barely glimpse his face because my eyes are drawn to the gun he's holding. Now I know what a rabbit feels like when it's caught in the headlights of a car.

"Move," he says, gesturing us inside with the weapon.

I want to comply, but my legs won't obey. My entire body feels like it's paralysed. I'm struggling for air, like a freshly caught fish flapping about on the river bank, mouth gaping open and closed in a desperate attempt to stay alive. Stacy is pressed tight up to my side, trying to hide the bag of towels behind us. The light now spilling from the open doorway casts long shadows that stretch out across the narrow expanse of clear ground behind us: Two, thin black silhouettes that are soon swallowed up by the darkness.

"Get the fuck inside," he shouts impatiently, grabbing my arm, pulling me into the room.

So this is it. This is how our lives are going to end. I stumble forward in a sort of semi-conscious state, now reconciled to our fate. No knight in shining armour is going to come racing to our rescue, no handsome prince sitting astride a white steed is about to charge up to the door and sweep me away to safety. Obscurely,

248

the last thing I notice before being dragged inside is how pretty the light looks glinting off the puddles of water that have formed along the narrow lane. I don't think my brain really registered the significance of the fresh tyre tracks cut into the muddy verge.

A single fluorescent tube, dangling from two thin chains is swinging in the breeze coming through the open door, bathing the long wooden table sitting beneath it in light. There are four empty, steel framed chairs placed around the table at varying angles, but on the fifth, the other side of the table, facing straight towards us, Liam is sitting bolt upright. His face is bruised and he looks tired, his eyes filled with a mixture of despair and fear. Standing behind him, his hands resting on Liam's shoulder as if he's holding him down, is our assailants partner. He's wearing a thick black overcoat that appears at least three sizes too big for his scrawny frame. I don't want to, but I can't help looking to his face. He's quite a bit older than his accomplice: Maybe mid-forties, with hollow cheeks and two or three days of stubble.

"Liam!!" Stacy shouts, desperately trying to hold back the tears.

"He's fine," the man holding the gun to his head says.

Part of me wants to face him down, look him in the eyes and see if I can detect a modicum of decency buried somewhere inside him. But I can't take my eyes off that bloody gun. My brain skips ahead, conjuring up a thousand horrific images of what those things can do.

The door behind us slams, Stacy instinctively grabs my arm and I almost jump out of my skin. Although the interior of the hut is reasonably roomy, it suddenly feels very claustrophobic. The space is filled with a crescendo of noise from the relentless drumming of rain on the tin roof overhead. The pungent aroma of dead fish hangs in the air, the stench clinging to the walls, seeping from every crack in the wooden slats. To our right, a solid wooden shelf holds a set of antique metal scales, the wall behind it is covered in photographs of proud fishermen holding their catch aloft. To our left, buried in the shadows, a waist high counter sections off the last four feet of the cabin. Everything other than than the gun is caught in the periphery of my vision.

"What the fuck is this?" The man who ushered us into the hut has wrenched the bag from Stacy's hand and thrown it onto the table. He pulls the towels from inside, spreads them across the table and waves the carrier bag above his head as if he's expecting something magical to fall out. "Do you think you can mess us about?" he shouts, throwing the empty bag across the room. He spins round to face us. "You must have a fucking death wish." Globules of spittle spray from his mouth as he drags Stacy towards him by the lapels of her jacket. "I'll shoot your fucking son dead in front of you before I kill you."

"NO!!" Stacy screams, trying to pull away.

He's close enough that I can smell the stench of stale tobacco on his breath. I turn my head instinctively, and when I do I catch sight of another figure buried in the darkest part of the cabin. Seated on one of the steel framed chairs in the gap between the counter, the figure stares silently back at me. Now I know why Mark hasn't been replying to my messages.

CHAPTER 39

I feel physically sick. My throat fills with bile and it's all I can do to stop myself from vomiting. Mark isn't moving, he's just sitting there, staring back at me helplessly. Blood is smeared across of his face. A deep, three inch long gash on his forehead just above his right eye is gaping open, raw, oozing sticky red liquid, most of which appears to have soaked into what was once a white cotton t-shirt.

"Where is it?" the thug screams, releasing Stacy's jacket only grab a fistful of her hair and drag her across the room. I don't want to let go of her hand, but he jerks her away so sharply that I can't hold on. "Last chance," he says, forcing her head onto the table. He pushes the barrel of his gun against her temple.

I manage to scream, "Don't touch her. Leave her alone." A last, desperate attempt to delay the inevitable. But even to my ears the words sound pathetic and weak. I don't want this to be how I leave this world; a pathetic female accepting her fate without putting up even the slightest resistance. Surely I have more in me than that? And just as I manage to summon up enough gumption to go on the attack, the door behind me bursts open and a gust of cold wind fills the room with icy rain. I only know someone has entered the room when I hear their footsteps on the floor.

"What the hell's happening?" The man holding Stacy says, releasing her head as he straightens upright to look over my shoulder at whoever is standing behind me.

I so want to turn round, but I'm rooted to the spot. I can sense their presence, close enough that I imagine I can feel their breath on the back of my neck.

"Put the bloody guns away," Tony says, closing the door and stepping from behind me.

At this point I should be mentally skipping round the room and thanking any God willing to listen for answering my prayers. The police have finally arrived, albeit just in the nick of time, but they are here. Outside, an entire unit of armed officers have surrounded the building, waiting for the signal to make their move.

If only that was the case. It doesn't take a genius to work out something is very wrong. Tony sounds nonchalant, and neither of our assailants appear perturbed by the sudden intervention.

The man standing on the far side of the table removes his hands from Liam's shoulders and takes a step to the side. "I thought you said..." but before he can complete his sentence a deafening explosion fills the room. The gun falls from his hand and he stumbles backwards into the wall, clutching his throat in a hopeless attempt to stop the blood spurting from the wound in his neck. Before he has fully collapsed to the floor, his accomplice raises his weapon, pointing it in my direction, his face a mixture of uncertainty and bewilderment. I close my eyes, waiting for the pain that's about to arrive. I hear the shot and smell smoke, but there's no blinding sting, which is what I imagine it feels like when a bullet hits you. When I open my eyes the young thug is laying spread-eagled on the floor of the cabin, a small, thimble size hole in the centre of his forehead trickling with blood.

"Tony," Stacy cries, pushing herself up from the table. "I thought he was going to..." she breaks into a fit of tears as she steps towards him.

Tony pushes her away before she can throw her arms round him. "Get over

252

there," he says, pointing with his gun towards the far side of the cabin, the opposite end to Mark. "Both of you." He shoves my shoulder and I stumble towards Stacy. "And you, you little prick."

Liam jumps out of his chair and runs into his mother's waiting arms. "I'm so, so sorry," he says, hugging his mother.

Tony ambles round the table, pausing momentarily to glance at Mark. "Made a mess of you didn't they?" Tony remarks casually, before continuing round the table scratching at his head with his free hand.

"What's going on? Where are the police?" Stacy screams.

"Get on the floor. All of you," he shouts, waving the gun at us. He's now standing over the skinny guy he shot in the throat. I can just about hear the horrible, gurgling sound as the man struggles for air. Tony pulls out the chair Liam was sitting on, and slumps into it beside his victim. "I suppose I owe you some sort of explanation," he says, looking at Stacy. Without pausing, he drops his gun hand and fires another shot into the head of the prostrate man. His eyes register no emotion, he could just as easily have been swatting a fly. "It's nothing personal sweetheart. If that little prick hadn't got greedy..." he turns his gaze to Liam, "well, who knows how this might have turned out."

I didn't think it was possible for my heart to beat this fast. It is the weirdest sensation, because although it really does feel like my heart is about to explode, every other part of me feels completely numb. It would seem my brain has stopped functioning properly as well: the only sound I can hear is Tony's voice.

Stacy slides to the floor, pulling Liam down alongside her. I'm still standing, frozen to the spot. Stacy grabs my hand and drags me down with such force that my legs buckle at the knees, and my bum hits the boards with a resounding thump. The shock, or the pain, brings me crashing back to reality. We are all about to die!!

"Liam?" Stacy says.

"I really am sorry, mum. I didn't know..."

"Don't give her all that crap about getting forced into it," Tony shouts. "You knew exactly what the crack was. Easy money for a sprog like you. But you just couldn't help yourself, could you? You had to get greedy. Well, now everybody has to pay the price."

Stacy turns her head, stares into Liam's eyes and says, "What's he talking about?"

"I...I...can't..." Liam can't look at her, instead he buries his head in Stacy's chest.

"Little Liam has been making himself a tidy sum over the past year," Tony says, wiping some blood-spatter from his trouser leg. "It was the perfect set up. Every few weeks these two," he waves his hand at the two dead bodies, "drive down from London for a day's fishing, and while they're here they drop off a little package, which they hide in the woods. At first, I was going to pick it up, but then - a couple of months after we recruited Liam - I started sending him to retrieve the goods. I suppose I've only got myself to blame; pure laziness on my part. The temptation was just too much for a teenager from a broken home. Wasn't it boy? Couldn't keep his fingers out of the pie. You might have got away with stealing a small quantity, but you just got a bit too greedy, didn't you?"

Stacy looks stunned. Her mouth is hanging open, her features locked in a look of sheer horror as she slowly digests the full ramifications of what she's being told. Even if she wanted to speak, at this moment I don't think she could.

Tony rises to his feet and takes a step towards us. "And then it all went tits up. First, they catch that idiot Michael Totter spying on them when they're making a drop. Okay, he had to be dealt with, but why bury the body in the woods so close to home. I mean, what the hell were they thinking? When I came round to your house that day," he waves his gun at me, "and I saw that red neckerchief that your bloody dog brought home...well, I knew it was only a matter of time before the body was discovered. I'd already sussed out that little Liam had started helping himself, so I thought I'd kill two birds with one stone, as it were."

I recall the red scarf Harry dropped on the kitchen floor, and the thought of him rummaging around Michaels Totters' corpse sends a shiver down my spine.

"We knew there was a very big drop planned," Tony continues, "so it seemed like a good time to bring things to a head. I picked up the entire stash and told them when I went to collect it there was nothing there. I thought if we offered up Liam as a scapegoat, that would be it. I assumed they'd pick him up, probably torture him a little, and when he didn't cough up, they'd just kill him. Instead they come up with the ludicrous idea of driving him out to that barn and putting a rope round his neck, presumably in the hope of scaring him into a confession. I assume they left him dangling there to contemplate the error of his ways with the intention of coming back later so he could spill his guts. What did you do Liam? Struggle a bit too much? Accidentally kick the box out from under your feet?"

"He could have died." Stacy screams.

"Yes, he could have. If you hadn't been such a caring mother," his voice takes on a sarcastic tone, "he almost certainly would have done. What a perfect outcome that would have been."

"You are sick." The words spill out of my mouth before I have a chance to think about the consequences.

"Hmm, maybe you're right. But I'm the one who has a stash of cocaine worth half a million safely tucked away. Not to mention the money we've already made over the last year or so, and I'm the only one who's going to walk out of here alive. I will miss the sex though," he says, smiling at Stacy. "That was an unexpected benefit of getting close to Liam."

"Fuck you." Stacy literally spits the words out.

"Yes babe, you did, and it was very nice while it lasted, but all good things have to come to an end."

At the other end of the room, Mark starts coughing. Tony peers across the table, craning his neck to stare into the darkness. Satisfied, he continues. "He was another unexpected bonus," he says, gesturing at Mark with a nod of his head. "Sort of ties things up nice and neat."

"What's Mark got to do with this?" I'm nervous as hell, but I realise the longer we can keep him talking the more chance we have of getting out of here alive. Right now I reckon our odds are about a hundred to one, and that's probably optimistic. Plus, I really do want to know exactly where Mark fits into this fiasco.

"Good question. We only discovered his true identity a couple of days ago. Apparently he's a private investigator. Obviously not a very good one by the state of him." Tony allows himself a little chuckle. "Stop me if I get any of this wrong," he says, smiling at Mark. "He was hired by the parents of some kid who died of an overdose. Been trying to discover the source of the drugs for a couple of weeks from what I can gather. To give him his credit, he did end up here, so maybe he's not all that bad after all."

The thundering rain on the tin roof above our heads has finally begun to dissipate. The low hum of the wind clawing through the cracks and crevices of our shelter now fills the void with an eerie symphony, interrupted by the occasional ping from isolated droplets of rain hitting the tin.

"We were only certain about him when he was spotted breaking into your house the other night." Tony continues. "It seems, having worked out that Liam was an integral part of things, he came to the conclusion that as Stacy was his mother, and you were her best friend, there could be a chance you were all involved. Am I close?"

What? Mark broke into my house!! It was him who shut Harry in the wardrobe. The revelation stabs at something deep inside me. If this is true, Mark was never interested in me, he was just pretending to like me so he could worm his way into my life. I'm surprised how much it stings. And then I feel guilty for having even thought about that at a time like this. I can barely see Mark because he's hidden in the darkest depths of the room and the edge of the table is obscuring my view, but I do see him nod. "Something like that," he mumbles.

"Anyway, I tipped off the brother's Grimm, and they grabbed him the other night." It's all he can do to stop himself laughing. "The funny thing is, without

Mark here, the final piece of the puzzle would be missing."

"You won't get away with this." Mark manages to choke the words out. "Just let them go."

Tony frowns. "And how could that possibly work out? No, sorry, but it's all far too neat like this. A little drug ring that just got way out of hand. The police are going to discover six bodies. Three of them," he points at us, "got in out of their depth. The private investigator – in a bid to save you – bursts in and carnage ensues. When the shooting is over there's nobody left to tell the tale. How does that sound?" he asks proudly.

"Like you're psychotic," Mark says. "her neighbours have seen you going in and out of her house in the last few weeks? It won't take the police long to connect you to Stacy."

Tony nods. "Yes, I was concerned about her son," he says with mock sympathy. "You know how these adolescents can be a handful, and as the local bobby I felt it was my job to keep an eye on him."

"And you think they'll buy that?"

"I can't see why not. When they search Stacy's house they'll find just enough drugs and cash to confirm their suspicions." He takes a pair of black leather gloves from his coat pocket and slowly rises from his chair as he puts them on. He squats down and prizes the gun from the the hand of the young man he shot in the head. He places it on the table, produces a rag from the same pocket, and begins meticulously wiping the weapon clean of prints. "Untraceable," he says, holding the gun up, waving it in front of Mark. "I assume you didn't bring your own." He doesn't wait for an answer. "No, of course you didn't. You're way out of your depth," he adds with a confident smile.

"You're okay with killing women and children are you?" Mark doesn't sound like he's about to give up any time soon. "It's one thing killing a couple of drug dealers, but two innocent women and a kid, you really think you've got that in you?"

"Needs must when the dev...." Tony stops mid sentence, a look of pure surprise and alarm in his eyes as he sees Mark rushing towards him. He aims his gun and I shout, "NO!" but the word is engulfed by a deafening, bang. I jump to my feet just in time to see Mark spin, and collapse to the floor. Before Tony can fire again, from nowhere, Harry leaps out of the darkness. When the next shot rings out, I feel my legs buckle.

CHAPTER 40

Harry

It took my last ounce of energy to finally force my way through the hole, and by then I was too tired to do anything except slump onto my side. When I opened my eyes, Mark was staring back at me. My first instinct was to attack, and if my body had complied I almost certainly would have done. Thankfully, it took several valuable seconds for me to recover. That gave me just enough time to re-evaluate the situation.

Mark was sitting on a chair, hands tied firmly behind his back. His head was turned at a strange angle, looking at me in astonishment. We exchanged a long, bewildered stare that seemed to last forever, but was probably no more than a few seconds. He was covered in blood and his face showed signs of a severe beating.

"They're here."

"Just remember to keep calm. Where the hell is Tony? He said he'd be here by now." The voices came from the other side of the counter.

I sniffed the air and struggled onto all fours. Two, no three people. One of them Liam. I had to resist the urge to shake off the excess water clinging to my fur. I was hidden in the shadows, obscured from their view, but I didn't want to risk making any more noise than necessary. I'm not certain how long I lay there wondering what the hell I was meant to do now. It was Mark who showed me the way. He began moving his fingers and jerking his arms, beckoning to me. It took me longer than it should have done to work out exactly what he was trying to do, but I put that down to fatigue on my part.

The rope wasn't very thick, but it was extremely tough. They'd tied his hands so tight the rope had dug into the flesh. I presume the grazes round his wrists were caused by Mark struggling to free himself. I took the rope between my teeth, carefully at first, and began twisting my head from side to side. I'd barely begun when I heard the cabin door open and Megan and Stacy were ushered inside. Now I was torn between rushing to their aid or persisting with my attempt to free Mark. It wasn't an easy decision, but eventually I realised any attempt at a rescue on my own was bound to fail.

They were undoubtedly the worst few minutes of my life. The shots sent little shock-waves coursing through me: every threat made me want to race from cover and attack. But when the last thread of rope finally broke away and Mark pulled his hands apart, I knew at least we had a chance.

I don't blame Mark for what happened next. Even if we'd had more time, it can't be easy to formulate a plan when you're partner is a dog: Albeit one as intelligent as me. When he leapt from the chair it came as a complete surprise. I will never forget those moments that followed and how he was willing to risk his life to save the others. The bullet hit Mark and sent him spiralling to the floor. Tony wasn't expecting me to leap from the shadows though. The look of stunned surprise plastered across his face was the last thing I recall seeing before I felt the sting. By then it was too late for Tony, I was already mid-air, jaws gaping open ready to clamp round his wrist. I bit as hard as I could, and immediately tasted blood. He screamed, dropped the gun and swung his arm in a long arc. I imagine he resembled an Olympic discus thrower attempting their final throw. As I was propelled through the air I caught a fleeting glimpse of Megan, staring in disbelief as I whistled past her with ever increasing velocity. Tony was shouting and swearing, but there was no way I was letting go. My teeth were clamped on his arm firmer than a limpet clinging to a ships hull. My long, canine teeth grated against bone at one point, causing him to scream pitifully. As he span for the third time, desperately trying to launch me against the wall, the weight of me hanging from his arm made him stumble and we both collapsed to the floor in a heap.

I presume it was Stacy who brought her foot crashing down between his legs because Megan already had me in her arms. I couldn't understand why she was crying, "No! Please no!" as she rocked me in her arms. I did think it was odd that I couldn't feel any pain, just an overwhelming urge to close my eyes and fall asleep.

CHAPTER 41

This is strange. The last thing I remember is Megan crying my name, but surely that was just a second ago, so why do I feel like I've just woken up from a very long sleep. What's even weirder is, there's a bloody halo round my head. Something very peculiar appears to have taken place without my knowledge. My body doesn't feel like it belongs to me. Also, once I've given my eyes time to adjust, it would appear I'm in a cage of sorts. I'm surrounded by thin steel bars and I'm laying on a blanket that is unfamiliar. A very loud buzzing sound fills the entire room; if we were outdoors I'd be expecting to see a helicopter coming in to land.

When I finally manage to lift my head and begin trying to reconnoitre my alien environment, I can't. It's quite dark, but also I can only see what is directly ahead of me because the bloody halo is obscuring anything in my periphery. I blink twice and try to move my head, without success. There is a loud clank when I turn to the left, and the same when I try the other way. It's only when my eyes have adjusted to the darkness and my brain has started to function properly that I finally begin to comprehend what this all means.

At the far end of the room I can see two cages - presumably similar to the one I'm trapped in – that appear to be stacked on top of one another. In the lower cage, fast asleep, is a huge Alsation. If anyone had told me that a dog could be responsible for creating such a hideous noise I would have laughed in their face, but this animal has taken the art of snoring to the next level. In the cage above - looking decidedly pissed off at having to endure the cacophony at such close quarters – a tiny, beige Chihuahua is attempting to cover it's ears with its front paws. At least now I know why the smell is vaguely familiar, for some reason I'm at the Vets. I should probably give the situation a little more consideration, but I just want to sleep.

The next time I wake up there is light pouring through the window, and I'm no longer stuck in the cage.

"Hello boy," Megan says, but her voice sounds strangely different.

I wag my tail in response, and a sharp pain shoots up my spine.

"He'll be a little drowsy for an hour or so." I recognise the voice: The veterinarian who I saw last time I was here. "He's going to feel some pain so make sure you manage to get him to take the tablets at regular intervals." he says, gently lifting me from the bench. "The hood needs to stay on for a couple of weeks. Other than that, he should be good as new when he's healed up."

"Thank you so much," Megan says.

And now I know why her voice sounds different; she's been crying. I hope they are happy tears.

We haven't gone home, instead we've ended up at Yolanda's house. The short walk up the path was a struggle because for some reason I'm finding it difficult to walk properly.

When we go inside it seems like half the village has turned out to welcome my return. Dorothy Barnstaple and Helen Pierce are the first to come over and make a fuss of me. Mel is here, but she's taken Megan to one side and they are whispering out of earshot. Sitting at the large dining table, Leah Derby is chatting with Daniel.

"So he's going to be alright then?" Helen Pierce asks as she ruffles the underside of my neck.

"Yes, yes he's going to be fine," Megan replies absently, but I can tell she's distracted.

Things only begin to calm down when Yolanda appears with a tray full of cups and saucers. One by one they all take a seat at the table and begin pouring. It's only when everyone is seated that I notice Stacy isn't here.

"And how are you dear?" Leah Derby asks, gently patting Megan's hand.

Megan shrugs. "Oh, you know..."

"It will take time," Leah says, giving Megan's hand a little squeeze. "I just can't imagine how traumatic it must have been. And to think, Tony Skinner...whoever would have believed such a thing?"

"How are Stacy and Liam?" Daniel asks, peering over the top of his cup.

"Safe. That's about all I can tell you. Stacy just wanted to get Liam as far away from here as possible."

"Are the police going to be prosecuting Liam?" Helen Pierce asks, in a rather accusatory tone.

Megan's face gives nothing away, but I can tell the question rankles. "Honestly, I have no idea. Personally, I hope not. I think they've both been through quite enough."

A chorus of agreement rumbles round the table.

"Do they know when the funeral will be?" Yolanda asks, changing the subject in the most dramatic way possible.

Funeral!! What funeral?

Megan shakes her head. "No, they haven't told me yet."

"Did he have family?" Dorothy Barnstaple enquires.

"I really wouldn't know," Megan says sadly. "I'm sure when everything has been arranged the police will contact me. If it hadn't been for Mark..." Megan pauses and places a hand to her mouth. She swallows before continuing. "All I know is, if it hadn't been for Mark none of us would have made it out of there alive. He sacrificed himself to save us."

What!! Mark is dead!! I really don't know why this information hits me so hard. I was proved right the night he broke into our house and locked me in the wardrobe. And there is still the fact that his scent was so strong at the snare where Winston had been trapped. He killed him, I know he did, so why was he willing to risk his life to save us? None of it makes any sense.

"Best not to think about that now," Leah Derby says, gently patting Megan's hand. "He was a true hero, and there aren't many of those left."

Several of the people at the table mumble their agreement.

"So Mark thought you and Stacy were involved in some sort of drug ring?"

265

Yolanda asks.

"Not quite. He knew Liam was involved, and I think he had his suspicions about Tony. He must have been watching Stacy's place for a while and what with Tony being a frequent visitor, I presume he made an assumption about Stacy. Obviously I got dragged into it because I'm such good friends with Stacy."

"You know what they say about assumption being the mother of all fuck-ups. Excuse my French," Yolanda says.

Megan smiles, and nods in agreement. "Yes, I just wish he'd spoken to me about it. Maybe things would have turned out differently."

This information has left me extremely confused. Before that night at the cabin, I knew exactly where I stood with regards to Mark: I hated him. But that night, when I chewed through the ropes binding his wrists, I think we bonded in some way. After all, we were both in a similar predicament, and we only had each other to rely on.

"Whoever would have thought something like this could happen in our little village," Dorothy Barnstaple says, looking suitably shocked. "And I gather the police still have no idea where Skinner hid the drugs. Almost half a million pound's worth, I heard."

Megan shakes her head slowly. "The police don't, no."

Everyone at the table stares at her in astonishment.

"Are you saying..." Mel begins.

"No," Megan quickly shakes her head. "No, I'm not saying I do, but there was something Liam said to us before the ambulance and police arrived..." She

266

suddenly holds up her hands. "Look, I'm sorry, I shouldn't have said anything. It's probably nothing, and I really shouldn't be talking about it until I've spoken to the police."

Yolanda throws her arms out wide. "You can't drop a bombshell like that into the conversation and expect us to..."

"Oh, look who's here," Mel says, jumping up from her chair, stopping Yolanda mid flow. She's looking out of the window, waving her hand vigorously. "It's George."

My ears prick up at the mention of George. It's a while since I've seen him. Yolanda gets up from the table and I follow her into the hallway. I can see the vague outline of George through the frosted glass as he approaches the door. Yolanda opens the door before he can knock, and Winston rushes past his owner and comes bounding up to me, furiously wagging his tail. Aside from the fact I can't get anywhere near him because this bloody plastic hood is getting in the way, I'm so stunned by his appearance that I can barely move.

When the humans have settled at the table again, I lay next to Winston on the rug, eagerly awaiting an explanation. Thankfully, I don't have to wait long.

"I bet you're glad to have him home," Mel says.

George nods, and reaches down, letting his fingers glide along Winston's back. "Very," he says, but even when George is at his happiest his face still resembles an irate gargoyle.

"So when exactly did you know he'd been found?" Mel asks.

"Mark came to see me the day after Winston disappeared," George says sadly.

267

"Told me about finding poor boy trapped in that snare, and that he'd taken him to a rescue centre. He didn't go into much detail, but he said it was best if we say nothing about it to anyone else because there were some dangerous people operating in the area, and if they even suspected that I'd seen something...well, he reckoned they wouldn't think twice about coming to finish me off if there was even the slightest chance I might have seen something I shouldn't have."

"And you didn't think about mentioning this to anyone else?" Helen Pierce says. "When we were all running round searching for Winston and worried out of our minds about you."

"Couldn't take the chance," George says solemnly. "Mark took me to see Winston a couple of times, and the old chap seemed happy enough. Sorry if I put you to any bother."

"You didn't," Leah Derby says, and everyone at the table except Helen Pierce nods in agreement.

How bad do I feel right now? Mark was there, just as I suspected, but he was saving Winston.

"Well he looks happy enough now," Yolanda says. "And Harry seems to have made a remarkable recovery considering he's been shot."

Hmm, I did wonder. I'd like to think I was being brave by not making too much fuss at the time, but I think the embarrassing truth of the matter is, I passed out.

"So do the police know how long all this has been going on then?" Dorothy Barnstaple asks. "Drug gangs using our village as an outlet for their wares I mean."

Mel laughs. "Only you could make it all sound like an illegal Tupperware party."

The rest of the table titter quietly. Dorothy just sits there, looking slightly bemused by the joke she's obviously not getting.

"They haven't told me much at all," Megan says. "And I don't suppose they will until they've completed their investigation."

"Unless Skinner starts talking, that could take quite some time," Daniel says. "I would imagine he's trying to hold out for some kind of deal. Corrupt police officers don't tend to fare well in prison." He pauses before asking, "Do you think he really would have gone through with it if Mark hadn't stopped him? I mean, killing two innocent women and a teenager in cold blood..." he shudders. "Doesn't bare thinking about."

"I'm sure he would have. After all, he didn't think twice about killing those other men, and he obviously knew them quite well." Megan shakes her head and casts a long, lingering look at me.

The following hour passes quickly. I am quite content to lay on the floor listening to the flow of conversation as Winston persistently nuzzles his nose against my thigh. To be perfectly honest, after my ordeal, I'm just glad to be alive, and having Winston back is a massive bonus. Although, I will probably be counting down the days until this contraption is removed from round my neck because I have an itch that I can't possibly get to, and it's starting to drive me insane.

I've almost dozed off when I hear Megan say, "Anyway, it's time I was getting

269

back. Are you sure you're okay with this?"

"Of course, he's no trouble at all." Yolanda says, reaching down to ruffle the fur along my spine.

Okay with what? Have I missed something?

"I've got to make a move too," Mel says, rising from the table.

"You be a good boy, Harry." Megan squats down beside me. "You're going to stay with auntie Yolanda for a few days."

I don't want to stay with auntie, bloody Yolanda. I want to go back home with you. Back to our house. Why the hell is she leaving me here? I jump from the floor and try to follow, but Yolanda has hold of my collar so, struggle as I might, I just can't get away. Instead I start whimpering, which might not do much for my macho image, but I reckon with getting shot and all I have a few credits in the bank.

"Go on, he'll be fine," Yolanda urges when Megan turns back.

And then, just like that, she's gone, leaving me sitting here listening to the simpering platitudes of the remaining group.

CHAPTER 42

Megan

That was difficult to say the least. There was a moment when I thought I'd lost him for good. That's what makes this harder, I don't want to leave him, not having just got him back, but it has to be done. If only there was a way of explaining things to

270

him, maybe I could make him understand, then he wouldn't have looked at me so pitifully as I walked away.

The moment I get home I make the call.

Greg answers on the second ring. "You got my message then," he says. I can sense the tension in his voice. "Thanks for calling back." He pauses, and I wait, listening to the inaudible sound of the cogs churning as he desperately tries to think of the right words. "You do know I wouldn't ever have hurt Joanne, don't you?"

Yesterday Greg left an extremely long explanation on my answerphone, as to what happened on the night he went to see my grandmother. At one point it sounded like he almost started crying. He admitted confronting her about the house, but said she gave as good as she got. None of this came as a surprise to me. Apparently the argument got quite heated at one point, and Joanne had come over dizzy and had to sit down. Greg said that was when he decided to leave. He insisted he'd asked Joanne if she was alright before he left, and that she'd told him to 'sod off', which sounded exactly like something my grandmother would say.

I'd listened to the message several times over the last twenty-four hours, and – if I understood anything about my ex at all – he was telling the truth. Also, the hospital had called to inform me that my grandmother's fall was almost certainly caused by a minor stroke. Apparently – and she hadn't mentioned any of this to me – she had suffered two similar strokes in the last six months.

It seemed the argument with Greg was almost certainly a contributing factor, but he wasn't directly responsible for her death.

"Maybe," I say in answer to his question. I have no intention of letting him off lightly. "But if you hadn't gone to see her..."

"I know. I know, and I've thought about nothing else. I really am so sorry Meg'." I hear him sniff, and hope he's wiping a tear away. "If I could change things..."

This time I interrupt. "Well you can't, Greg. What a wonderful world it would be if we could go back and erase our mistakes. But that doesn't happen in the real world. In the real world you have to man up and take responsibility for your actions." Fifteen love. "If we could turn the clock back there are one or two things, or should I say, people, that I certainly wouldn't let into my life." Thirty love. "But then again, perhaps you did me a favour; I mean, let's be honest, Greg, you were always going to fuck up at some point, so best you did it sooner rather than later." Forty love. "I won't be saying anything to the police about your visit to Joanne. Enjoy your new life with your child-bride. I don't expect to hear from you again. Goodbye Greg." Game, set and match.

Now to make arrangements for what I suspect is about to happen.

It's eight-thirty. It's a cold, miserable night, even for October. Ten minutes ago I put another log on the fire and since then I've been sitting here hypnotized by the sight of the flames gently licking at the wood. Harry should be laying at my feet, and because he's not the house should feel empty, but that isn't the case.

I risk another sip of wine and fidget nervously in my armchair. I'm determined to stay in the moment and not let my mind wander, but that's almost impossible.

There has been so much trauma packed into the last week or so of my life that I could be forgiven for not being able to keep the ghosts out. I know that mustn't happen. It's imperative I stay alert.

Eight-forty-five comes and goes, and just when I'm starting to think maybe this has all been a waste of time, I hear the gentle knock on my front door.

I couldn't be certain who I was going to find on the doorstep. This could easily have been a complete waste of time, but when I see Daniel standing there it doesn't come as any great shock.

"Just thought I'd pop round to see how you're coping," he says. "I hope it isn't an imposition."

"No, not at all." I gesture him in.

Daniel is dressed in a black raincoat and dark trousers. He pulls the hood back as he steps over the threshold, half turning to steal a glance behind him. Down the lane, little puddles of freezing water glisten in the moonlight. "It's bitter tonight," he remarks, wiping his feet.

I let him pass, welcoming into my home like an old friend. His mouth turns at the corners, a smile of sorts. and I follow him into the kitchen. "Would you like a coffee? Or, I've got a bottle of wine open if you'd prefer."

"Coffee's fine, thank you."

Daniel takes a seat at the table while I make the coffee I know he doesn't require. "How come Harry is staying with Yolanda?" he asks, trying far too hard to make it sound like idle curiosity.

"I have to leave early tomorrow. It's just a lot easier letting him stay overnight,

273

rather than rushing about in the morning to drop him off. Sugar?"

"No. No thank you. Nothing to do with these missing drugs then?"

Straight to the point. I wasn't expecting that. "Missing drugs!" I turn slowly, trying to retain my composure. Daniel is no longer seated, he's now standing, slowly slipping his fingers into a pair of black leather gloves.

"Shall we cut the pretence," he says, his tone now cold. "You know where the drugs are, don't you." He takes a step around the table. "We can make this very easy, Megan. I just want my property back, and you get to carry on with your life."

I'm not stunned by his admission., but I carry on the pretence just the same. "What do you mean, your drugs?"

"Oh come on, you didn't really think that moron, Tony Skinner was working on his own did you? It's only a matter of time before he cracks under the pressure and starts squealing to the coppers, and by then I want to be a long way from here."

"You! You were behind all this?" I retreat instinctively, slowly withdrawing until the lower half of my back connects with the work surface. I really didn't think he could scare me, but right now, he does. His change in persona is so dramatic that the long speech I'd spent half the evening planning gets stuck in my throat.

An awkward, forced smile forms at the corners of his mouth. "We had something good going, but I knew it wasn't going to last. As soon as Tony got that kid, Liam involved, I knew we were on borrowed time. All good things come to an end." I must look petrified because he adds, "I really don't want to hurt you Megan. But I will, if I don't get back what's mine."

Finally I find my voice. "You will anyway," I manage to spit out. "You have no

274

intention of letting me go. At least four people are dead because of you."

"Four? Oh, you're talking about that idiot, Michael Totter. That really wasn't anything to do with me, that was all down to those two muppets we were using. And you can't hold me responsible for what Tony did." He takes a step closer, his eyes now seem dangerously vacant. "I'm not a man given to bouts of violence, but unless you tell me where I can find my property, I'm afraid you are going to suffer quite badly."

Behind him, in the doorway, Mark's frame fills the space. His left arm is supported in a sling. "I don't think so," he says, and steps into the room.

That night, when Tony shot Mark and Harry, I had to make a choice who I wanted to go with. I chose to go with Harry instead of travelling to the hospital with Mark. Once I knew Harry was going to be alright, I went straight to the hospital. They informed me Mark had been taken to London where they were used to dealing with gunshot wounds. As soon as I'd made a statement to the police, I went to see Mark. By the time I arrived he'd already been operated on. The surgeon had removed a bullet from his shoulder and he was recovering in a private room. It was then that he told me about his suspicions that Tony Skinner wasn't operating on his own. He suspected Daniel, but there was a chance Tony was also in cahoots with one, or maybe more colleagues. Going to the police with the allegations wasn't an option. That was when we concocted the plan. Mark also spent over an hour apologising for letting himself into my house and locking Harry in the wardrobe. I would have given him a much harder time if it hadn't been for the fact that he had saved our lives, and his insistence that he had done it with the best of intentions. I wanted to feel far angrier than I was. I tried to imagine it was someone else telling me they'd been sneaking around inside my house, just to see how that felt. But it didn't work.

Before I picked Harry up this afternoon, I had spoken to Mel – the only person I now fully trusted – and told her exactly what the situation was. The plan went as expected. Mel prompted me to mention the drugs and sew the seed. She played her part perfectly, even to the point of interrupting Yolanda - when she started questioning me - by jumping out of her seat and making a big fuss about George's arrival.

It was Mark who suggested it might be for the best – for the time being at least - if everybody believed he was dead. If he was right, and Daniel was involved, the news of Mark's demise wasn't going to cause any great trauma to the locals. The only other person who knew he was still alive was George. If we were right, once Daniel suspected I might know where his drugs were hidden he wouldn't waste any time coming for me. And so, here we are.

Daniel looks suitably shocked. "But...you...you're supposed to be dead," he stammers.

Mark takes another step and pushes my wooden table to one side with his one good arm. The legs scrape across the floor tiles, filling the room with a grating sound. "Lay one finger on her, and you're going to wish I was," he says, his eyes burning with an intensity I don't think I have ever witnessed in a person before. For some peculiar reason – in the midst of this impending danger – this blatant act of machismo stirs an unexpected feeling deep inside me.

276

Daniel stands, rooted to the spot, a rather bewildered expression on his face. Daniel looks at me, then Mark, trying to assess his options.

I'm sure the fact that Mark is incapacitated plays a major part in Daniel's next move. Like a cornered rat, he takes the only course of action left open to him. He reaches inside his jacket pocket and produces a long-bladed knife, holding it out proudly in front of him as if he expects Mark to back away.

I think it comes as quite a shock when Mark just smiles and says, "I was hoping you'd put up a bit of a fight."

Daniel regains his composure quickly. There is a only the briefest hesitation before he lunges forward, thrusting the blade at Mark.

I'm sure that what follows might appear quite impressive to a bystander, but I am terrified. Mark takes a step to one side, moving with all the dexterity of an accomplished ballet dancer, and jabs out with his right hand. His middle three fingers are arrow straight as they catch Daniel in the throat. Daniel collapses to the floor making a strange gurgling sound, and before he can react, Mark brings his foot crashing down on the hand that is still desperately clinging to the knife. The sound of Daniel's wrist bone cracking is sickening, and the scream that follows sounds like it should be coming from a child rather than a grown man.

If I were to obey the primeval feelings performing somersaults inside me, I'd be heading round the table and throwing myself into Mark's arms. But I'm determined not to fall into that trap. Instead, I step away from the figure writhing on the floor at my feet and make the call to the police.

CHAPTER 43

Harry

Order has finally been restored. It is now over a week since I had to spend the night at Yolanda's house – which proved very enlightening by the way. Around half-past-nine that evening the village lit up with flashing blue lights and a lot of commotion. Yolanda kept me locked in the kitchen, so I had to wait about an hour before I learned exactly what had transpired, and then it was only the bare details. Over the course of the following few days I discovered exactly what had taken place at our home that night. Once I got over the shock, I have to admit to feeling quite smug. I had Daniel pegged as a bald twat the moment I met him. It feels very comforting to have been proven right.

Long after all the excitement had subsided, and following several very long, tedious phone calls – one of them with Megan, which wasn't so tedious – Yolanda finally relented and let me out of the kitchen. I managed to glean from her conversation with Megan, that Yolanda would be keeping hold of me overnight as Megan was busy giving a statement to the police. I would have quite happily spent the entire night sulking if it wasn't for two extremely surprising revelations.

At ten-thirty, Mel turned up.

"Are you up to date?" she asked Yolanda before she'd even got through the door.

"About Daniel, yes. I couldn't believe it. Why didn't Megan say anything?"

"She couldn't, not until she knew for sure."

"And you didn't know?"

"No. Not everything. But she did ask me to let you know about Mark. He's alive."

Yolanda's jaw dropped open, and just for a moment she seemed lost for words. "But...How? What the...?"

"Wait until tomorrow. Megan will tell you everything."

She wasn't the only one who was stunned by this news. I felt a really strange swirling in the pit of my stomach; a lightness that made it feel as if I was almost floating. I was still floating when Mel dropped another bombshell.

"Oh, and I don't suppose you've heard the latest news about our missing postman. Poor man has been in hospital for the last week or so, apparently he was bitten by a dog and it turned septic." Mel holds a hand to her mouth to stifle a laugh. If she notices Yolanda's cheeks flushing bright red, she doesn't say anything. "I shouldn't laugh really, but one of the nurses who treated him is a friend of mine and she reckons there was no way he was wearing anything when he was bitten. Can't imagine how that could happen."

Yolanda poured herself a very large brandy the moment Mel left.

Oh, I nearly forgot, the police have finally arrested someone for stealing dogs in the area. Apparently they are a middle-aged couple who live on a farm about five miles from here. They had seventeen, yes, seventeen dogs in the barn when the police raided the place. They have been advertising them for sale all over the country, and making a good deal of money from it by all accounts. I hope they lock them up for life. At least we can all sleep a little easier at night now.

In other news, Megan has talked to Mark on the telephone every other day this week. She is still twiddling with her hair when she talks to him, but she isn't quite ready to commit herself to a relationship. From the little snippets of conversation I've managed to overhear, I gather Megan can't quite forgive him for breaking into our house and locking me in the wardrobe. For my part, I intend to make my feelings quite clear at the first available opportunity. I think both our lives would be better if he were a part of them.

Joanne's funeral took place yesterday. It was the saddest day. I wasn't allowed to attend, but I spent the morning stuck to Megan's side trying to soak up some of her pain. I like to think it had some effect because when she got back from the funeral she let me sit beside her on the sofa while she flipped through a thousand ancient photographs. She only cried four times.

No news on the Greg front. I hope it's the last we've heard from him because I can't deal with all these mixed emotions. I know he tried calling at least twice because Megan has a special ring-tone that only sounds when it's Greg calling. She didn't bother answering either of his calls.

Biggest news of all, I finally managed to trap Houdini. Two days ago I was watching him from the kitchen window while Megan was upstairs taking a bath. He was busy burying nuts in the flowerbed along the edge of the fence. Every few seconds he'd stop, poke his head into the air and scour the surrounding area as if he were prepared for an attack. He obviously underestimated my superior Ninja skills. I sneaked up on him and sprang from the grass, trapping him inside my plastic hood, pinning him against the wooden fence panel. The little sod bit me on the nose and ran off chattering away to himself triumphantly. I am currently on a course of antibiotics.

The End

Printed in Great Britain
by Amazon

39462489R00155